DEAD NED

THE MACMILLAN COMPANY
NEW YORK · BOSTON · CHICAGO · DALLAS
ATLANTA · SAN FRANCISCO

DEAD NED

The Autobiography of a Corpse
Who recovered Life within the Coast of Dead Ned
And came to what Fortune you shall hear

by

JOHN MASEFIELD

NEW YORK

THE MACMILLAN COMPANY

1938

PRINTED IN THE UNITED STATES OF AMERICA
AMERICAN BOOK—STRATFORD PRESS, INC., NEW YORK

TO

MY WIFE

"And since it's only Ned,
Who was alive and is dead,
There's no more to be said."

DEAD NED

I AM GOING to set down my story, while I remain young enough to tell the truth.

When the tale is finished, it will go into a banker's strong-room for one hundred years. If it should survive that time, then, it may be opened and read, by whoever finds it and has the patience. I have altered all the names, and purposely confused the places. Of course, I know well that no man can hide the past; much of what is buried (even if by genius) can be dug up by labour; but I mean so to bury my past, that the digging up shall take time, of which no mortal has much to spare. At any rate, whoever digs for me, will dig a hundred years hence, when all now living will be elsewhere.

My life has been in three scenes, one of great happiness, one of horror, terror, shame and disgrace beyond all telling, and then, one, a long one, of an interest, a steady joy and peace for which no words of mine suffice. I do not know enough of this life of ours to be able to explain, why the second scene was allotted to me. I was a young man at the time, wicked, no doubt, with the usual folly of the young, but not so wicked, as I see myself, as to deserve such fate. Without that second scene, the third could not have been; this, too, I know. Wise men in the land where I have lived have told me, that I was receiving punishment for something done in a past life. One or two of them have said that I was being prepared by destiny to a new fate, and that all, to whom life is to be full, or significant, must first pass through a furnace of suffering. It may be so.

One told me that I was blessed among men, to have gone through a Hell in my life-time. That, too, may be so. He said that fire cleanses, and that sorrow purifies, and ennobles. I know that my fire did not cleanse me, nor my sorrow ennoble. The fire smouldered in me for years, filling me with smoke of blackness and bitterness; my sorrow made me angry, cynical and savage. It gave me hatreds which even now are hideous in me. However, if I start with the results of events, I may never come to the events.

My father was a physician in London. He was a tallish, bustling merry man with a delightful face, kind, smiling and eager. I remember him best as he was during my mother's life, when he was in the height of practice. He was then very trim in his dress. He wore usually a suit of pale purple, with gold buttons, each engraved, and having lace at wrists and throat. Like most physicians of the time, he wore a curled, powdered wig with a small pigtail, also tied in purple. He kept his things in camphor. To this day, I cannot smell camphor without the feeling that my father is in the room. He was a very elegant man, with charming manners. He was much sought to, when I was young, by people suffering from disease in the kidneys.

My mother was a shortish, bustling, merry woman, plump, red-cheeked, and with beautiful dark brown hair. There was a portrait of her, by a famous hand, not very like, I used to think, being too solemn and stately. Now that I have recovered it, after long search, it seems to me to be truly like. The thing that I remember most clearly of her was the merriment in her eyes, and her charming little nose. I will not say that it was a snub nose, yet it had something of the charm of a snub. She had had two children before my birth, a girl, Margaret, who died of measles when I was three, and a girl, Caroline, who died of scarlet-fever when I was four. I seem to remember Margaret; she is hardly more than half memory to me. Caroline I recollect clearly, because she once poured a can of very hot water over me, as I sat in my tub, being bathed. The time when Caroline scalded me became a mark in my life; I could date events as before and after that scalding. I suppose that that was due to some sin in a past life, too, a pretty bad one probably, for the punishment was sharp, and not yet forgotten. There were no other children after my birth.

I saw nothing of my mother's grief, when her daughters, my sisters, died. I was packed away into the country when they were ill, and did not return till some weeks after their deaths. I know, that those deaths were great griefs to her.

My mother was a beautiful dancer. At one or two Assemblies, I saw her dance. She was also a sweet singer, and like my father, played much upon the harpsichord and sang for some ten minutes every day. Sometimes, even now, I hear some of the songs they sang. It never fails to move me to the marrow when I do. There was one, with a sweet tune, which she often sang. It had a refrain, "My little babe, let be," of which I was very fond. At a Concert at the Rooms yesterday, a young woman sang it before me, much such another as my mother she seemed, only younger. Perhaps it was her singing of the song and bringing back my past, more than anything else, which has set me to the writing of my tale.

There are relatives of my mother still alive. I saw and

talked with two of them a fortnight ago. If they had
thought that I was I, they would have swooned. But I am
Dead Ned; I do not exist; I am never talked of; I am forgotten. Sometimes I wonder if Ned ever existed. Does a
skeleton in a cupboard exist? Sometimes I feel with the
wise men of my adopted land, that I have been caught in
an illusion, that all life is an illusion, till the soul can per-
ceive the reality behind it.

When I was still very little, perhaps six years old, we
moved our home from a street into a square, which had
trees, flower-beds and a pond of water in the midst of it.
It was then as it still is, a fashionable square; the house
was much bigger and more splendid than that we had left;
and the people near us, in bigger houses than ours, kept
great state. At one house, a painted coach drew up, every
afternoon, at half-past one. There were negro page-boys,
with gold caps and bright scarlet cloaks, who opened the
doors and ran down the steps as soon as the coach arrived.
Then the two negro footmen climbed down from their
perch behind the coach; one opened the coach door, one
stood near the coach door. Both wore gold hats and scarlet cloaks. Then, from the house, a very magnificent negro,
with scarlet turban and cloak, and a scimitar in a scarlet
scabbard, came majestically down the steps, bearing a little dog in a scarlet basket, which he placed in the coach.
He then stood beside the second footman, with his scimitar drawn, while a little old woman, dressed in black silk,
and carrying a cane, walked across the broad pavement to
the coach door, attended by two negro women, each of
whom carried a scarlet rug. She was very old, with suspicious black eyes, and a skin all yellow and wrinkled. She

entered the coach, the women wrapped the rugs about her, bowed, curtsied and drew back; the footmen closed the coach door, bowed, and took their perches on the coach. The man with the scimitar saluted with it, and the negro coachman whipped up and away they drove, for exactly one hour. At half-past two, they returned, and the process was reversed; the old woman came out, and the dog was carried in after her. I cannot tell you what pleasure this bright pageant gave me daily. The old woman was a West Indian Nabob's widow, they told me; the negroes were slaves. Sometimes, my mother said, that in English law they were not slaves, but free; because in England all men are free. I used to glow with pride to think this. She said that the negroes were men whom the English had bought to save from being killed, that if they had not been bought they would have been killed, but that we sent ships to buy them and carry them to the West Indies, where they made sugar for us. Ah, my Mother, I was to see something of that matter with my own eyes.

I used to pass that house of the negroes almost every day. In the front window on sunny days a macaw was to be seen. They used to wheel its perch there, so that it might have the benefit of the sun. I used to beg to be allowed to stand to watch it, as it twisted about in its odd way. Sometimes one of the negro pages would bring it sugar, fruit or a nut, and I would admire its sideways look, its delicate craft, and its tongue like a little wooden carrot. This bird was green and blue and yellow; there were other parrot-birds in the house, but none so pleasing to myself. One day I was to see something of these things, too, in the lands from which they come.

I remember also very clearly a great stir about what my father called the New Treatment, and how it behoved him to go to study it. So we all went abroad, over the sea in a ship to a place called Holland where there were lots of tulips and canals, and then to a place called Sweden, where there was a man with a wonderful face under a shock of white hair. His face seemed to shine with goodness. He asked me in a queer English what I was going to be, when I was a man, and I said: "A doctor, like my father."

I began soon to study, for my father said that youth was the time to learn. I had lessons in Latin grammar from the clergyman of the parish, and learned a little French from one who had been exiled from France for some offence given to the King. Soon I was a big boy attending daily the Academy of Dr. Theopompous Calamint, who would not much care to hear what became of me. My father was, by this time, one of the most sought-to physicians, for his particular skills, in all the world. His door was beset by carriages all through the morning. We used often to talk together of how, when I too was a physician, we might work together. He was a charming companion to me; he would talk of physical matters to me in ways that made them as interesting and exciting as poetry. I learned much from him. I learned also to sing and to play the harpsichord; sometimes we all sang together. I suppose that no boy has had a happier life than I, in all the wide world. As for games and sports, there were plenty of those. I rode, I fenced, and ran. As to thoughts, I suppose mine were those of such boys as myself. I believed that the rich were rich and the poor poor, by divine appointment. I felt that goodness was a code to be learned, and badness a thing to be avoided, and that if you learned the code and made the avoidance, why, then all was and would be well. I knew that my parents were good people. I knew that my father would become one of the Royal physicians and be knighted. I knew that presently I, too, should become a doctor, learned in the miracle of the human body and pledged to a lifelong struggle against disease.

Long before I left Dr. Calamint's, my father thought it wise to make me his apprentice, as it was called, so that I might the sooner qualify for the practice of medicine. In this way, I passed some happy years, learning a little of humane letters from Calamint, and picking up much of my profession from my father. I looked at bones, I cut up dead birds and animals, made up some simple medicines, bandaged cuts, helped to set limbs, poulticed abscesses, attended at certain operations, and learned at first-hand much curious lore about kidneys. I always feel, that if Life had not changed, I should have become my father's shadow, doing his cures at second-hand.

Presently, I left Dr. Calamint's and became more helpfully my father's assistant. I was eighteen, and beginning to have views of my own. I was beginning to revolt against the kidneys, and to think lungs pleasanter and hearts more important. Then, after a brief illness, my mother died of pneumonia, which put an end to all the first and happy part of my life. My Fortune changed, that is, my father's Fortune changed; and I was still linked to that.

They say that the death of a child breaks a heart, and the death of a wife a home and husband. Certainly my mother's dying was the death of my father's heart and

brain; all that he had later was a sort of posthumous ex-
istence, unlike anything known to me. Five days after my
mother's burial, he told me that he was giving up house
and practice and going abroad. For myself, he said, that
he had been seeing his old friend, Dr. Josiah Copshrews,
of St. Lawrence Herbary, in the City, to ask him to take
me for the remainder of my apprenticeship, and that Dr.
Copshrews was willing, but wished to question me a little
first, to find out the extent of my knowledge. I was to go to
see him that day.

The news came suddenly and heavily, yet there was
something of relief in it. Neither of us could have faced
much more of that house and way of life with the main
support and life of it gone. I knew, though I was but a boy,
that my father could not stay there, that he did well to get
away, for some months at any rate, and that if he were not
practising, I should have to find a new master and teacher.

Within a few days, our home was broken up. Our furniture was either sold or put into store, and my father, having sold his practice and settled his affairs, bade me good-
bye, and passed almost out of my life. He went first to
Paris for a few weeks, then to Blois, to perfect his knowledge of French; then, meeting with a companion, a man of
learning, who wished to go to Rome, he set off thither,
writing to me from time to time, but telling me little, and
bidding me ply my studies. I knew that my father and I
would never be much to each other thenceforward.

I, in the meantime, was the apprentice of Dr. Josiah
Copshrews, about whom something must be told. The second, or frightful part of my life had now begun.

St. Lawrence Herbary, in the City, is a well-known par-

ish. It took its name from the Herbary, which surrounded
my Master's house, and had saved it from the fire of London. The Herbary had been encroached upon since those
days by buildings of different kinds, but there was still a
garden, containing herbs of frequent use in medicine, such
as the mints, pennyroyal, podagra, the white poppy, and
some others. Dr. Copshrews, being a doctor of the older
school, took much pleasure in this garden, which was well
looked after by an old Welsh lady, Mrs. Ann Morgann,
who was a good herbalist, and queer character, who ruled
the Doctor's house for him.

Josiah Copshrews was an old man, over seventy, with a
great practice in the City. He was a man of wide, strange
and unexpected learning, great piety and much severity
of life; he touched no meat in Lent, drank nothing but
water, and would not lean back at ease in any chair, "since
it would be a pampering of the flesh." He was a tall, gaunt,
bony figure, with a kind of twitch or muscular distortion
in the face, almost every few minutes. He was conscious of
the twitch, and used to mutter "God bless us all" whenever it happened. He was a man of the utmost sedateness
and precision in his appearance and manner. He wore always black, with white ruffles at the throat and wrists,
and an elegant little white wig, with a tail tied with a
black bow. Like some of the older physicians, he always
carried to the bedside a silver pouncet, or pierced box, containing aromatic vinegar or smelling-salts. His manner in
daily life was always professional and smacking of the
sick man's bedside; he seemed always to be on tiptoe, with
his head a little on one side, as though taking a shrewd
look and summing up the symptoms. He had early de-

cided that noise was hateful to most sick people. "Noise," he said to me once, "is a symptom of health and of life. Sickness is inability to make or endure noise; I speak, of course, of other things than mania." In his eagerness to save his patients from this annoyance, "and it is a great annoyance, Ned, my boy, a sad, sad annoyance," he used to wear always shoes made of a kind of felt, which were silent upon the floor and could not creak. It was thoughtful of him, and some may have been spared a little annoyance thus. I remember one old lady, a patient of his, who once said to me: "I do wish you'd tell Dr. Copshrews to wear leather shoes, like other human beings, and not keep gliding about like a ghost or a deaf mute." When in thought about a case, he had a habit of pressing his two hands together and resting his chin upon the finger-tips. He then looked like some kneeling figure in stone upon a tomb of the time of James the First. The students of medicine apprenticed to the physicians and surgeons of the City knew this trick of his; they called him "Old Sacred-to-the-Memory Jo."

He did look like a stone image, I confess. His face was the most bloodless I have ever seen. In between its twitches it was a rigid face; so that many, who did not know him, thought that he must be inhuman; but in this they were wrong. No man known to me has ever shown a charity more complete, or a sympathy for suffering more generous. He was a widower, and had a wastrel son, who caused him constant grief. He had a big practice, and must often have made large sums from his profession, but the son was a rodent ulcer, and his own devout, tender, thoughtful, discriminating charity was daily like the sun-

light upon many poor souls. He was one of the very best
men I have ever known. I have been touched to see, within
these last few days, that his tomb in St. Lawrence Church
is still kept decked with a few flowers placed there by
some who keep his memory green.

Living at the Herbary with Dr. Copshrews and his two
apprentices was a sad wrench after being at home, but
there could be no doubt that it was of benefit to me as a
student. At home, I had been with my father, seeing few
but wealthy patients, nearly all of one type, and that re-
pulsive to me. Now I was in the midst of a big general
practice, meeting every kind of ailment and accident in
every week. I had less time for book-work, and I had no
time and no associate for the charming talks with which
my father had beguiled the evenings. I was a pugilist in
the ring with disease all day long, and at night might
often be called out again.

The time passed, as a young man's time does, not too
happily, the skin being not yet toughened to the world. I
did not much like the other two apprentices, but we could
bear with each other. I liked Dr. Copshrews. When he
found that I worked hard, he praised me. It was one of his
generosities, to praise. It is a rare and, when just, a noble
thing to praise; few people praise enough; all ought to
praise whenever they see something that can be praised.
Once in a century a man may be ruined, or for the time
made insufferable by praise; but surely once in a minute
something generous dies for want of it. I once heard someone say: "The occupation of Heaven is praise."

I heard from my father from time to time; he had been
at Rome and at Venice, and was slowly journeying back to

Paris. When I had been with Dr. Copshrews rather more than a year, there came a long gap in my news of him. I was not alarmed, because he had never been a regular writer, and because the posts were often much disturbed, letters were lost or stolen or cast away; still, this gap was longer than any that had come hitherto.

Then it chanced that a Dr. Gillivor, a friend of my Master, dined at the Herbary one day. He had been in Paris, and had but just returned. He told me that he had seen my father there, and added: "But I suppose you will have heard all about him." On my saying that I had not heard much, since my father was not a good letter-writer, he told me that he had reason to believe that he was going to marry a widow there, a Mrs. Rackage, who had come to Paris with her almost grown-up son, Dennis Rackage, to launch him on the Grand Tour. Dennis had gone off, with his tutor, while she, liking the life of Paris, which is ever perhaps more human than anything offered to widows in England, had stayed on there. I had not heard anything of all this. It was important news to me. If my father married, then, surely, I might expect the less from him. I had always thought that the chances were that he would marry again; but it was a shrewd blow, none the less, to think that now I stood alone in the world.

I must tell a little of my possessions. I inherited from my mother, that is, through my mother's father, my grandfather on her side, a sum of money over which my father had no control. It amounted to £1400. On my father's advice, I had lent this upon a mortgage, and received for it about £87 a year, which sum my father's lawyers controlled and accounted for. They paid Dr. Copshrews certain sums; they paid such bills as I incurred for clothing, shoes, books, instruments, and for pocket- and travel-money. What was not spent in the year was saved for me, to be paid over on my coming of age. My father had not told me one word of any Widow Rackage; he had said only that he had found life in Paris agreeable and might make a prolonged stay there. I heard no more from him, though I wrote at once to wish him joy. Then, one day, while I was busy in the dispensary, mixing some draughts for patients, I heard my name called, and there was my father, with a woman on his arm. He said, that he wished me to meet my stepmother. That was my first sight of the Widow Rackage; I many times regretted that it was not the last. I dropped my mixing work, to welcome them, and soon had a good look at the lady, and decided that we should not agree. Men and women are divided by Nature into certain camps and clans, which seek each other out wherever they may be. You find your wife or your friend in your camp or clan. It is idle for you to look for either outside the bounds of those communities. I had a good look at the Widow Rackage, and knew that she was not for me. She was very good-looking, in a drooping, rich, drowsy style. She was black-haired, with great, black, languishing eyes. Her face was highly coloured; her whole appearance was of vivid colour. She had this rich red-brown complexion and glossy black hair. In an age when many still kept to the fashion of powdering hair, her strong colour attracted attention; she looked vivid, like a splash of scarlet on a palette. She was of the medium height. Her teeth were not so good as one would have expected. In fact, after the first shrewd look at her, I judged

that she was not a vital person, but something of a weed.
Still, she was handsome, and had her charms. She moved
very gracefully; her voice was sweet, drowsy and allur-
ing; she could sing, she could play the harp, she could
amuse. In her youth, she had attracted many men; and
had enjoyed her power; but I imagine that her followers
soon left her, for the reason that she was without much
life, and lazy. I felt from my first critical look at her, when
I saw or suspected all that I afterwards proved to be the
truth of her, that her stars should have made her a favour-
ite wife in an Oriental Sultan's harem, where she could
loll upon a sofa all day long, with a dish of sweetmeats at
her side, and slaves fanning her. Lord, I did hate that
woman; forgive me for it. If the stepmother hates her
stepchild, God knows the passion is returned. Like many
women who have had some success as a charmer she had
her insolence, as though a word were more than enough, a
favour almost too great. There she was now, my stepmother, suddenly thrust upon me as such, without a word
of warning. I blamed my father at the time, for springing
such a surprise upon me; he might, I thought, have warned
me; he might have arranged, at the least, a quiet meeting
between us. But nothing of that happened. He had married in Paris, and now was passing through London, to
the village of Cholsington, some miles from London, where
she lived. He had landed at Dover, had posted to town,
and was now upon his way. She hoped that I would spend
the next Sunday with them. They were going to live at her
house, the Manor of Cholsington, during the absence, and
in the minority, of Dennis abroad. When Dennis came of
age, the Manor would be his, of course, and they would
move elsewhere.

Within a day or two, my father and my stepmother were settled at the Manor. On the Sunday, I went out to see them there. Cholsington was then a pleasant village, with a fine church near the cross-roads, and many pleasant orchards, stretching away down to the river. The Manor was a big red-brick building, built directly upon a grassy lane, which ran away among the fields on both sides. The house had been built in the latter days of Queen Anne; the garden lay behind it, and beyond the garden were fields, reaching to the village. It was strange that the builders should have placed it directly on the lane; it was a fine house; one would have expected it to lie more remotely in grounds and gardens of its own.

As I passed to the front door, to knock, on that, my first visit, I noticed a man standing at one of the windows. He had seen me before I saw him. I knew afterwards that he must have been expecting me and looking for me; and I was struck as I passed by the very sinister look of ill-will in the fellow's eyes. I knocked at the door, and, as nobody opened, knocked a second time, and was about to knock a third time, when this man opened the door to me. He was dressed in decent black, which I somehow knew had once belonged to his late master, the dead Mr. Rackage. His face was bony and coloured like old bone. His eyes were grey and rather far apart, and his look was one of contempt and loathing for myself. He opened the door, as I have said, gave me this look, but made no enquiry as to what was my pleasure. I asked if Dr. Mansell were within.

"I will ask my mistress," the man said; but at this moment my father appeared and welcomed me.

"Wait, Ned," he said, "before you come in. This is Mr. Henery, the factotum here."

Dr. Copshrews had always insisted that I should watch faces with great closeness. He said that careful observation must always be the doctor's safest guide. I looked at Mr. Henery, and I must say that he gave my father as evil a look as he had given me. I had no doubt, that during Mrs. Rackage's absence in France, Mr. Henery had had some pretty pickings there, which were now ended, or likely to be. He gave me, on the whole, as cheerful a welcome as you might expect to get from a death adder.

I went in to greet my stepmother, whom I found languid and ill-disposed.

In those long-ago days, people prided themselves on having visited Paris. It was much, still, to have gone the Grand Tour, but much more to have stayed in Paris, seen the French King, and the incredible manners of the nobility. That, in those days, was reckoned by some people, as something like the stamp of life; without it you were either dead, or not made in God's image. Certain things must ever confer distinction among men, the things change from time to time, and that one thing has changed among us. Revolution has now destroyed the French King and his nobility; years of savage war have changed our views of the French. But in those far-off days of peace and folly he or she who had been in Paris looked down upon the stay-at-home, and affected a dress, a manner and a languor by which they could be recognised. They often assumed airs which seemed to say: "We who have been at the French Court are not as others; we are superior, and expect to be worshipped as such."

My father was almost without that vanity; he showed it only in trifles in his dress. My stepmother had it to the full. She had the languor, as though she were too exquisite a plant to live in such loutish air, having once breathed at Versailles or at St. Cloud. She had the manner, as one who has seen a play may affect the manner of a player. She had the dress, of one who would buy what she was sold.

There she lay languishing on her sofa, with her eyes half-closed, and her white, plump, and rather useless hand plying a fan. She smiled on my appearance and held her left hand idly to me. She did not rise. I think that she meant me to kiss the outstretched hand. I shook it, instead, and saw her compress her lips with disdain as she drew the hand away. She smiled up at her husband, and said in French that his young *étourdi* was wanting in manner at present and smacked too much of the apothecary. I knew French rather better than she, as it chanced, but I said nothing, then. Presently, Mr. Henery called us to our meal.

We went in to the dining-room. There were portraits on each side of the mantel: on one side, the late Mr. Rackage (in a red uniform, with a sash and a gun), on the other, his wife, my stepmother, as Flora, with a cornucopia of flowers. On the wall behind me, was a portrait of a young man, with fair hair and strangely pointed ears; he had rather a look of insolence. Later, I came to feel that it was more of a sinister and deadly look. This, as I judged, was my stepmother's son, Dennis. Over the mantel was a French mirror, in a fine carved gilt frame. In this mirror, I caught frequent sight of Mr. Henery's snake-like eye, now upon my father, now upon myself. There could not be much doubt of how he regarded us. My stepmother affected a want of appetite; it was considered ill-bred, I had

heard, for women to eat much in public; they ate their
real meals (often very hearty ones) in private. The conversation between my stepmother and my father began
in French, with a reference to myself as *"ton pauvre
étourdi."*

   "Madame," I said, *"il parle Français, ce pauvre."*

   She turned crimson with vexation, and spoke in English thenceforward.

   I felt that she had determined, long before coming to
England, not to allow me to share my father with her, or,
perhaps, not to let any reminder of my mother reach him
through me. I judged that her plan had been to make my
father dissatisfied with me, as a lout, not fit to visit at the
Manor; to try, in short, to make him ashamed of me. She
was not a clever woman, and could hardly hide that that
was her plan. She now began another approach to this
scheme, with some skill. Her aim, throughout the meal,
was to speak to me, as though it were great condescension
in her to speak to me at all. I judged that she was determined to show me, and to show her servants, that, though
she had married the father, she had not adopted, and never
would adopt, the son. I was to be made uncomfortable
there, so that the servants, especially Henery, might take
their cue, and be rude. If she were cutting and contemptu-
ous enough, and the servants insolent enough, why, then,
I might avoid the Manor thenceforward. However, I could
see that she was a little afraid of my father, and dared not
go so far as she had wished. We tilted from the first, but
had not yet learned to be downright rude to each other.
She would begin thus:

   "My son, who is now at Rome, writes that his fencing-master is very well contented with him. It is so important, do not you think, that a gentleman should be a master of the fence? To whom do you go, for your fencing?"

I saw that she meant to confound me, imagining that I should have no fencing-master, and no taste for such an accomplishment. I said that in the City we went to the Salle of one Esteban, a Spanish fencer, in Gracechurch Street, who had been fencer to the Sultan in Constantinople. Her next sally was:

"My son, in Rome, finds the Italian dancing-masters so much superior to the English, he wonders that any English people can be content . . . But perhaps you are too busy at your mixing pills to care for such things as dancing?"

I said that all young doctors learned to dance, that it was most important, that they should cross a room with grace, and have an ease of bearing; and that my teacher, near the Fields, was an Italian from the Theatre at Milan. She asked, then, if I would not much love to go upon the Grand Tour, that Dennis always wrote of the supreme importance of such a tour, to form a manner, and to give just views. She, for her part, could not see in what other way such advantages could be had. I said that I hoped, presently, to tour, to see the foreign Universities and Schools of Medicine, and perhaps to take degrees there. She replied that "That was such a different thing; that brought in vulgar considerations of personal profit." I replied that it did no such thing; that it was an effort to advance man's knowledge, in ways beneficial to all. All the time, Henery was gliding about the table silently, with his viper eyes on us. There was something about the tilt of his head forward, that made one feel that his main task in life was to overhear. His ears seemed bent outwards, so that he might listen at keyholes. He was probably usually able to control his feelings, so that they did not show; he was a secret man; and later in our life together he did hide them, but on that first visit of mine he was ruffled out of his usual control.

I have thought over all that household many, many times, and have seen things through their eyes to some extent. I have partly understood, and partly pardoned. I can now see how hateful I must have seemed to this woman, to whom life (real life) was one flighty, social gathering after another, preferably in a new dress, and who wanted liberty to bend her new husband to her ways of thought. I know, too, something of what Henery felt towards us. We were interlopers. He had been, they said, a faithful servant to Mr. Rackage, now dead. He had had considerable power and trust during the late Rackage's life and his relict's widowhood. Doubtless he had looked forward to a year of mastery there before Dennis came of age. Now, suddenly, Mrs. Rackage was married to a doctor-fellow, a terrible comedown from the late Rackage, and the doctor-fellow was there, the new master till Dennis returned. But now the new master brought in his son, not even a doctor-fellow, but apprenticed to one, a creature who mixed pills and let blood and dressed the itch. And now this creature, such as would never have darkened the doors of the Manor in the old days, was at table; he had to serve him, while he planned with his father how that old Henery might be got rid of.

How Mrs. Rackage had caught my father I could not, at

the time, imagine; any more than her friends could imagine how he had caught her. I was presently to know sorrow and to crave for consolation. I knew, then, that two lonely souls, however unlike, however certain to make each other wretched, will draw to each other from that loneliness of the soul. If you are walking the bitter nightmare, it is any companion, for God's sake. I have often longed to be able to go to them and to say : "I was harsh and a fiend to you. I understand partly, now." Often, later, I was to say to myself (concerning them) : "You acted thus and thus because you were broken-hearted." I was broken-hearted myself, then, and had learned some glimmerings of what is meant by forgiveness of sin.

After the meal my stepmother said that she had to lie down. She did not hold her hand to me this time, but gave me a curt nod, and said that perhaps I might be able to come to the Manor later in the year, meaning that she would not ask me again. My father asked me to stay for a few minutes, as he was coming out with me. We walked along the grassy lane and down its slopes to the river. There was some constraint between us. A year of absence had changed our relations, and now this new wife had made them difficult. When we were in the sunlight, which shows up all the truth in faces, I saw that he was not looking well. He had eaten little at our meal, and now that I saw him I recognised that he was aged and anxious. I said :

"I don't think you look too well. Are you feeling well?"

"No," he said, "I have not been feeling well for some time, though there is nothing organically wrong. Perhaps some of this gadding about in foreign places has been

more tiring and upsetting than I supposed. But a quieter
life here will soon set me up."

I had meant to say something about his marriage and
about Mr. Henery, but it was not possible. I could not get
the words out. He did not say anything about them either.
In between us came the ghost of my mother and the image
of Mrs. Rackage; there was to be no more intimate talk between us again.

He tried to talk about my studies, and said that Dr.
Copshrews had spoken highly of me. "But I am sorry," he
said, "that you are to be a general practitioner. It is more
fascinating to take one organ as your province, and rule it
as a King, than to come as an ambassador to every organ
in turn. But perhaps you will take to some particular
study?"

I said, that I had been much perplexed by hearts and
lungs, and wished that I could know more of them. I could
see that he was vexed that I could not care for kidneys;
hearts and lungs were trumpery matters to him, hardly
organs at all, perhaps.

"That is how you young fellows begin," he said. "Hearts
and lungs. You do not know the meaning nor the value of
either."

On leaving the Manor house, we had turned westwards
along the grassy lane. When we had gone about five hundred yards, we came upon a low brick wall, to our left. All
that country was then quite new to me; I had never been
there before. The wall was topped with railings of twisted
iron, painted blue. Through these one saw a neat and pret-
tily-kept flower-garden, of the precise, formal, Dutch type,
brought in by the Dutch King. Beyond this, standing well

back from the road, was a handsome red-brick house, with a strange structure on the roof; a sort of raised platform, with what looked like a cannon of peculiar make.

"That is Hannibal House," my father said; "an old Admiral lives there. The thing on the roof is his telescope. He is an astronomer."

We walked on together, and presently took boat and fished for jack, but without catching any. It was not a happy afternoon, but it was the type of most of the afternoons that I spent with my father thenceforward. There were not many such, of course. My stepmother did not wish to see me, and even if she had loved me, Dr. Copshrews could not spare me for more than one day in a fortnight.

Still, I went there when I could, to see my father, who did not seem able to recover his health; he was not the man he had been. Always when I went there, I had to feel the hatred of Mr. Henery. There was nothing that one could object to or speak of. He was silent, he was seemingly obsequious, his eyes would be downcast and his ears all attention, but the cold poison of his thoughts of me ate into my back at a meal, when he was serving, and seemed to strike at me like a snake's tooth when he opened the door for me. The sidelong evil of his eyes seemed to follow me home. I was the master's son, but he was the mistress's dog and meant to bite me if he could.

Nearly always, when I went there, we would walk to the river and go fishing from the riverside tavern, the "Angler's Rest." We always passed the Admiral's house. I always looked at it, and spoke of it. The Admiral had called upon my father by this time.

"He is Admiral Topsle Cringle," my father said, "an old man, very crotchety, who came to some fame years ago, destroying pirates. He lives there with his old sailor servant and so forth. He is rather a character; and is said to be a miser."

I asked in what way he was a miser, for the house was so trim that it did not look like the house of a niggard.

"It is the rumour of the parish," my father said, "that he receives his rents for his house property in gold, and stores it in his house. Did you ever hear of Edmond Quichet, or Keachy, the pirate?"

"No," I said, "never."

"Nor I," my father said, "but he was the man whom Cringle destroyed. It was a long time back; forty years ago, or wait, it must have been more. Yes, more than forty. But see, here is the Admiral. Good day to you, Admiral."

Coming towards us, on the grassy lane, was the figure of a small yet alert old man, who gave one the impression of some valorous cock-robin or weasel, who would tackle anything or anyone at any time. I have seldom seen so much good spirit put into so frail a bottle. He was frail and pale; he did not look well; his old man's skin looked unwholesome, but there was a kind of mastery in his walk and in the jut of his hat which showed that he would never say die. He wore a plain, neat suit of black, with a sword. Something in his walk showed me that he had pain in legs and shoulders; he was not giving in to that. His eye was on all things, I thought.

"Ha," he said, to my father's greeting, "Dr. Mansell, I see."

"And my son," my father said, thrusting me forward.

The Admiral took a shrewd look at me. "And what do you do, my lad?"

"I'm to be a doctor," I said.

"When I was your age," he said, "I used to think scorn of doctors. But, by George, you get us later in life. Some part of me is wanting one or other of you all the time. Could you take me to pieces and put in new works and get me to go again?"

"I'll try, sir," I said.

"By George," he answered, "that's what you all say. You'll try. You never say you can't. By George, none of you amateurs'll lay a finger on me, no matter how sick I am. An old sailor lives and dies in harness. But you are going a-fishing. I'll not keep you. Come in on your way back and tell me how you have fared."

We parted at that, but had not gone far, when we were hailed by him.

"I forgot," he said, "that I am engaged this afternoon. You must come some other time."

My father said that we should be happy to do so. When we were round the bend in the lane, my father said:

"That is an example of his crotchetiness; he liked you; then, when he thought that having us in this afternoon might interfere with his nap, he changed his mind. Did you notice his frost-bitten fingers?"

"Was that frost-bite?" I asked. "I have never before seen the result of frost-bite."

"That is frost-bite," my father answered. "And though it is always carefully covered with his hat or his wig, his left ear is gone in the same way. He said that he was sent to the North Atlantic to be ruined outside, and then to

Africa to be ruined inside. I am sorry that you aren't to
see him ; you would have liked to see Hannibal House. His
ship, in the pirate days, was the *Hannibal.*"

We went on to our fishing. On our way back, we were
met by the Admiral, who seemed to be waiting for our return.

"I was hoping that you would pass," he said. "The
friend who was to have been with me has sent word that
he cannot come. So come in, will you, doctors both, and
perhaps you will tell me what is amiss with my leg?"

That was the beginning of my acquaintance with Admiral Topsle Cringle, but for whom my life would have
been different indeed.

I just pass quickly over the next few months. I saw my
father and stepmother once or twice in each month. I
went, because I wished to see my father, but shrank from
going lest I should mar the happiness of his marriage. At
each visit, I heard more about Dennis, the faultless son,
now no doubt fully formed by foreign travel, and the nice
observation of what is choicest in civilised life. He was
soon to be at home, and soon after that to come of age, and
be the lord of the Manor. As that day drew nearer, I felt
the insolence, or veiled hatred (for he was never openly
rude, only insufferable) of Henery, to grow even greater.
He would delay opening the doors to me, when I called.
He would delay to serve me at meals, or serve me with the
worst and the skinniest bits. He would delay to answer
me, in a way that I could scarce endure, but always with
that aped obsequiousness and downcast eye. Later, I
would catch his cold eyes upon me, grey as poison, and bitter with loathing of me. Hatred is usually returned, I

think, whenever it exists. I hated that creature as I hated that house.

I am sure that my father was very unhappy. He had married in the despair of loneliness, or because his health had so failed as to impair his judgment of persons. After my mother, that radiant, merry soul, Mrs. Rackage must have been unendurable. She took him into crowds, where the empty find and the solitary forget humanity. It was at that time, too, that she introduced him to a sprightly French noble, here on some mission for the French Court, who persuaded them both to some venture of investment, which promised wealth and honour, as well as the gratitude of a King. Well, the heart-broken, in failing health, do not always act with sanity.

Dennis, we were told, was on his way back from Italy. He did not write many nor long letters, but a letter came from Grenoble to say that he was on his way to Paris. We expected him daily thenceforward; but I made three or four visits to the Manor without meeting him. No more had been heard from him; Mrs. Rackage was anxious and talked of sending to our Ambassador, to ask him to enquire. Then a note came from the missing son, to say that he had been detained unavoidably by affairs of moment. A young man of twenty was not likely to be involved in affairs of moment. "Affairs of *the* moment," my father said to me. My stepmother was much pleased at his delay, much as she longed to see her son.

"I expect," she said, "I expect that the Embassy has made use of him to unravel some intrigue. He must by this time have a distinguished acquaintance in Paris. He may well be of the greatest use to our Ministers. He has a great

instinct for politics; he always had. I do look forward to
hearing of it all from him. Ever since he was a child, he
has taken an interest in affairs and weighed the play of
parties."

I said nothing, having been assured that it was not the
play of parties which weighed with him so much as the
parties of play.

Once or twice, during those months, I went with my
father for brief visits to the Admiral. I suppose that altogether I may have passed one hour in the house. I liked the
old man, though I must say that he was as crotchety as a
swarm of bees.

It was at this time that my father began to suspect that
his investment with the noble would prove to be a total
loss. He feared to talk of it to me. God knows, I did not
urge him to talk of it. Once, as we walked together, he
said:

"Joe Copshrews likes you and speaks well of you. That
is high praise, Ned. How soon will his two apprentices
leave him?"

"One at Christmas; one a year from Christmas."

"And they are setting up for themselves elsewhere, you
say?"

"Yes."

"What I should like to see," he said, "would be yourself
in partnership with old Joe, when those two men leave
him. He is getting on, and needs a partner. Only, you see,
Ned, things have not gone very well with me of late, and
though Joe Copshrews was never a money-seeker, I fear I
cannot any longer offer what a partner in that practice
ought to pay...."

"I have plenty of time still to serve," I said. "It isn't time to think of all that yet."

"Time soon passes," he said, "and men pass even sooner. I would like to talk to old Joe. By the way, do you ever see his son, Dick Copshrews?"

"No. He never stays with his father."

"Is he still a Turkey merchant?"

"I don't know quite what he calls himself at the moment," I said. "He is a wildish fellow, with expensive tastes, they say, but with a charm."

"The charm of the worthless," my father said. "He always had that. I'm afraid he isn't much good. 'He sups up, as it were the east wind.' I fear that he may be one of the reasons why old Joe will want money in the firm."

I knew, from this, as well as from one or two little signs, that my father's affairs were going ill; thinking it over, I felt that perhaps Dr. Copshrews was sometimes pressed for money at that time. My father went on for some distance without speaking, then he said:

"Are you still all for the heart? A young man generally gets a twinge or two there."

"I'm very much for the heart," I said, "but as for twinges, no, sir."

"Do you still see the Morsoes?" These were old friends, once our neighbours in the Square.

"Yes, sir. I see them from time to time."

"Patty Morsoe must be a good-looking girl."

I blushed at this, for she was a very good-looking girl, and entirely delightful, so delightful, that the twinges had been charming to me.

"You see, Ned," my father said, "one must begin to

think of your establishment. I ought to have thought more of it. However, the French business may pull round. I saw Monsieur de Lamenois a few days ago; he said that he was assured that the factions will be cleared away by Christmas, and everything straight by mid-summer. I must just hope for the best, I suppose. It has all been the turn of the cards; things have gone contrarily for me."

"Oh, but you must not mind, sir," I said.

"I do not mind for myself," he said, "but I do mind for you. It did look so very tempting. However, if things do mend, there will be little need for either of us to trouble further about ways and means; we shall both be rich."

Like many young men, I had for some years questioned my father's judgment in many things; since his remarriage, I had come to think that he had no judgment at all. I saw now that he would be ruined. I could not prevent that now; the deed had been done. I wondered what I could do to provide for him, later on. I should be a practising physician before two years had passed. I knew, from what my friends had told me, that the beginning years of practice may be very difficult; still, as one of them had gaily said: "There is always life for a live one." I should succeed, and earn enough for us both. As to Mrs. Rackage, I felt that Dennis might look after her; I had no wish to support her. Sometimes, I thought, that perhaps I might be called on to maintain Dennis, too. All report said that he was a wild young man. I had expected to see him at home in September; he did not come, then. He wrote to say that he had been detained by important matters. I was at the Manor when the letter came, and could judge, from the faces shown, how likely the plea was; the two faces,

my father's and Mrs. Rackage's together, showed me just
what sort of a youth this Dennis was. "He will be with us
soon," Mrs. Rackage said. My father compressed his lips;
he was not so sure. My father was right. Dennis did not
come soon.

He stayed on in Paris till his mother began to fear that
she would have to go to fetch him. Then, as I learned, there
came an appeal for money to bring him home, and a dispute between my father and my stepmother as to the giving of the money. My stepmother was for sending it direct
to her son. My father, who knew that Dennis had already
received two such sums for his return journey, and had
deflected both to other uses, probably female, urged that
this sum should be sent to a factor, and kept from the
young man's hands. The dispute was sharp, but my father
carried his point, with the result that Dennis could no
longer stay in Paris, and had to return. This dispute was
the first real rift between my father and his second wife;
the money involved was Rackage money; the will that pre-
vailed was Mansell will. I thought that the quarrel would
rankle long; it did.

My father had but a shadowy knowledge of Dennis. He
had met him, but the instinct of the two had been to avoid
each other. The old man did not want the new son, at any
rate, not just at once. The young man did not want a new
father till he had had time to see what sort of a fellow he
might be. They had met, had been polite, and had then
held off and been shy. I had no wish to begin the topic of
Dennis; my own position in the new household was too
uncertain for that. One day when we were walking together, my father said:

"It is a fair house, the Manor, isn't it?"

I agreed.

"I fear," he said, "that it will not long remain so. This young man, Dennis, will fling all over the moon. It would be good, if we could find him some employ abroad, though there one has no control of him."

I said that in a few months, he would succeed to the Manor estate, and that then there could be no control; he would be his own master.

"Yes," he said, "but his mother thinks that when he succeeds, the position will steady him. She thinks that he has an instinct for position. It may be so."

He shrugged his shoulders, in a way he had, which made me feel that he knew my stepmother to be a goose in all her judgments of her son. Presently Dennis returned.

I was coming back alone from the "Angler's Rest" late one afternoon; it was sunset, with bright sky behind me and glow in front. As I drew near to the Manor, to hand in a jack I had caught, I saw coming towards me a strongly-built young man dressed in an outlandish rig of pale blue, with lace at collar and throat. He was flaunting with a swagger, elegantly poising a long cane with tassels. I had never seen anyone walk with a carriage so affected and foppish. Two little boys were watching him from the hedge with wonder and amusement. This was Dennis, I knew. Here he was. He recognised me, indeed, he had been told that he would meet me, and had come out to get it over. We met in the lane and shook hands. My first impression of him was favourable. I thought that he was not an ill-looking fellow, except that he had acquired this extraordinary manner. He had an outward ease and pretence of geniality. But after five seconds, I knew that he was sinister behind that very shallow mask.

"So you are here at last," I said. "I hope that you had a fair journey home."

"Pretty fair," he said. "I suppose you have never been abroad."

"Oh, yes," I said, "three times, but not very lately."

"But I thought you were a medico or something."

"Yes, but even so."

"God," he said, "and you can come to a place like London, after being in Paris!"

"Yes," I said ; "but have not you?"

"Yes, worse luck," he said. "It is a filthy place. I thought it was bad, but, Lord, it is worse than I thought. Now tell me, are there any girls here? Where are there some girls? In Paris, there are pretty girls at every turn. Here, you either have an old gin-bulk, or a father lying in wait, to make you marry her. What do you do for girls?"

I said that he could never lack for girls, if he wore that blue suit in public.

"Ah, you like it?" he said. "It is the last thing, in Paris, this. George, to think that I might be there now, instead of here."

"You'll get used to it," I said. "It may seem a wrench at first, but you'll settle down."

"Never," he said. "No country-squire-life for me. You medicos ought to know what is on in town. What fights are on?"

I said that I did not know of any.

We had somehow turned from the Manor and were walking slowly towards the Admiral's house. On the platform on the roof, were two figures, casting loose the telescope, for a look at the tiny crescent of the new moon. The figures were the Admiral and Will, his man.

"Ha, the Admiral," Dennis said. "That old fraud still alive. He is said to have £20,000 hidden in that house somewhere."

I said that people said much that had no foundation, that it was very unlikely that he would store such a sum in a house that had not even a watch-dog.

"No watch-dog," Dennis said. "He has that sea-servant, Will, who would fight his weight in wild-cats."

Somehow, the sight of the Admiral on the roof, had convinced Dennis that he would go no farther. He swung round for home; we sauntered back together.

"It is a bit of a strain, you must admit," he said, "to have to make up to a new sort of father at my time of life. You might tell your father that I don't intend to be ardent or domestic or filial or whatever they call it. I think it's a damned nuisance, having this upset, and the less we both do about it, and the less we pretend, the better. I shan't interfere with his domestic bliss, if he won't interfere with mine. But if you could tell him this, it would come with a better grace from you, besides, I might not do it quite as civilly. He has interfered between my mother and myself, in a way I don't approve."

"That is possible," I said.

After a few minutes, just as we were at the house, in the very last of the glow, he said :

"Well, I will be getting into an evening set out. I must get to the 'Bunch of Fives' this evening or I shall die of the fan-tods. In Paris, there would be an Assembly, **or** some rout at the Palace or the Embassy. Here one must go to the 'Bunch of Fives'."

I thought that he might have gone to his mother, in one of his first nights in England after a year abroad, but, as I learned later, he went to the "Bunch of Fives," a big, flash, sporting tavern near Charing Cross, where there were racket courts and a boxing ring. It was a well-known place; the bloods and the hawks went there.

At Christmas time, my father caught a chill, which kept him for some weeks in bed. Unfortunately, many people in London that winter had the same complaint, with fever and great debility, so that my master and I were more than busy. I could not get away to see my father till the sickliness abated with the warmer weather in March. When I did see him, I was shocked by the change in his appearance. He was grown all old and frail and shrunken; but within the shrunken body his nature seemed curiously sweet and living. Dennis had gone again to Paris, I learned, as the presence of my father angered him, and his riotous behaviour angered my father. He was living riotously in Paris, but at any rate his uproar was at a distance there. He was to be there until the end of the summer, my father said.

However, my father, after some weeks of frailty and pottering about with a stick, took again to his bed, as a very infirm old man. I was not told of this at once, for my father could not write, and my stepmother, being either lost or vexed, did not. When I did hear, through our old housekeeper, Mrs. Morgann, I went over at once, and did not at all like the case. I was not my own master then, and could not get away to Cholsington more often than once

in ten days. I felt, that my father could not live through
the summer in any case. I should have loved to have had
the care of him, but that could not be. I was grieved to
think of him in the care of that stupid, idle woman and the
dreadful Henery. But I was at the disposal of Dr. Copshrews, and with our practice as it was, and our only
other helper going, I had to be in the City. On one of my
visits, I was told that Dennis had been sent for, "to be near
his mother," and I must say that my heart sank when I
heard the news; it meant that they had given up all hope
of my father living, and were already preparing for the
funeral.

When next I could go to Cholsington, I found that Dennis had arrived, but was gone out. My father, I found, was
very weak, but inclined to sleep. He asked me to leave him
for a while, as he felt that he might sleep a little, and had
not had a good sleep for a long time.

"You go out for a walk, Ned," he said. "Then tell me
how the river looks."

I said that I would go for a short walk towards the river
and then return. I had to be at my surgery at eight that
evening, in case of a call. It was fine sunny summer
weather, not very hot, but all things full and happy, and
murmuring with flies. I always rode and walked with a
holly stick which I had cut years before; it had polished
with use to a texture like smooth old bone. I took this with
me now, for the fields so near London were never very safe
in the summer-time, on account of the footpads. I had
never been attacked, because I was young and had a look,
perhaps, of not being worth attacking, but it was always
reckoned wise to have a cudgel, if not a sword or a pistol.

I set off, alone, sadly enough, for I was fond of my father, and knew that he would not last out the morrow. I had some misgivings about going out of the house, even though he had wished it. I was grim enough in my sorrow. He had been a good man, and a good physician, who had relieved a lot of suffering. Now here he was helpless, soon to die. What was the meaning of it all? What was this life? And what was this Death, to which we all drifted? I had seen a lot of Death that year, but I had had no answer to my enquiry. Now one great thing more in my life was to be torn from me, and I should have no father any more. I was sad and bitter. I was even very bitter against my stepmother who had caught him in his loneliness, had ruined him, and had poisoned all the end of his life. What sort of thing can Life be, I asked myself, that can be so subject to Fortune? And what sort of thing was my father? What my mother had made him, or what now lay dying in the Manor? I walked savagely along to the river, and could not bear the sight of it, as it reminded me of days when my father and I had fished there, so I turned to walk back, and leaned for a long time on a stile, wishing that some footpad would creep up behind me and knock me over the pate with a black-jack or a crow, deep into my brains, and end my troubles for ever. I envied the cows in the field, for they were only bothered by the flies, and would soon, soon, be beef.

I got no help from the prospect of the fields. Presently I set off for the Manor, thinking that probably my father had sent me out, so that he might die alone: that he would die without me, and that I should never speak with him again. My way led past St. Marches, which is the parish church of Cholsington. I remember that I meant to pray there, if the door were not locked. I remember, too, that I thought: "In a few days from now, my father will be buried in the churchyard there. I shall stand by, while he will be put into the ground, and what hope shall I have of a joyful resurrection?" I knew that I should have none, no more than the cow that would soon be beef. It was a black and awful afternoon to me. Remember, I was troubled, and had seen much of the misery of death that year.

Presently, I left the fields for the road. I went slowly and sadly on for St. Marches Church, thinking, as I was to think very often in the months to come, that life is a black business, by no means worth the having.

There is a bend in that road some distance from the church; perhaps five hundred yards from it. As I drew near to this bend, I heard suddenly, from beyond it an angry outburst of noise of men, the cheers of men charging, the cry of: "Out him, boys; out him; put his light out," and the exclamation of one taken by surprise. The cries mixed at once with a noise of scuffle. I knew at once that the footpads were attacking someone.

Now, I had always heard that footpads dread an outcry more than blows. Blows they are hardened to from childhood; an outcry may raise the parish and bring them to the gallows. Instantly and instinctively, I started running towards the noise, shouting: "Hey, hey, hey. Thieves, thieves; drop it." I had my holly stick ready for a smack at someone; I was round the bend in no time.

There I saw three men attacking the Admiral. As I came round, a horrible dwarf, who was behind him, tripped him, brought him down, and kicked him as he lay. The other two struck at him as he fell or lay, but in their excitement, and with the Admiral twisting about like an eel, for all his age, I don't think they hurt him much. I ran straight at them, shouting: "Come, Billy; come, Tom," and other nonsense. One of the three thieves turned at once to deal with me. He was a cool-looking customer, who had been in tight places often enough. He had a sort of bludgeon in his hand and was very ready for me. But at that instant someone answered my shouts from one of the houses up the road. Instantly, the three thieves left their prey and ran for it, through gaps in the hedge, into the field and away. I suppose the whole affray took only a very few seconds. I had and have vivid memory of it all, especially of the three men; one cool man, of a compact, medium build, ready for anything; the second, a big man, burly and stupid, with a bush of black stubble on his jaw; and the third, the dreadful dwarf, with a face with a maggot, with no teeth, and a wheeze rather than speech: "Tear him up, boyth; tear him up, dear boyth." However, there they all were running for life. I remembered the saying, "A bridge of gold to a flying foe." I shouted at them, and saw them hurry on, in different directions. I turned to help the Admiral, who was sitting up, dazed and shaken, but full of fight.

"Ha, Ned, my lad," he said. "Help me up. We'll bring them to book."

I had an arm round him, to help him up, when he gave a whimper of pain.

"There goes my knee again," he said.

Dennis came running up. Half a dozen men were running to us.

"By George, Ned, my lad. You went for the three of them," the Admiral said. "See there," he said to the men about us, "there go the knaves. I'd have been in a bad way, but for this Ned here, who tackled the three of them."

He was excited and rather breathless; the knees of his breeches had split, and he was very dusty. I dusted his coat and supported him. We were in the centre of a crowd by this time.

"They got me by surprise," he said. "Jumped out of the hedge on me. I got a bat on the shoulder. My game knee's gone again. This lad, Ned here, Dr. Mansell's son, isn't it? He tackled the three. I'm all right again."

"Just try, sir, if you can walk at all," I asked.

"Not with my knee," he said. "No. I'll have to be taken. But after those three birds, someone."

Somebody said that Joe and Arthur and some of the young fellows had gone after the thieves.

I said : "We must carry the Admiral home and look at this knee. Give me a hand, Dennis," I said. "Clasp and cross hands, so as to make a seat."

"Not Dennis, no, thanky," the Admiral said. "I've a lot too much respect for my stern to put it on any hand of his, thanky."

Dennis gave him, and me too, an evil glance and stood aside. A man in shirt-sleeves, who had been working in a garden, clasped hands with me; others helped the Admiral on to the seat and supported him there. We set off for the Admiral's house. At that point, we were not very far from it, by the field-path. As we went along, all the story passed from mouth to mouth. When the descriptions of the men were repeated, some said :

"Why, those were the men I saw in the churchyard; a little man, with his feet in bandages, not in proper shoes; one of them a big black sullen fellow."

The Admiral, from time to time, said:

"I'll bring those three birds to book, if they have to carry me to give evidence. It might have gone hard with me, for they had me down, but for this lad here, who went for the three of them. This Ned, here, is a doctor, to heal people, but if he'd been a fighter to smash people, by George you'd have heard of him."

Presently, the Admiral stopped us, and said: "Has anybody gone to Lambert?"

Lambert was the village constable, a very honest, good man, whose wife kept a shop or store in the village.

One of the men said: "I believe young Spilltimber went to call John, sir."

"That won't do," the Admiral said. "One of you; Peter, there; run across the fields to John Lambert and tell him I was set upon. Tell him he must get some horsemen to ride out at once over the hill, to get those three men. He can't fail to catch them. Tell him to order any horsemen in the Fair. Tell him I said so."

Peter said: "If you please, sir, I'm not sure where I'll find Mr. Lambert with the Fair going on."

"Well, search till you are sure," the Admiral said. "Off with you. Those men have only a short start and they've got to be caught. One horseman can take the three of them. What do you stay for? Run."

Peter ran; we lifted the Admiral and went on.

I suppose news spreads almost as quickly as light. How it spreads I never can tell, but it goes across a countryside, to the remotest spots, as though on the wings of the wind. We were only half-way to Hannibal House when the Admiral's household met us, his servant, Will Coxwain, Mrs. Coxwain and Polly, their daughter. All had heard that the Admiral had been laid weltering in his gore by armed assassins.

"Come on here, Will, confound you," the Admiral said. "Take over from the doctor here. He's carried me all the way from church."

"I trust you're not badly hurt, your honour," Will said, taking over from me.

"Hurt, no; my game leg's gone again though. You'd better take me to the arm-chair by the fire. Now, Mrs. Will and Polly, don't pull those faces. You're not going to bury me this time, however nice you look in black."

We dropped most of our crowd at this point, for the Admiral told them to top their booms and up killick, that is, to clear out. We four got the Admiral into his arm-chair by the fireplace. He was, by this time, showing signs of wear. He had been hit, batted and flung, as well as taken by surprise. Tough old bird as he was, he was glad to sink into the chair and call for a dram, which, by the way, he did not drink when it came. Instead of drinking from it, he held it, as though it were a sceptre, giving him authority to rule.

I said : "Sir, you have had a fall, and I thought that one of those ruffians hit you in the side. Would you let me run over your ribs, to see if anything is broken?"

"No, thanky," he said. "I'll have no amateurs running over my gear. I'll have in Gubbins, my own surgeon, later, thanky. But you, Will, and Mrs. Will and Polly here, you

look at this young fellow. Those dogs had me down, by
George; caught me fair by the lee, with the watch on deck
asleep. You young fellow, you Ned, or Mansell, or whatever your name is, you haven't done with me yet. He ran
up as those dogs got me down and tackled the three of
them. They'd have laid me out and stripped me to a bare
gantline, but for him; but he tackled the three and made
them fly. By George, boy, we'll have those three on Tyburn
tree this very autumn assize."

I said: "I only shouted and raised an alarm; and now,
if you won't let me look to the bones I will go. I must go, in
any case, to see my father."

"Ah, yes," the Admiral said. "I've been sorry to hear of
your father. But see here, Ned, come in to-morrow and tell
me how he is."

I came away after that, attended to the door by Will,
who said:

"I am sure, sir, we servants can't thank you enough for
what you have done for the master, and then to tackle
three ... Three is long odds, sir."

I said that they had run when the alarm was given; they
had not fought.

"No, but still, sir, three to one is three to one."

After the door had shut upon me and I had turned towards the Manor, I found Dennis waiting for me.

"How is my father?" I asked.

"I haven't been at home," he said. "I do not know how
he is. But you have had a stroke of luck, if you know how
to play your cards. He has neither kith nor kin. If you give
him a little soap and sawder, he'll perhaps leave you some

of his plunk; he's as rich as a Nabob. He's got £20,000 stowed away in that house in gold alone."

"Nonsense," I said. "No man would stow gold in a lonely house like that."

"The fact is well known," Dennis said. "He collects all his rents in gold, everybody knows that. He's got a secret room in the house and puts the gold there."

At that moment I saw some men returning from the chase of the thieves; I called to them:

"Did you catch them?"

They said: "No, they got clear away down the hill the other side, and had too good a start."

As I walked on with Dennis, he returned to his talk of the Admiral.

"Those chaps to-day knew all about him," he said. "It's quarter-day, or very near it; they knew he's been drawing his rents. His pockets were stuffed with it, as you could see. Didn't he bulge with gold, when you lifted him?"

Now his pockets had been full of gold, there was no doubt of that.

I said yes. He had seemed to have money on him; and I wondered why Will had not been with him as a guard on the way home.

"He's a secret old bird," Dennis said. "He has his claws into me, worse luck, or I'd be putting in for a mention in his will. He is an old miser, who'll cut up very warm, and if I could be at the cutting I would be. I'd not miss a shot at all that plunk for want of a little soft soap. I'd rather get money by being polite than by giving purges and vomits, but tastes differ, it seems. However, you may not have much chance of seeing the Admiral much longer."

There was something of a threat in this last remark which I could not quite fathom.

When we were about one hundred yards from the Manor, we came round a slight bend into sight of it. As we turned this bend I knew within my heart that my father had died. On the instant I saw Henery come round to the front of the house with a package of crape, which he proceeded to tie upon the door-knocker. My father had died some quarter of an hour before, while I was in Hannibal House.

Few can die without almost breaking the heart of someone; there is little solace at the time of death. It was a shattering blow to me, for I had somehow been hoping that presently I should come to some happier way of life, in which my father and I might see more of each other. Now he was dead.

I could not go to the Manor more than once again before the funeral. That once was enough, perhaps, for I found Dennis drunk and my stepmother passing from tears into hysterical screaming, and then back to tears again. Somehow, the Admiral learned on which day I should be there, and contrived for a letter to be there to meet me. It was a wise, kind and manly letter; it was a dear comfort to me then.

It was a time of much summer sickness; I remember that I found it difficult to find a man to take my work, while I rode over to the funeral. My father was buried in the St. Marches churchyard. Few were at the burying. His old friends had hardly seen him since my mother died, and he had made few friends since. Mrs. Rackage's friends sent their empty coaches to the churchyard, "out of respect," as it was called. Dennis was not at the funeral. He had gone away the night before, they told me, "so as to be out of the way." I had hoped that he might be away, yet when I found that he was not there, I had the unreasonable thought, that he was a scoundrel to be away from his mother in her grief, whatever he may have thought of her second choice.

After the funeral I went back to the Manor to hear the will read. I knew, by this time, that my father's fortune was gone into the bottomless pit of the French adventure; there was nothing left, except books and furniture, and all this went to his widow, including my mother's portrait, as I supposed. I had his gold watch and two rings. You must not think me mercenary or heartless. Many things in my youth made me savage; this was one of the things; and I want you to know the worst of me; I fear it is the greater part of me.

When the will was read and the men had gone, I was for going, too; but Henery came in and said:

"The mistress asks you not to go till she has spoken with you."

I said that I would go to her.

He replied that she was coming down at once. I waited for some time, but she did not come. I rang the bell, meaning to send a message to her, to ask if I might see her at once, as I had far to go, and much to do before bed. No one answered the bell, though I rang three times. I went out with a candle to the head of the basement stairs and called. No one was below; all had gone to the bailiff's across the garden, to cheer themselves up after that day of funeral. As no one was there, and it was necessary for me to go, as sick men would be needing me in the city, I went to my stepmother's room. I found her in bed, with a case of cordials at her side; the room smelt of these strong waters; she was weeping, in a maudlin way, and wiping her jewels, of which she had a good store in cases on the bed. She had not combed her hair in that day of grief; her face was partly made-up, partly rubbed-off, or wept-off. Her room was in the worst state of untidiness, with clothes, wraps, stockings and shoes littering everywhere. She tried to be cross with me for entering there, but I told her that I had no choice but to go, and wished to take my leave. I had meant never to see her again, unless pressed to do so. I had expected to be allowed to go without any invitation, but in her grief and loneliness, her sorrow, confusion and semi-drunkenness, she said she hoped that I would come for Dennis's coming-of-age a fortnight later; she hoped that I would do that. I said that I might be able to come in the morning, early, just to leave a little token and come away. She had been my father's wife; I could hardly refuse her that; but I felt savage at the thought of buying a little token for this man. I said I hoped that her grief might pass.

"No," she said, "it won't pass. I shall go from it, before it goes from me. I've that in my side now that must kill soon. Then I shall be at rest."

I thought she meant that her grief for my father was soon to kill her, but as she might have meant that she was ill, I asked her if she would not see a physician, who might recommend some course likely to benefit.

She replied that she thanked God that her heart's life was more to her than her body's welfare; that her flesh

might ache or break, for all she cared, since her heart's
darling had gone, almost as soon as she had had him.
From this passionate outcry, she passed suddenly to a
mood of much shrewdness. She asked if there were things
of my father's which I might like to have. I said that, no
doubt, there were books and personal belongings, such as
walking-canes, surgical implements and so forth; as well
as one most precious thing, my mother's portrait. I had
thought that she wished me to have these things. So she
had, but in her own way.

"Very well, then," she said, "I will have these things
valued, and if they be not above your compass, your lawyers shall pay me for them out of your yearly allowance."

I was somewhat startled at this: however, I was all for
having the things.

"Very well, madam," I said, "if you will have them valued, and will let me know the amounts set upon the things,
I will see what I can afford."

"You cannot expect me to go to the expense of the valu-
ation myself," she said, as though I had been trying to rob
the widow.

"No, madam," I answered, "I will cause my lawyers to
do all that."

"I think not," she said. "Since cruel Fortune makes me
the seller, the valuing must be done by my agents, that is,
if my son decides that it shall be done, for, of course, all
that is now mine will be his."

I must say that the thought of Dennis owning my
mother's portrait was more than I could relish.

"Well, madam," I said, "if you will presently discuss
it with your son, or let me do so, I shall be grateful."

She began to shudder here and asked me to put a rug about her. Her shuddering shook her presently into another burst of weeping. At the end of it she seemed ready for another bout of business with me. No doubt we should have had it, and passed from it into a dispute unworthy and miserable, but at that moment we heard, coming up the stairs, a slow and stealthy footstep. Someone was creeping slowly up the stairs, waiting almost at every step to listen. I was not certain that there were not two people.

"What is that?" she asked, in a low voice. "Who is that on the stairs?"

"Hush," I whispered, "it may be Henery, or one of the other servants coming to know if all is well."

The footsteps, at this point, made a little rush, followed by a stumble and an ejaculation; then there was another stealthy pause. After another little rush, which brought the feet to the landing, there was a pause and a sigh of relief. I heard the voice of Dennis saying:

"Oh the dangers of those crags and presserpushes. But I beat 'em; I got up 'em."

"It is your son," I said to my stepmother.

Going to the door with a candle I looked out. He was standing on the landing, holding on to the banisters at the top of the stairs and breathing with drunken heaviness. He carried a riding switch in his hand. I had the impression that he believed that he had just ridden up the Alps. He was dressed in an extreme of foolish fashion. Can you imagine a suit of clothes so extreme that it can take to itself a human body and compel it to display it? This suit had taken him; he was its slave, bent to its folly, cramped to its whim. He was scented with essence and with powder, rather dirty, for he had fallen, and rather stinking, for he had been at a ring, among smokers, and had drunken much spirit.

"Dennis, dear," his mother cried, "come in and talk to me."

"I'm coming, as soon as my horse has got his wind," he said.

He steadied himself and took some deep breaths. Then, as though urging on a tired horse, he switched his thighs and called: "Get up, now," and so went unsteadily past me, into the bedroom. I followed him there. He went about the room whinnying at the tumbled clothes, but at last brought himself to a stop at the foot of the bed. Here, some memory of events came to him. He lurched a little and said: "Funeral go off all right, hey?" This question won no answer, so he repeated it in a different form: "The solemn 'casion settled?" As this had no answer, he seemed to feel that something was amiss. "Mother," he said, "you ought to get a new maid a man can look at without spewing." He was uncertain on his legs. Looking about him, he saw an arm-chair heaped with his mother's clothes. He lurched to this and fell into it. "Got into it, first try," he said. "Thing never done before. I made forty-five to-day, backing Pugg against the what-you-call."

He seemed to be settling to sleep, after this. Mrs. Rackage was weeping.

"Dennis," she moaned, "come here and kiss me."

"All right," he said, rising unsteadily. "I will go as far as that."

He made some short lurches towards the bed and did at last reach it. He kissed her, and seemed inclined to sleep there.

"Dennis," she said, "it's a sad thing, when a man comes home on the day of a funeral to kiss his mother smelling of drink."

"A damn sight better than garlic, Mother," he said gaily. "But I never could argue with a lady. It's a thing the *monde* forbids. The Pugg was in form this afternoon. In the very best style. Just as you were going off to the solemn 'casion, he knocked the what-you-say just into a cocked hat. I shall buy you a new husband with the winnings."

I had to go back to my work, so I said: "Good night, I must go."

"Good night," Mrs. Rackage said. "You will come, if you can, to the Birthday, will you not?"

I said that if I could, I would.

Dennis looked up at this. "Yes," he said, "he must come to the Birthday. I've a special reason for his coming to that."

"It will have to be early in the morning, then," I said. "If I might come to an early breakfast, it ought to be possible for me."

"The earlier the better," Dennis said. "It could not be too early, before breakfast, or anything."

I thanked him, and then thought to ask if I could help him to his room.

"Help me to my room," he said. "Who needs help? I hope I've not sunk so low as that yet. Help me to my room, he says. Tirry, my jock, go help some of your sick ones in the city."

There was no chance of staying longer in the room without starting a brawl, so I came away. As I went down the stairs I heard a crash in the room, for he had upset his mother's dressing-table with all its dressing-set of blue and white oriental china. He fell on top of it, I hope.

Outside, in the lane, was Will Coxwain, with a note for me from the Admiral, which I read by the lantern. It apologised for not having been present at my father's funeral, but said that he had been shaken by the thieves and was not able to use his knee yet. He hoped to see me soon. Something made me ask Will if he had been waiting there long.

"A good time, your honour," he said. "I don't visit at this house. I was waiting for you to come out."

It was a strange phrase, which stuck in my memory.

"Look, Will," I said, "I cannot write an answer to this now. Will you thank the Admiral for me, with all my heart, and say that I shall be writing to him to-morrow? I shall not be here again until Mr. Dennis comes of age. I shall be over early then." (Here I named the day.) "But I will not fail to look in and pay my respects to the Admiral then."

"You may depend upon it, sir," Will said, "that the Admiral will be glad to see you. He thinks the world of you, sir, for what you did, and so do we all."

"I suppose they never caught any of the three men," I said.

"No, sir," Will said. "They let them get away, it's my belief. They could have caught them if they'd a mind to. But it's the bearing witness against them to the death that people are afraid of. But the Admiral would have spoken against 'em. He's one of the old sort, sir."

Whatever sorrows and bitterness a doctor's life may hold, the chances are, that one day of general practice will bring him someone to whom Fate has been more cruel. I found it so, in those days, and perhaps learned to try not to be sorry for myself. I had expected some word about my father's belongings; none came to me. Soon it was time to consider what gift to buy for Dennis.

After thinking of a pocket-corkscrew, I decided on a scarf-pin with the image of a bull-dog's head upon it. He could wear that with applause, I thought, in the circles he frequented, at the "Bunch of Fives" and in the Bear Ring, up Black Dog Alley. With this in my pocket for him I rode over to Cholsington, left my horse at the inn and walked up to the house. I should have said that we were very busy at that time; it was understood that I was to hurry back to the city before the doctor went out upon his rounds at half-past ten.

I had started from the city very early. It was striking eight by St. Marches Church when I knocked at the Manor front door. As usual, I was kept waiting some little time, so I rang and knocked again. Henery opened to me with his usual cold insolence. We did not wish each other good morning. I asked if Mrs. Rackage were in. "My mistress is not yet risen," he answered, and opened the door into a sitting-room to the right of the front door. Dennis was standing in the room. Henery came in after me and closed the door behind him. Dennis was dressed for riding, and held a riding-switch. He was just beneath the portrait of his father.

I mentioned the portrait a little while back. I looked at it now. It showed the late Rackage in a red coat, holding a fowling-piece. In the morning light it showed up well. I glanced from father to son, and thought how like they were, and what sinister faces they both had. I had sometimes thought the faces sullen. Now, as I looked, I felt that there was something worse in them than sullenness; there was something dangerous; there was a threat. Sometimes, I have seen this threat in leaf or berry; now here it was in faces.

No one could have failed to feel that something was wrong; something evil was meant. The two looked at each other, said nothing, then looked at me.

I looked at Dennis and said: "I congratulate you on your coming of age, and wish you many happy returns of your birthday." I had not wished to say any such thing. I said it, though it went against the grain to say it. His pale face seemed to grow a shade paler and a sort of gleam of sweat came out on his brow. He switched his legs once or twice and licked his lips. Outside in the hall there was a noise as of a trunk or box being shifted; it seemed to tumble down the last few stairs right into the hall. Dennis seemed to draw assurance from the noise. He licked his lips again and beat his legs. At last he spoke.

"You know I'm of age. That means this place is mine. I'm master here. There are some precious traps of yours and your father's here; they're being put out of doors now. Get out of doors with them and don't come here again. Is that quite clear?"

"Perfectly," I answered. "But your mother was my father's wife. I should be glad to take a formal leave of her. I am glad to be quit of you on any terms."

He sweated rather more on the brow at that. "My mother agrees with me," he said. "She wishes the connection to end. She wants no leave. My orders suffice."

He walked swiftly to the door at that; Henery opened to him. Standing at the door, he called to the garden lad, who was in the hall.

"Have you got that box of things, Joe?"

Joe said: "Yes, sir."

"Fling it out of doors into the lane, then. Get it out."

It was a little too heavy to fling, as it contained mainly books; Joe had also a poor man's sense of the value of good things; he was not going to inflict wilful damage upon a well-made trunk. He lifted the box down the steps into the lane, and then came back into the hall.

"Your things are out now," Dennis said. "Now follow them, or shall we put you?"

"You had better not try to put me," I said. "You'd be called to an account which might upset your plans."

"Get out, damn you," Dennis said.

It was not a pleasant scene. In the door were Dennis (something like a fat wolf), and Henery (like a viper). In the hall was Joe, who had been plainly warned that I was to be flung out by force. Beyond Joe, just round the sweep of the stair, were Martha and Tryphena, the two maids, all ears and eyes. I do not doubt that all of these last-named three took the view of Henery, that I was an interloper, following in the steps of my interloping father. I said that I should be pleased to know whether Mrs. Mansell, my father's widow, had caused those of my father's effects which she wished to sell, to be valued. Dennis, who was very white and twitching at the nose, seemed to sputter, but did not answer.

"She may answer my lawyers perhaps," I said.

It is a grim thing to be pitched or ordered out of a house.

I suppose few who are so ordered go with dignity; probably I did not. I went with a flaming rage, which could
have cheerfully murdered. I had some thought of smash-
ing Dennis in the face, though it would have been fighting
three against one. I looked him in the eye, and for all his
sputter knew that he was afraid. I passed him and looked
Henery in the eye. He looked back, and at the end of his
look gave a little nod with his head, as though to say:
"Now you know who is master." I think that he made
some half-gesture, after I had passed, as though to seize
me, and hurry my going, which Dennis checked. I looked
next at the lad Joe and at the two maids, as they at
me. Then I was outside the door, which Joe slammed
behind me.

There I was, put out and shut out, with my father's
trunk in the lane in front of me. I went down the steps to
the trunk. It was a small leather trunk, which I well remembered. I had seen Joe lifting it, and knew that it was
heavy. I kept my back to the house, for I knew that the
maids and Joe were watching me from one window and
Dennis and his man at the other; I could hear their laughter. I should have said that it was a bright October morning, now that the morning haze had lifted. The lane was
dusty. The big elm, exactly opposite the front door, had
one little low branch covered with bright yellow leaves;
all the rest were still green. I noticed that and shall remember it till I die. To one side of the elm tree was a pent-
house, in which a farm-cart stood. It had shafts of a faded
scarlet colour, some rusty iron-work and chains. I remember that a little black-and-white kitten came out and
smelled at the chain and then whisked away. I stood as a

man stunned, watching all this from dead in front of the front door.

Presently a little boy whom I knew came along the lane. He was sucking the seeds of scarlet hips.

"Bill," I said, "if you are passing the Stevenses' cottage, will you ask Tuck to come with a barrow to take this trunk?"

Bill stared at me; he stood still, sucked his seeds, and stared.

"Yes, Mr. Ned," he said, at last.

He went on, then, still sucking seeds, but he looked round again to stare. What had happened to me? All this time, the eyes in the house were on me; they burned right into my back. Glancing to my right, after Bill, I saw the gardeners and farm-men, craning over a gate to watch me. I was the late master's son, kicked out by the rightful master; there was a joy in that. They stopped Bill to ask what I had said to him.

I was watching this, to my right, while the maids in the house giggled behind me and my ears burned and my blood boiled, when I heard the noise of wheels and voices to my left. Looking in that direction I saw the Admiral, being driven by Will Coxwain. He kept no horse, but hired a pony and cart from "The Three Toms" inn, near the church. He had hired these now, and there he was. They drove up to the door and there halted. Both the Admiral and Will had their eyes fixed upon me from the first moment they first saw me. I do not doubt that I was looking strangely.

"What's all this?" the Admiral asked. "Why are you like this?"

"I've been asked to leave," I said. "I'm just waiting for a wheelbarrow."

"Asked to leave," the Admiral said. "I don't understand. Who has asked you to leave?"

"The heir," I said.

"What, this morning? On his birthday? Do you mean that he turned you out?"

"Yes."

"Well," the Admiral said, "that doesn't explain the wheelbarrow. What is the wheelbarrow?"

"I asked for one," I said, "to take this trunk of my father's books to the inn."

"Pitched the books out, too," the Admiral said, "this new heir of eight hours' standing."

At this moment the door was opened; Dennis and Henery were there.

"Good morning, Admiral," Dennis said. "I wonder you stay talking to this itch-curer here."

"It's no concern of yours," the Admiral said, "to whom I talk. I was coming to wish you the top of your tide; but since you've insulted my friend here, I'll wish you one in your snout from an Irish hand and three with a boot in your transom. Bear a hand, Will, and get the doctor's trunk on board. And you, Ned, my lad, get in with me and drive me home to breakfast. You'll stay with me, henceforth. Leave this young dog to the rooks who'll presently pluck him."

Will, who had been standing at the pony's head, took my trunk, shifted a case of wine that was in the cart, and stowed the trunk beside it.

"That's one good thing," the Admiral said, "the heir

doesn't get that dozen of port we brought him. That'll go home with us."

I explained that my horse was at "The Pruning Knife," and that I had to ride back to the city.

"Right, Will," the Admiral said, "just nip along to 'The Pruning Knife,' for the doctor's horse; we'll go back the way we came."

I had climbed in beside the Admiral, had taken the reins, and had turned the pony-cart. Will went off to the "Knife" to fetch my horse.

As we turned, Dennis, who was white with vexation, called : "Please don't trouble to call again."

The Admiral laughed. I drove on ; the old pony stepped out. I felt that Dennis had lost the round after all.

"Not he, by the Lord Harry," the Admiral said, as we drove, "not he. A man who fights three against one for me isn't going to be flung on the road by any young whipper-snapper who smells like the swell-mob. Turned twenty-one five minutes since, and wants to be lord and master, does he? He'll not be master of much a year hence, the way he's shaping. Pitch you into the street, bag and baggage, as though you were the boot-boy caught filching sugar. He made his mistake and so he'll find. But enough of him."

I said : "I hope, sir, you find yourself none the worse for the tussle the other day?"

"No, none to speak of," he said. "My knee hurts a little, but I'm used to that. I'm sad they didn't catch those three birds, for we make good rope in England, still; and three better lads for rope don't breathe. I'd have caught all three if I'd had a horse there. I've not seen you properly since that day; but I'll see you now at least. But there is Jimmy from the inn. Just pull up at the gate, Ned, will you? Jimmy'll take the pony back. And give me your arm, for my knee is none too safe. I got hit with a wad or a rammer-head or something thirty years ago. I don't rightly know what it was that did hit me. But it's been a sad annoyance, one time or another."

I pulled up at the open gate of Hannibal House, where a strange, roguish, clever-looking man, named Jimmy, took charge, and helped the Admiral out. I gave the old man my arm and walked with him up the brick walk to the door. The sun was bright on everything. The little brass guns on each side of the door shone like gold. The ferocious, bearded, swarthy figure-head of Hannibal, which had once dipped into so many strange seas, had been newly-painted "proper" as the heralds call it, with a flowing scarlet cloak and golden cuirass. As we drew near, Mrs. Coxwain opened the door to us.

"Ha, Mrs. Will," the Admiral said, "as soon as Will comes with the horse, let him bring the Spanish Admiral to my room here. Then we'll have breakfast at once." He led the way to his sitting-room, where there was a fire, to which he went at once. "By George, I feel the cold," he said. "I used not to, but now I do."

I said: "It is a brisk morning, sir. It froze early this morning a little."

"Yes, but I feel it more; much more than I did. It's this damned Anno Domini, that gets us all," he said. He left the fire, came over to me, and took both my hands, looking earnestly into my face. "I'd have been a lot colder if you hadn't run up when you did," he said. "You saved me from those three."

"Sir," I said, "I really did nothing. I didn't fight. I ran up and made a noise, and they turned tail. I don't think they would have harmed you; just snatched your watch and purse and bolted."

"No, no, Ned," he said, "those men weren't going to leave a witness. I gave myself up for lost, though I don't lose heart readily. They meant to kill me. And I was down and the wind knocked out of me. That middle-sized man was a killer. I knew I was done for. You saved my life."

"I'm very glad I was there and able to help, sir," I said, "but I did nothing, except yell. The middle-sized man would have licked me, if he'd only stood."

"He'd have licked me if you hadn't come, I know," the Admiral said, "and put my light out, what's more. But here comes Will with the Spanish Admiral."

Will had come on with the horse almost as quickly as we had come with the pony. He had slipped on a white apron and gloves, and there he was with a big silver tray on which stood an uncorked old wine bottle which diffused a fragrance all over the room.

"Ha, there's the Admiral," the Admiral said. "None of your damned commodores and post-captains have that perfume of Araby the Blest. I got that years ago from a Spanish Admiral. Not much of it left, alas, but then, there's not much left of me."

"I hope plenty still, your honour," Will said.

"Not too much," he answered. "But how much of this, have we? Is it as much as a dozen?"

"Fourteen bottles, your honour."

"It'll last my time," the old man said. "Fourteen Christmases and fourteen New Years Days at half a bottle apiece. I might stretch it out as long as that. But come now, the doctor cannot wait. Will, go call all hands on deck. Fetch your wife and Polly here, and bring more glasses."

While Will went to fetch them, the Admiral said: "That's Will Coxwain, my servant, a man of gold. He'll be your servant for life, because you saved me that time. And he'll only have one grudge against you, that it was you and not he that scattered the ruffians. He'll be jealous of that just as long as he lives; but he's your friend, Ned, and you'll find he'll stick in any weather, like an old tarred hat. He's a good man."

"Was he in the *Hannibal* with you, sir?" I asked.

"No, no, Ned," he said. "He doesn't go back as far as the *Hannibal*. Why, the *Hannibal's* ancient history; not many old *Hannibals* knocking about now. But here come the lasses that love the sailors. Come on here, Mrs. Will; come in here, Polly."

Will came in with the two women; one of them was his wife, a tall, very pale woman, with strangely beautiful dark brown hair, which one could not help noticing. She had an intelligent face, with a look of extraordinary good humour; it was this good humour, I suppose, which had kept her hair from turning grey, for she must have been fifty, and had not one grey hair. The other woman was their daughter, aged about twenty; she was a strongly-built, fresh-coloured girl, with a look of great gaiety. She was inclined to giggle now, but was abashed by the Admiral and myself.

"Here you all are," the Admiral said. "Now, dress-up to the deck-seam, and hear all, fore and aft. This gentleman is Dr. Mansell, who saved my life the other day; tackling three, unarmed. Now I want you, Mrs. Will and Polly and Will, here, to shake hands with him. No mock modesty, no blushing, now. The fair loves to welcome the brave. To it, now, Polly." It was something of a trial to them, but they did it with a good grace and simple feeling. "Now," the Admiral said, "now we'll down the Spanish Admiral in the best of all healths. One and all is our motto." He went to the tray and filled five glasses with the wine, which sent its warm sweet heady perfume about the room, as though all Spain were blossoming there. He handed glasses to the company, then lifted his, and said: "Let's drink to Mr. Mansell and our better acquaintance." They drank to me with a real warm enthusiasm, calling my name. I thanked them, and said that I'd done nothing but shout, but that I would like to drink to the second part of the toast, so we drank.

"And now," the Admiral said, "now that we're better acquainted, I want to say this. Dr. Mansell here saved my life. He is to come in here just as he chooses and when he chooses. If he wants a meal or a bed, there'll be either for him here, at any time. I don't see many people, but I'll see the lad who tackled three. And now, as the doctor has to hurry away, let's have breakfast along. But I want the doctor to promise first, to come in to a dinner here on one day in each week."

I said, that for the next year I should be at the work of Dr. Copshrews, and could not be sure when I could come, but that I gladly would come when I could. I thought that probably he would not want to be bothered with me. Young as I was, I knew how little a general invitation may mean. I supposed that we should have this one rather merry breakfast, and then see each other perhaps once in a year or so. He was old, I was young; and we lived at different ends of the town.

I soon found that he meant what he said, about my being welcome and wanted. He wrote to me afterwards, in a strain that made me feel that I ought to go. I thought it absurd, to be praised for what I had done; but it was no good telling him that I had done nothing. He believed that the three men would have killed him if I had not come up. Well, perhaps he was right. They might have. A bat on the head, meant to stun, may well kill an old man, or a young one for that matter. I, for my part, was sure that they had not meant to kill him, but that if I had entered the battle they would have killed me. I have always held that luck is more frequent among soldiers than military skill. But putting all that aside there was a reason for the Admiral's interest in me. Age is touched by youth. This old, crotchety, solitary sailor, after living all his life in the loneliness of sea-command, or the loneliness of the country, did suddenly feel, through my presence, that he had somehow missed something. I found, within a few weeks, that he was eager for me to be there. He was looking on me almost as a son. This was a joy to me. I was lonely, too, as only a young man in a city can be. It was a joy to me to have this house, to which I could come to certain welcome. It was not a home, of course, but the welcome was very real.

In the winter, with the days so short, I could not go

over often, but by the end of March I found that I was there two or three times in each month. It was at the end of March that the Admiral told me that my stepmother had died in Paris of one of the spring feverish complaints, which had overstrained her heart. She had gone abroad soon after my father's death, to winter abroad, as she said, because she could not stand the English winter. I do not doubt that the real cause of her going was the riot of Dennis, who made the Manor very quickly no place for a lady. I could not mourn for her. She had, as I reckoned, robbed me of my father and of my inheritance. She had never sold me my mother's portrait, which now passed from her direct to Dennis. This hurt and angered me more than I can well say. She and her son did me much evil: I have not learned to think tenderly of either of them. I have been told that this is a sign that I shall suffer from them in another life. Grant me the night of nothing, rather.

She had been buried three weeks when I first heard of her death. I suppose I ought to have written a note of condolence to Dennis; I did no such thing. Those two had brought nothing but unhappiness to me; that one of them was out of life altogether, and the other (as I thought) out of my life, was a satisfaction to me.

I was told at Cholsington, where rumour often spoke untruth, that when Mrs. Rackage asked Dennis to go to her in Paris, at her first falling ill, he delayed, so that he might see a prize-fight, in which he was one of the backers. The fight was between a black boxer known as the Jouncer (to whom Dennis was patron), and a white man called Young Noll; it made a great stir in London, for the black beat the Englishman. I know that Dennis attended the fight and that Mrs. Rackage died in Paris before Dennis arrived. She was buried in Paris, I heard, and so she passes from the story. I suppose few thought of her again.

For myself, for a young man whose prospects had been much blasted by this unlucky second marriage of my father, I was not unhappy. I liked my profession. I very much liked old Copshrews. I found a wide variety of practice and interest in the daily work of the consulting- and dispensing-rooms. I was able to watch the work of all the ablest living surgeons, and to meet all the brightest and most thoughtful of the young men studying medicine. I belonged to a club of these; we met twice a week for discussion and distraction at a tavern long the haunt of medical students. I had time for some reading, and for the examination of subjects, but perhaps not so much of either as I should have liked. I had friends, too, and the enchanting Patty Morsoe. On the whole, for a young man, I was happy, busy and interested, a little bitter for my years, perhaps, when I thought of the Rackage marriage, but still, on the whole, compared with what was soon to come, in a state of blissful happiness. Who knows Eden till he loses it?

Certainly, in that spring, it was a joy to me on a free day to ride away out of the city, off the stones on to the turf, to a welcome at Hannibal House; it was real welcome, too. People talk a lot of rubbish. They say that it is bad for a man to be liked and praised. Believe me, more are ruined by the want of liking and praising than by having too much of them. I know that that cheer of praise at Hannibal would often carry me gladly through a hard week.

I must give some short description here of Hannibal
House and its inmates.

First, then, as to the house.

It stood in its garden, well back from the grassy lane.
It was a comfortable, pleasant-looking, longish house of
red-brick with white window-frames. It was older than it
looked. Its late owner had re-faced it, to make it conform
more to the Dutch fashion then in vogue. It had a ground-
floor, and a main upper-floor, with great attics under the
roof. It was straightforward in its design, like a ship. A
long corridor ran along the back of both the floors. Most
of the rooms opened from these corridors, and had windows to the front of the house.

Over the front door was the figure-head of the frigate
Hannibal, in which Admiral Cringle had come to fame.
On each side of the door stood a brass three-pounder gun,
in a wooden carriage; each gun always shining like gold
from Will's hand. In front of each gun was a garland, or
pyramid of little cannon-balls, each painted red.

The house, inside, was something like a ship. It was
simply and sparely furnished, and kept very clean. The
floors of the corridors were scrubbed daily and left without matting. Perhaps the first impression made on the
visitor was that the house was bare. The rooms had few
things in them; all there was neat, clean and useful. I
speak here only of the rooms on the lower floor, because
at that time those were the only ones I had seen.

The Admiral spent most of his day in his sitting-room
at the house's northern end. Over the mantelpiece in this
room was a biggish painting, some seven feet by five, of a
frigate under easy canvas firing a bow-gun as she set forth

from the Downs. Whenever the sun had southed and begun to wester this picture had a good light upon it, so that one could see the red inner frames of the open gun-ports and the delicate gear upon the topsails. As she bore the figure-head now over the front door, there was no need to ask if she were the *Hannibal*. In the foreground of this picture, was a boat containing people who waved fare-well.

I very soon found that this picture was the very apple of the Admiral's eye. I could not go up to it, to look at it, without his coming also. Then he would say, for the hundredth time:

"Ah, the old *Hannibal;* there aren't many ships like her now in the world, the more's the pity. Ah, she was a fine ship, the old *Hannibal*. Joshua Budd painted that for me. He knew a fine ship when he saw her, did Joshua. He said that he'd painted dozens of ships for their captains (it was a thing often done, then), but never any ship like the *Hannibal*. He knew his business, too, old Joshua. See, they are hoisting the fore-topgallant yard, and he has put a lad in the cross-trees lighting up the gear as it goes up. He had been at sea in the old *Ramillies* before she was lost, that time. Ah, I knew every plank and every nail and every bolt in that old ship. Look at that bow; there's an entry; and the run, too. Ah, she was a ship, indeed, worthy of the name of ship."

Then he would tell me that that was how she looked when he set sail in her to suppress the pirates. "The men in the boat are all portraits, too; well known at Deal. The man with the sketch-book is Budd himself; the man standing up to wave is Dick Budd, Joshua's younger brother;

he became an architect, later, and built the bridge over
the Thames at Windlesham."

On the table at the other end of the room was a model
of the *Hannibal*. The Admiral was very fond of this, and
allowed no one else to touch it. He dusted it daily with a
pair of bellows, a little feather broom, and a tiny Turkey
sponge on a crochet needle. On the table with this model
were other relics of her; a case containing a piece of her
copper, crusted thick with barnacles; an ink-stand made
from some hard foreign wood which had been used as her
bitts, so he told me; and two little garlands of grape-shot
piled up in pyramids, each shot painted red as in the garlands outside the front door. Later, I was to know these
better.

There was another room near this sitting-room on the
other side of the front door. The Admiral called it his
office. It had a table and some chairs as furniture. On the
walls were some drawings of the *Hannibal;* two of them
the draughts of her builders, the other a pencil sketch of
her laid up with her topmasts struck.

The Admiral loved to talk of these, too.

In the dining-room, still farther along the ground-floor,
were some big coloured maps of the West Indies, the
Americas and Africa. These had been made, he said, for
the King of Spain, and had been taken by him from a
pirate in the West Indies, who had had them from the Governor of Veragua, on his voyage home. They were very
beautiful pieces of engraving, and were now framed in
some of the *Hannibal's* wood (from her gun-deck). He
had carefully ruled upon them in scarlet ink all the tracks
of the *Hannibal's* courses in her famous voyages of sup-

pression. The *Hannibal's* bell was mounted in a teak bel-
fry on the mantelpiece in this room.

Still farther along the ground-floor were the kitchen
and the Coxwains' sitting-room, which opened from it
with the larder, pantry, scullery, all at hand.

South of the house was a kitchen garden, kept in very
good order by Will and Jimmy. At the back of the house
was an uncared-for shrubbery, in which escaped flowers
blossomed; a gate opened from this into the fields.

I have described the house and surroundings carefully,
for all these things were of moment to me later.

It was rightly called Hannibal House, because every
room on the ground-floor had some mark or relic of the
Hannibal in it. The house kept the old ship's memory
green. One could not be with the Admiral for half an hour
without hearing her mentioned. He had had a varied
service up and down the world; but nothing in it had compared with those triumphant years in her. I was green in
the world then and had never before met with one who
lived in the worship and the memory of a first success. I
have met with such since, of course; it is not an uncommon case.

In one house known to me a dearly-loved wife had died
at twenty minutes to eleven. All the clocks in the house
were stopped at that time, and pointed to the fatal moment as long as the widower lived. In the Admiral's house
the reckoning seemed to have ended when the *Hannibal*
paid off and had her topmasts struck some forty odd years
before. He had had his first success in her. She had confirmed his early belief in himself; she had brought him
fame, promotion and a handsome sum in prize-money. In

talking of her, he talked of what he thought he might have been.

Now am I right in saying that the Admiral's clocks had stopped with her? Ought I to reconsider that? Certainly, he had sent his mind back to her, so that his young man's fervour was lit by his old man's passion. An interest in her was a road to his favour, that is, a temporary favour. Early in our friendship I pleased him deeply, by asking: "What became of her?"

"Dammy, Ned," he said, exploding, "they let the worm into her. They let the copper wear off her. One of these captains, aged twenty, whose father had a vote or something, did that for her. When that poop-ornament had ruined her, they promoted him and broke her up. But I heard of it in time. I got Josh Budd to make those drawings of her before she went to the knackers. I got her figure-head; and when Sir William went to the Admiralty, I got that model of her that they had in the attic. She was a ship worthy saving relics from, the old *Hannibal*. The old *Cannibal,* people used to call her. She was a ship . . ."

After this prelude or exordium, I must say something about the Admiral.

First, then, about himself. He was the youngest son of a rich country rector with a large family, of which he was the sole survivor. He had gone to sea at an early age, had gone to the West Indies, and had done well. "Anyone did well there," he said, "if he kept alive at all."

He had always been careful of money. In the Indies, like many sailors, he had made large sums of prize-money. This money he trusted to his elder brother, who was a sugar-planter in Jamaica; the plantations prospered and brought him a big return. Then, when some relatives left him house property in London, he sold his West Indian property and bought other houses near them; all this investment prospered. He liked to talk of his thrift. "I'm not careless of money," he would say. "I never was. Money is the important thing in English society. I saw that when I was only a shaver. You may talk of Blood and Breeding, but if they've not got money, they can whistle for their supper and their dinner'll be wind. My grandfather was with the King in exile. There was Blood, the Blood of the Stuarts, and Breeding, too; why the Darley Arabian was bilge to it; but my grandfather said the King often hadn't enough to eat. Besides, if you're not born to Blood and Breeding, and yet have money, people will reckon you have both. Money is the main thing. Money you can get, if you know how to keep it. And with money you can say your say and be listened to. I've never wasted a penny since I knew it from a farthing. I hope you're the same."

I said that I had to be careful, for I had not much and meant to be independent.

"By the Lord Harry," he said, "it's all in that; being independent. Being your own master and not caring to call the King of France your cousin. You keep to that, boy. Paddle your own canoe. That's better than pulling stroke in somebody's else's barge. I was one who saw that early, thank God. I put pennies together and made 'em breed; now I can sit under my own vine and under my own fig-tree, like the man in the Bible."

From this the reader may judge that the Admiral was something of a miser. That would be an unfair judgment;

he was frugal; he was thrifty; he was accustomed to a life of hard simplicity. The reader should remember, too, that he had been starved of all those affections which give men happiness in spending.

From what my father had told me, I had expected to find him a man of science.

It is true that he had a telescope mounted on a platform on the roof. I soon discovered that he was no astronomer. The telescope had been left to him by an optician with whom he had dealt, and whose glasses he had recommended. When it had reached him from the executors, he had said to Will: "What the devil are we to do with this, Will?" And Will had said: "Would you not rig up a little platform on the roof, sir? You would have a fine view of the moon with a glass like this, on a clear night." He had probably given Will a sharp answer for presuming to advise him, but he had altered the louvre, or cupola, on the roof to a little platform, on which the telescope was mounted; and there, in clear weather, when the moon was making, he passed many happy hours. He was ever making charts and plans of the moon; he showed me these, all drawn in his niggling way, with notes in his neat little writing. Sometimes, I thought that he was charting the moon, from some notion, that after death he might be sent in some new *Hannibal,* to look for pirates in her. Will had a much more scientific notion of the moon than he, and Mrs. Will knew more than the two of them put together.

I cannot say that he was a man of science in the matters of his own profession. It seemed to me, that he was only really clever in those matters which had served him in the *Hannibal.* He had some books of voyages. These were nearly all those which had helped him in his cruises after pirates; they were voyages to the West Indies, the Spanish Main, and the Western Coast of Africa. When I came to know him better, I found that he had at one time been interested in naval gunnery; but then, again, only as the gunnery would have helped the *Hannibal* in her famous cruises. He had then wanted light guns with long ranges; "chasing guns," he had called them. For one so thrifty, he must, at one time, have spent a good deal of money with a certain Dr. Tompion in casting and trying brass guns of the kind. Later on, I saw models of these in the bedrooms. He did not like to talk of these things. "I had all the weight of the profession against me," he would say. "They called my guns 'pepperers.' 'It isn't pepperers we want, it's smashers,' they used to say. But if I had had pepperers of the kind I could have given them, I'd have saved them hundreds of good men and untold pounds in money. 'Pepperers' they called 'em. I'd like to have some of those damned poop-ornaments being peppered by some of them, as we were in the *Hannibal,* and unable to reply. They might have changed their tone about 'pepperers.' "

I suppose he was always a little unforgiving towards his opponents in the Service. Who forgives where he cannot understand? I only knew him in his old age, when infirmity had made him crotchety. He was uncertain in his temper because his body was an uncertain machine. He suffered a good deal. He was sensitive to the weather, much more than he liked to admit. His bruised knee bothered him before rain set in; his shoulder ached in drought; and other twinges caught him at odd times, in his arms and in his liver. Being a valorous soul, with no idea of surrender, he carried on as though these danger signals showed no damage. He paid for his defiance with a good deal of pain, which he bore like a man, and with a good deal of incapacity, which he rebelled against with venom. I soon found that he had a way of ruffling, even when nothing was ailing. Will Coxwain called this "the Admiral's park" (or perquisite) ; he told me that commanding officers often pretended to be vexed, even when they were pleased. "It would never do," Will said, "to let the people think they had done well; they might give up trying."

I did not discover all his peculiarities at once. After several visits and some raps over the knuckles, I came to know the danger signs, the topics to avoid and the times to stand clear. Do not think that I was a time-server or self-seeker. I was neither. I thought that he overrated what I had done for him, and told him so. He said that he was the best judge of that, thanky, and dammy, he would do as he chose. He and his were kind to me. I liked them all and was grateful to them. I liked him more and more as I came to know him better, but I was not unjudging; Dr. Copshrews always put me to probing through symptoms to the man.

And this brings me to what must be one of my last points about the Admiral. There can be no doubt that he had done very well indeed, at a very early age. My own judgment is, that this intense experience came to him too early in life. He had been sent out, while still a boy, to fight the devil incarnate in wildernesses under the line, where Law was the wild man's whim, and Death struck daily between breakfast and supper. It may be that experiences of that sort are so deep, that they null the brain, so that it receives no later impressions. After those two cruises, though often employed at sea, he had not again been successful. Thinking him over now, so long afterwards, I feel that he was like many English men of action, who are so often just adventurous, brave boys, who never grow up. Such men may succeed in independent commands by boyish dash and singleness, and yet be great failures in problems more important, when they work under a commander as one of a fleet, and have to subordinate their talents to some great design which they cannot understand. His early independent command unfitted him for subordination. He preferred independence, and let it be seen. I know that his admirals had found him too independent; and perhaps, a little limited and stupid; certainly, they had shelved him, quite early in life, and he had retired into the memories of his successes in the *Hannibal*.

Now, after some weeks, when I had paid several calls at Hannibal House, and had come to know the four inmates a little, and had seen the rooms on the ground-floor, I was asked to spend the New Year's Eve there, to see the New Year in, first at the church, at a watch-night service, later with a bottle of the Spanish Admiral. Dr. Copshrews granted me the night of absence, and I must say that I looked forward to it, having been away as a guest very seldom since my old home broke up. So away I went, in fine, brisk weather, and for the first time in my life went upstairs to the Hannibal House guest-room. It was an important occasion to me, because it was my first introduction to something very strange, which has affected all my later life.

Let me describe the guest-room a little.

It was the end room to the north of the house, just over the Admiral's sitting-room. Unlike the other rooms in the house, it was rather full of things; the Admiral had put into it many relics from the past, all of much interest to me. In cases and on shelves were some of Dr. Tompion's model brass cannon, the "pepperers." I suppose that there were twenty of these of different shapes and sizes; all rather spindly and narrow, and all mounted on little wooden carriages. There were several trophies and stands of arms, mostly swords and tomahawks taken from pirates. There were narwhal and walrus tusks, engraven with the outlines of ships, which had afterwards been coloured red and black; there were sharks' backbones worked and polished into walking-canes; beef-bones cut into what Will (who laid out my clothes for me) said were sail-makers' rubbers; and a snuff-box (which he told me to notice particularly). It looked like a box of dark, polished wood, but Will said that it was made of sailor's salt beef, and that it had been made for the Admiral while in the *Hannibal* by his captain of the foretop.

On the walls near the windows were curious painted maps or charts (as much picture as map), all taken from pirates, Will told me. After Will had left me to dress, I looked at them with interest. They had little paintings on them, of ships under sail, dolphins plunging, mermaids disporting, a Wind puffing or Neptune riding on a whale. Compasses on all of them radiated lines and bearings. The coasts showed many smoking mountains. The harbours were pictured in insets. I loved the titles: "A Prospect of the Anchorage of Cabeza de Toro, in the Indies"; "A View of Las Palomas, from the Rip-Raps"; "A general View of the Port and River of Little Momboe, in the Costa d'Oro."

Between the windows was a glass case containing twisted, spiky and shining shells, and two big masses of coral, one white, one scarlet.

The low winter sun was shining into the room on to the inner wall. It fell brightly upon a curious picture there, so brightly, that for a moment I had the illusion that I was looking not at a picture, but on the scene itself.

I remember that at the first glance I had thought that the picture represented pyramids or the minarets of some eastern port. Now that the sun lit it up, I saw that these pyramids or minarets were strange conical peaks, some red, some grey, rising out of tropical forest above an anchorage. There were ships and canoes in the water; the huts upon the shore made a small town. The people on the shore and in the boats were negroes. For one instant, I could almost have sworn that they moved.

I will not say that this was a good painting. It was somewhat crude and stiff; but there was something about it, in that light, which held me. I felt that the painter had seen it, and had recorded it with a depth of thought and feeling which struck all who saw. The frame bore a square of parchment, stuck on with a black gum. This title bore the words, in faded red ink:

THE SIXTEEN PEAKS
Edmond Quichet

As an idler will, I counted the Peaks, but could only find twelve. "I suppose the rest are either behind these or too much to one side," I thought. I went on with my dressing, and in a few minutes the winter sun was off the wall, and I thought of the painting no more.

Now, until that time, I had had no intimate talk with the Admiral; I had felt modest, he had felt shy. But on that New Year's Eve, as we sat by the fire sipping port, he seemed eager to talk. I have found that solitary men, however fond of loneliness and of silence, will sometimes long to talk; they will demand a listener, any listener. On this night of an ending year all the experience of his years already ended demanded outlet.

"Sir," I said, "when I first saw your house, my father told me that you had destroyed a pirate called Edmond Quichet or Keachy. In my room upstairs, there is a picture of the Sixteen Peaks by an Edmond Quichet. If it be not rude in me to ask, will you tell me if that were the same man?"

He sat up in a sudden way he had when about to answer rudely; for an instant I feared that I had been tactless and had touched on a forbidden theme. After a second or two of hard stare, he answered very gently:

"Yes, that was the same man. He painted the picture. So you've been looking at that, have you? Well, well, well. Les Seize Pics."

"Will you tell me where they are, sir?"

"By George, not many want to hear about them now," he said. "They are on the Coast; away down to leeward."

"Which Coast is that, sir?"

"The Coast of Dead Ned," he answered. "But you

wouldn't know it by that name. It's far inside the Bight, dead away to leeward there; you beware of it.

> "Beware, beware, the Bight of Benin,
> Few come out, though many go in."

"It seems a strange place, to judge from the picture, sir," I said.

"Yes, it was a strange place," he answered, "the Sixteen Peaks."

I could not make out from his manner whether he wished to talk or avoid the subject. He looked at me, as I thought wistfully.

"If Keachy painted the picture himself, sir," I said, "he must have been a man of talent. Was he a very wicked man, as pirates go?"

"He never was a pirate," he answered. "He was a very unusual man. What he did, was to stir up a confederacy among the blacks, to stop the slave trade. He was a very righteous man, if you ask me; but he committed the unforgivable sin, and so he had to go."

"What sin was that, sir?" I asked.

"He interfered with the white man's profit," the Admiral answered; "that's what Keachy did. Did you ever hear of the Matablancos?"

I said: "No."

"Well, they were a tribe," the Admiral said, "for all that I know, they may still be a tribe. Their name means 'Kill the whites.' They had settlements in the Sixteen Peaks, at one time. They didn't like the whites and wouldn't trade with them. There was a great stir once, when I was a boy, about a Captain Fidd, who tried to trade with them. They made him cook and eat three of his own fingers, as a warning not to come there again. I say it made a great stir: why, it shook the land, like Jenkins's ear. The slavers wanted us to send a fleet against them. But I'm glad to think, we never did. These Matas didn't make Keachy cook and eat his fingers; they took him in as a friend, and little by little, he got them to stop the kings from selling slaves to the whites. I tell you, those fellows, the traders, were wolves anyhow, and when their profits began to go, by the Lord, they were tigers. Mind, I call them traders: that's a grand name. They were slavers: they dealt in men and women: and there was hardly a money-grubber here that wasn't in that dirty trade in some way. And money came back to them fourfold. They sent out no-tions to the Coast, and got a profit on them; they took the slaves to the West Indies and got a profit on them; they worked the slaves on the plantations, and got a profit on them; they shipped the sugar to England, and got a profit on it; and they sold the rum to the Navy; and then rode in their coaches to Parliament, and made the laws about it. I was a sinner myself before I knew better, I and my brother. We did very well, planting sugar in Jamaica, till I went to the Coast and saw the trade close-to. I got out of it, then, and made my brother get out.

"Now the Coast is a thousand miles long, I reckon. You must not think that one man could stop slaving all along a thousand miles of savagery. But the Matablancos are or were a fighting tribe, bred to war and fond of it. They can-not marry till they have killed and aren't allowed to kill till they have had their war-test. There were swarms of them; hardly a man of them less than six feet tall; and each man a savage, with his front teeth filed to a point and his rib-bones done in white on his skin, to make him look like a Death. When Quichet persuaded those lads that the whites would not come, if slaving were stopped, the local kings, who lived by providing slaves, were very soon put out of business. The Matas went against them and wiped them out; they would kill every man, woman and child who did not do their bidding.

"Quichet and the Matas stopped any slave supply for four hundred of those thousand miles; he just killed the season.

"The first year, the traders said: 'Ah, this is a bad year, on account of the unsettled state of the country; we shall get double profits next year.' When next year came, they found that the kings who usually sent them their slaves were afraid of the Matas. The word went round that a white fanatic named Keachy, a Frenchman, had persuaded the Matas to stop slavery.

"The word went round that the profits were to stop, all the lovely fourfold profit, each bit of which depended on the other; my good Golly, what a row there was."

Since then, I have seen men and women threatened with a loss of profits, and a little understand the row there was. The Admiral paused, thinking of his past.

"Sir," I said, "why did this man wish to stop the slave trade? I have always heard, that the slaves are prisoners of war, who would all be killed, if they could not be sold."

"Perhaps," he said. "But those who say that do not say, what is beyond all question, that the slavers foment, foster and encourage the wars, solely in order that there may be prisoners to sell. Without the slave-traders there would be neither slaves nor wars."

"But then, sir, what would the Matablancos do?"

"They do not make war for slaves," he said. "They fight for glory as they call it, and for women and plunder. I never heard of their taking a slave; certainly they never sold a slave to a white man. They reckon white men as things pretty low in the scale. They say that a Matablanco is a lion, and the white man something between a hyaena and a dog."

"Yet this Quichet made friends with them?"

"Yes," the Admiral said, slowly, "he made friends with them."

"Do you know how he managed to do that, sir?" I asked.

"He was just the one man who could."

"Personal genius?"

"That's what we call it."

"But why did he want to stop the slave trade? The French are as much in that business as we are."

I had asked this question a moment before and had no answer. I did not get an answer now. The Admiral became thoughtful. "Anyone with any human feeling at all would want to stop that trade, if he once saw it. I had not expected anything like it. The poor wretches are chained and packed. They lie flat for six or seven weeks together touching their neighbours, with another layer, as like as not, only two feet above them, and another two feet below, and this in the tropics in a ship's lower hold. I've seen strong men swoon from the stench as they went round feeding them. And Lord, the dirty lies used to defend the trade, since the profit was so great. I've heard men say that it gave the negro the inestimable advantages of Christianity . . . a pity it doesn't bring more of them to the Christians . . . I saw the Christians at it, remember, and I say I'd rather sail with Satan than with some of those devils. But there they were, with their profits stopped. What were they to do? They couldn't fight the Matas; the Matas were a lot too strong. They couldn't touch Keachy; he was French. Something had to be done. They had to rig up some charge against Keachy which would bring our Government in against him, and do what they could to turn the Matas against him. These fellows, the traders, you have not seen them.

"We call all that stretch the Coast of Dead Ned. All the white people on it are done for; the Coast has done for their bodies, the trade has done for their souls. I was in the West Indies for a while, suppressing pirates, some of whom were very wicked, cruel men. But in the West Indies you come to something like Christianity wherever you land; you'll hear church bells, and a priest will bury you. All my pirates had something Christian in them; they'd a touch of a font in 'em. When you go to Dead Ned, you'll see what the world is that hasn't been and isn't Christian; it's a thousand miles of heathen Hell.

"I don't exaggerate much, when I say that every white man in all that thousand miles is not only a scoundrel but a damned scoundrel. No font there, nor touch of it. These men set to work to ruin Keachy. They arranged a raid on the English settlement at a place called Little Massa. I call it a settlement. It is a place at a river mouth, where slaves can be shipped. They called it a settlement, though it wasn't settled; a fort, though it wasn't fortified, and a factory, though nothing was made there, except misery for poor slaves. They caused some low-down savage of a king to raid the place, burn the huts, and two small ships waiting for slaves there, the *Anna,* pink, and the ship *Eliza Jolly,* both of Liverpool. Then they all swore that Keachy had led the raid, and that our trade ought to be protected. There were pamphlets and books about it: Parliament took it up. This is what was said: 'Is our Trade, at once the Nursery of our Seamen and the Backbone of our West Indian Possessions, to be at the Whim of one Man, and that Man a Frenchman, in a League with Savages? It is well-known that this Keachy's Allies are of such Malignancy to all Civility that None has yet wooed any of them to the Conveniences of Trade.'

"While they were at this, they got busy with the natives; they spread the news, through some of their savage friends, that Keachy was aiming at kingship of the Matas. They could count on a lot of the Matas hating a white man anyhow. However, the slaving interest here is enormously strong, with unlimited money; they contrived to make the Admiralty do something. They used to boast that they had the Press, the Pulpit and the Parliament all at their command: and they weren't far wrong. I was in some repute in those days as a pirate catcher. I was told to take the *Hannibal* and bring this Keachy into trial at Cabo Amarilho.

"Of course the Admiralty knew nothing. They said: 'There is this French fellow, Edmond Quichet or Keachy. He is said to be somewhere in the Matablanco country, in the Bight of Benin somewhere. He seems to be a pirate or something. Go and bring him in to be examined.'

"When I got to Cabo Amarilho, I had my first sight of the trade and the kind of men Keachy had against him. I began to see the kind of job I had. No one there knew the Matablanco country, nor even how big it might be. It might be three hundred, four hundred or five hundred miles across. It was all unknown land and uncharted coast, with great rivers here and there, some of them with fifty mouths, and all the land savage, tropical and forested. I was to find this Keachy there among his savages, who were said to eat white men as a general rule. Look at the map here. The wind blows in to the Bight, and the farther you go into it, the less the wind is; it grows fainter and fainter, and away to leeward here, at this patch of islands, it often dies away and leaves you becalmed, without a breath, in a heat like a furnace; no breath of air, the sky like brass, the sun blazing, and the sea steaming; all grey with heat, like this grey oil, with black shark fins sticking from it. There are more sharks than herrings there. When you are well in the Bight, you may not see the shore from the steam rolling up. You will hear the roll of the surf, and see a mass of grey steam, which may not clear more than for a half-hour in a day. Everything steams, and is wet and grows things. The coat you take off will grow moss, and the shoes you cannot bear will grow fungus. I was told to find Keachy and bring him in. It was no easy task. You cannot sail too near an uncharted shore, you risk your ship too much. You cannot send boats in to explore, for you risk your men too much; they get sunstruck. Besides, the natives are a match for any boats, in their canoes. And the whole coast is a bad one for boats, because of the surf, which is bad almost everywhere, and very bad indeed in some parts. It looks bad from a distance, but when you are in it, by the Lord Harry, it is awful.

"I went along from road to road, asking about Keachy. Ships there keep two or three miles out and fire a gun, if they wish to communicate; then the native canoes will come out. A man-of-war is not welcome to the natives; the captain of a man-of-war doesn't give rum and gun-powder to every naked savage who chooses to call himself a king. Still, some of them came and talked. I knew no native tongue, but there is a jargon on the Coast which you quickly learn. You talk in that. It hasn't many words in it, since the blacks only want rum, guns, cloth and gunpowder from the whites, and the whites only need slaves from the blacks. All the whites told the same tale. Keachy was killing the trade; Keachy had ordered the attack on Little Massa; Keachy had been seen at Little Massa, setting fire to the *Anna,* pink; and had been heard swearing that he would drive all the whites into the sea.

"Presently, as I went on, nearer to where he was supposed to be, the people told me less and less about Keachy, and more and more about the Matablancos. This puzzled me; for it ought to have been the other way about. I began to wonder whether this hatred of Keachy were not all the product of the trade at its centre at Cabo; none but the traders had mentioned him even there. Well . . . I went on. I received warning after warning of the Matas; how I was never to trust them, never to go among them without fifty armed men; how they were all treacherous, and cannibals; and poisoners; how they had spears from which no one could recover and magic which killed in a year, a week

or a day, whichever they chose. At a place called Dimbobo,
a Portugee told me that the Matas always ate their prisoners alive, 'and make them collect the salt first.'

"I kept thinking of the child who goes dancing into the
danger ground in the game. The child will sing:

> 'Here I come into Tom Tiddler's Ground
> 'Picking up gold and silver.'

and presently Tom Tiddler will rush out to catch him. I
was going into Tom Tiddler's ground. Which Tiddler
would rush out to catch me, would it be Keachy, or these
Matas?

"It was an important question. If it were Keachy, I
could manage him. If it were the Matas, who were said to
have 100,000 fighting men, it might be perplexing. I had
one hundred and forty-seven men and boys with me, and
about half of them were too sickly to do any good.

"The wind fell lighter and lighter as we went on and on
to the leeward; then we came to Bartolommeo, the island
there, and went ashore for news. Hell is cold compared
with Bartolommeo. Men who die there always come back
for their blankets. It's a Portugee place, so I went in with
a gift of port for the Governor, and there I had news of
Edmond Quichet from a ship's carpenter, who had escaped
from him in a canoe, about ten days before.

"He said that Keachy lived at the Sixteen Peaks, and
had fortified the river mouth with ships' guns. I asked,
why had he deserted? He said he hadn't liked the look of
things; the Matas had gone off on some great adventure,

at the bidding of their devils, and he feared the Cornudos would come down while the Matas were away. I asked who the Cornudos were? He said, a branch of the Matas, in feud with them over a fishing right; they wear horns on their brows, he said, just like Christian husbands. I asked, had Keachy been at Little Massa? He said, no, never, nor heard of it, probably. I asked, what strength Keachy had? He wouldn't tell me that. Then I asked, what did Keachy intend? He said, to trade in what the land produces, in exchange for what Europe can supply that is worth having. I asked, when would the Matas be back? He shrugged his shoulders; *qui sait?* Anyhow, he had had enough of life on Dead Ned, and wished to be out of it and back in France. If he stayed, he was sure it would be one of two things, either the blacks would kill Keachy or the whites would.

"I asked, what defences there were at the river mouth? He said, very strong and well-guarded. He wouldn't draw a plan of them.

"It is a maxim that deserters generally tell the truth. But you have to think that the deserter may also be sent to spread false tidings. On the whole, I felt that this fellow told the truth; and I respected him for not betraying his man. I asked, did he dislike Keachy? He said: 'No one could do that; Keachy was a fine man; humane and good.' I asked him, if Keachy held a commission from the King of France? He said: 'Yes; naturally. *Oui; naturellement.*'

"This was perplexing to me, for if he were the French King's officer, I had no right to touch him. I doubted this answer about the commission; all the traders had agreed that he had none.

"I asked if Keachy lived in a ship in the river, or at one of the forts? He said: 'No; he lives on the red peak, in a cave; and has a tame king-snake as a bodyguard.'

"That was about all that I could get out of the carpenter. After I had sailed from Bartolommeo, I wondered if the man's wits had not been unsettled by the sun.

"It is not far from Bartolommeo to the Sixteen Peaks, but the wind is light; it took us four days. Presently, towards evening, we saw the Peaks far off. Don't think of them as crags or mountains; they are about four hundred feet high. We crawled along till about three in the morning, when we were becalmed. The officer of the watch came down to say that he heard firing from the shore; would I come on deck? It was a dead calm night with a half moon; a waning moon. There is always a certain gurgle and creak in a ship at sea; and we could hear the surf along the shore, too. But sure enough there was a popping and clapping of guns from somewhere ashore. It popped and died down, and then sprang up again. My officer thought it might be natives rejoicing; to me, it sounded more like a fight. It was just before dawn; that's the time they usually fight in those parts. Then, quite suddenly, it broke out hot and strong, with some big guns mixed with it; we could see a sort of glimmer from the flash of these. It went very briskly for half an hour, then died to a few shots, then ceased. We were still talking of what was happening, when we saw a glimmer of fire on the shore; it looked as though it might be a big bonfire.

"It was first a sparkle; then a big bonfire; then, in no time, a great blaze; oh, how it spread. You know the saying: 'It ran like wild-fire.' When the wind catches a spark where the jungle's dry, it will run a flame five hundred yards in a minute. All the forest there seemed to catch and to burn in a blaze in no time.

"We stayed there watching, till presently the fire died down and dawn came. We were there all that day and all the next, just becalmed, not a breath stirring except a waft or two from the shore with the smell of smoke on it; we could smell gunpowder smoke among it. There was no more sound from the shore; but indeed, the current set us away a little from where the shots had been.

"When the wind gave us a chance, I stood in, with colours flying, and fired a gun for a pilot, just to the west of the Seize Pics. As no pilot came, I anchored, and got into a yawl which I had had prepared; I was going to speak with this Quichet according to my orders. I had had a good look at the coast through my glass. I could see that the river disembogued there in some seven or eight channels; there was a bar on some of them, and a surf on the rocks in between them. The land seemed all jungle and burnt wood, still smoking; behind these were the queer peaks, red and grey and odd, with forest half-way up them."

He paused here, and looked at me. "I talk and talk," he said, "and all about sixty years back. The bottle's out too, now; which is a lot more important. I'll have up Will, with t'other bottle."

I said that I longed to hear the end of it. He said he would tell me, when the new bottle was opened. Somehow, the chain had been snapped; he was less ready to talk after Will had gone.

"The end of it," he said. "Well, there was hardly more

of it. The place had been attacked and burned by the
Cornudos. I saw some dead Cornudos with the white, jag-
ged horns tied to their skulls."

I asked: "When you found Quichet, sir, what sort of
man was he?"

"Dying," he answered. "Wounded by the Cornudos,
and dying."

"Was he in a cave, sir?"

"Yes, with two French lads; all at the point of death.
They were the only survivors, except the tame snake."

"Were the Cornudos still there, sir?"

"No. They had killed and sacked and gone."

I saw that the Admiral wished not to talk more, so I put
no other question; he saw that I was not going to ask. He
hesitated a little; then he said:

"Quichet was dying. He said: 'All in this cave is yours;
it is worth a king's ransom.' That is how I came to have the
picture."

"Will you tell me what he was like, sir?" I asked.

"Like? He wasn't like anybody. How could he be?"

"I do not know, sir."

"I've got his sketch-books; one of them has his portrait
in it. I'll show you that."

He was away for some little time, and returned with
three little books bound in canvas. "The ant's been in
them," he said. "We talk of the moth corrupting, but he's
nothing to the ant." Indeed, some of the leaves of each
sketch-book had been eaten away in a curious manner, as
though some tiny bird had been making a neat little nest
there. Much of the writing had faded away; there were
outlines of coasts, compass bearings, jottings of anchor-

ages with the guiding marks and depths of water, with notes of where the springs were. In one book, less faded, there were sketches of men and ships, done with the pen in a kind of India or cuttle-ink. "This is the book with himself in it," the Admiral said. He showed the drawing of Keachy. It was a little pen sketch, done in some idle minute with a few swift strokes; it showed a youngish man with a great mop of hair, and an expression hard to define, serious, yet with a whimsical look.

"He must have been a charming creature," I said.

The Admiral looked at me strangely. "Charming?" he said. "Yes. He had the two powers. He could compel, and he could charm." He turned the pages, to show some other sketches of the Sixteen Peaks. "There are one or two views at the end," he said. "He did them from the cave where he died." He turned the pages, licking his finger at each page in a way learned, perhaps, when he was a midshipman with a signal book. "There," he said, at last. "These are views from the cave. All that is the harbour and the spits where the batteries are. Then beyond, is the sea."

I looked at the views with interest. They had been done in a strange place all those thousands of miles away, by a strange man, who had died for his idea far from any friend or comfort.

"A strange man, Edmond Quichet," the Admiral said. "A very fine fellow in many ways."

He seemed suddenly angry with himself for talking about Keachy. He took the books and relics from me and carried them away. When he returned he seemed ill at ease. He went from window to barometer, and from the barometer to the fire. I had seen him restless like this before, but had learned never to ask how he did, for that angered him.

"One good thing about sea-service," he said testily, "it makes you a damned good weather-glass; my knee hurts when it's going to be wet; my skin tells me when it's going to be cold." He came to the fire and shivered over it. "One odd thing about the Seize Pics, a very odd thing; I see that old Brancker, the Dutch traveller who was there in 1680, mentions it; they get a cool land wind as well as the cool sea wind; that is, it isn't the sweltering hell that most of the coast is. There is a down draught from those mountains, they say; those Ghost Mountains."

"Tell me, sir," I said, "if the place is cool and has this wonderful anchorage, and if the Matablancos have gone away, why do not the traders use it?"

"It's too far to leeward," he said. "The wind blows you there, growing fainter all the time. You have to beat against it to get back. It's a six weeks' beat only to Cabo Amarilho. The trade on that coast is for slaves. If you loaded slaves at Seize Pics, you'd have to feed and water them all those six weeks, as well as the six weeks from Cabo to the West Indies, which would just double your Middle Passage and double your losses, too, for they'd be dying on you all the way. The trade don't mind the death, but they do mind the loss. Besides, the leeward coast has a bad name, even for that coast; men shrink from it. It's under a curse." He shivered again, and said that it was turning colder; he rang for Will to bring a boat-rug and wrap it round him.

I had never known the Admiral so ready to talk. After that day, I saw clearly that he regretted the talk. When

next I slept at Hannibal House I found that the painting
of Keachy had been removed. I asked him about it. He
said that these old paintings were often the worse for being put up in rooms not often used; he had, therefore,
taken it away. I had already noticed that he disliked talking about anything for a second time. "We talked of that
before," he would say, and change the topic. Of course
he would always talk about the *Hannibal,* that wonder
among ships; I had only to ask where the men slept, or
how fast she could go, or what was her best point of sailing, and he would talk freely; but about the Coast and Edmond Keachy, no, he had talked of them and now seemed
to repent, and even to dread the topic.

Apart from that I grew in friendship with him and liked
him more and more. It was a happy house. Much of its
happiness was due to the excellent Mrs. Will, who was the
merriest and the most hard-working woman I had ever
known. I never saw dust or dirt in the house. Wherever
she appeared good-humour reigned. Her big, pale, merry
face spread good-humour everywhere. Whenever I sat
with the Admiral I could hear the peals of laughter in the
kitchen at the end of the corridor. She was famous for her
good-humour; I know that many people hung about the
gate at the back of the house in the evenings just for a
chance of being made merry by her. It was her genius;
few people have a genius so harmless, or so well based on
kindness and goodness.

It was in the spring that my next promotion came. I had
ridden out there late in March, on a lovely, windy day,
when the blackbirds were building and the sloe was in
blossom. The Admiral seemed merrier than usual, and

eager to talk about my progress as a doctor. I said that I was getting on and enjoying it.

"Do you think you'll be able to cut me up, presently," he asked, "to find out where the old age is?"

I answered: "I hope, sir, there'll be no need for anybody to do that this long time yet. And I think your timbers are sound, if you ask me."

"Maybe," he said, "but the plank isn't what it was; rather a lot of creaks and groans. . . . Still, you shall have the job, when it comes to the point."

I said: "No, sir; I am much honoured by the compliment, but doctors shrink from treating their friends."

"They know too much, by George," the Admiral said. "They know what the brown mixture really is."

"No, no, sir," I said, "you mistake; besides, I'm not a doctor yet. I shall not be till the autumn."

"That brings me to the point," he said. "As friend to friend, now; are you dead set on being a doctor?"

"Yes, sir," I answered. "I nearly am one, now. It was my father's profession, and it is the one I have chosen and enjoy."

"So you've said, and so old Gubbins says: 'enjoy.' I don't see where the enjoyment comes; but I suppose there might be some, in a way. You really feel, that you want to be that, all your life?"

"Yes, sir," I said.

"Why?"

We were now in front of his sitting-room fire; the window was open and the draught was shaking the daffodils in a pot on the table.

"Why, sir," I said, "you were once a midshipman, ordered about, you said, by old masters' mates and lieutenants. Then you were made lieutenant, and longed to be captain. You said that all the time you were lieutenant, you said: 'I'll see a change made as soon as I ever get command.' Well, I am like that. I want to have command, after going through the lower stages."

"I understand that," he said, "and in a way, you ought to go through your course and ship your swab, and hoist your flag and the rest of it. But the thing I've wanted to say to you for some time now, is this. I'm getting on in years and I've got no kith nor kin. Money can't buy you those, if Nature doesn't do her share. Now, I've taken a fancy to you. I'm pretty well off, as the world reckons in cash and goods. You saved my life that time, tackling those three. I'm going to make you my heir."

"Sir," I said, completely overwhelmed, "this is too much. You overwhelm me with goodness. And I've always told you I never fought those men, only helped to scare them."

"I'll take my own view of what my own eyes saw," he said; "and there's my hand upon it. I may live a dozen years yet, to spite you."

"I hope you will, I'm sure, sir."

"I believe you do, Ned," he said. "I've noticed that about you; you aren't after my money, like some I could name. There's that whelp at the Manor, who says he's going to keep in with me, because I may cut up warm. Keep in with me, quotha. He'll best not try coming in here. But you shall have all I have, Ned. Only I want you to promise

me faithfully that you will give a home and a living to
Will and his wife and Polly, as long as any one of them
shall be alive. Will you promise that?"

"Sir," I said, "they have been so kind to me here, that I
would do my best to save them from want anyhow; but I
gladly promise you."

"Right, boy, and I believe you'll keep your promise, too;
which is more than you can say of some." He stretched
across, caught the bell-pull and rang. When Will appeared, he said: "Will, there; fetch your wife and Polly
along. Don't let them stay to dress ship, or they won't be
here till sunset. Tell them to lay aft as they are, and fetch
up a bottle of the Admiral—and glasses for the five of us."

When they appeared, the Admiral said: "Now, Will,
uncork and pour. Take your glasses. Now all hands. This
young gentleman, Ned Mansell here, is going to be my
heir. I've decided that and so it will be. He has promised
me faithfully that he'll give a home and a living to all the
three of you; so you need fear my death as little as I do.
This place and your life here will go on after all. So shake
hands all round, and let's drink to my heir."

We shook hands and then they drank to me. I was all
upset and startled, but contrived to say that now we must
drink to its being many, many happy years before ever I
was heir there. It was drunk and drunk again, which
ended the bottle; then we shook hands again and the party
broke up.

I came away soon after that. The Admiral had been excited and my own heart was so full, that I felt that I must
get away to think of it. It was so beyond all thought that
this old man should like me and give me all that he had.

It was said to be great wealth, too: land, houses and £20,-
000 hidden in the house; all rumour spoke of great wealth.
But I have never been very prone to believe good news. I
am a doubter. I told myself: "Rumour may be false, and
an old man's mood is capricious and may change before a
week is past."

It was my duty to write to thank him. He wrote back to
say that it was for him to thank me. He had always feared
lest he should die before he had found an heir; now, in me,
he had his wish; he knew that I would keep my word to
the Coxwains. He added, that he hoped I would come
over on the Sunday, as he had something to show me and
to tell me.

I rode over on the Sunday. Just as I got down at the inn,
to hand over my horse, I was hailed by Dennis. He had
heard somehow, that I was to be there and there he was to
meet me; he had the face to come up, in public, with an
open hand, as though he had not pitched me out of his
house only a few months before.

"Let me congratulate you," he said. "I hope it answers
your expectations. You seem to have played your cards
rather well."

"It won't do," I said. "Keep your dirty paw for your
dice-box."

I gave the horse to the ostler, and went past him. He
was crimson with fury, and was within an ace of striking
me. Henery was there, to see the fun, but that was all the
fun there was at that time. I heard Dennis splutter: "You
shall answer for this."

I found the Admiral ill at ease about something. After
dinner he told Will not to disturb us, but to leave coffee

and the port in the sitting-room. After we had enjoyed these good things, the Admiral said:

"You never were in my bedroom, I believe?"

"Never, sir," I said. "But I know that is over the dining-room."

"Well, I want you to come up to the room, if you will," he said. "I've got something there I want to show you." He led the way to the staircase, and called at the stair foot, along the corridor to Will: "Shift the cups and gear, Will." He then led the way up the stairs and along the landing to his bedroom door. The door, like most of the doors in the landing, and indeed in most houses of the time, was double. He opened both doors, invited me to pass in and then locked them both. " 'Safe bind, safe find,' Shakespeare says," he said, "and I've found it true. Only as a general thing, I leave the doors."

His room was a very gracious place, beautifully proportioned and spotlessly clean, but a monk wouldn't have had anything barer. There was no carpet; there were no curtains; there was no furniture except a grim little stand with a copper jug and basin on it. The stand was painted red. "That's a bit of the *Hannibal*," he said, "that old battered jug and basin were with me in all my going a-fishing."

The bed was a hard, little, seaman's cot-bed. There were no sheets on it, only dark blue blankets.

"So you think I ought to have sheets," he said, guessing my thoughts. "Only women and landsmen use sheets; not the deck department. But one of these days, I'll have to pamper the flesh. I begin to find the floor very cold to put my foot on when I turn out on a winter morning. I'm afraid I'll have to have a mat one of these days. But I'll do without as long as I can. That's the way of the sea : never lay up until you're dead, and then you won't want it.

"Now that the doors are shut I'll shut the window, too," he went on, "then I *know* that I can't be overheard." When he had done this, he turned to me and asked : "Are you still willing and eager to be my heir, boy Ned?"

"Sir," I said, "that isn't the way to put it. I ought rather to ask, are you still thinking of making me your heir, all without deserving, as I am?"

"Yes, Ned, I am. And it's something well worth a young man's being. I'm not one of these harum-scarum sailors, all for rum and the girls. Never was. What might you suppose being my heir would amount to?"

"Sir," I said, "whatever it may be, it's infinitely above any possible desert of mine."

He weighed this remark, with his little, shrewd, ferret eyes fixed on my face, and nodding his head slowly.

"No," he said, "but what have you heard about my wealth, eh? That I'm an old miser with a house just crammed with gold, eh?"

I said, yes, that there had been stories that I'd heard, but that they were no concern of mine, and that I had not paid any attention.

"Well, some day you shall know the truth about that matter, too," the Admiral said, "that is, if there be any truth; there isn't much in rumour, I say. But come on in now to the powdering-room."

He lit a candle and opened a door at the end of the bed-rooms, into one of those powdering-rooms, in which, in those days, the wigs and head-dresses were powdered in the messy way then in fashion. If it were not done in a room apart, the powder, which was blown on to the hair by a kind of bellows, went everywhere, and dusted the furniture white.

"This place," he said, "was in the hands of a Catholic family when it was built. In those days of persecution, the priests had to hide; they had a hiding-place here. Do you see that innocent old forged nail? Turn it round and pull it a little out."

I did so. With a very little noise of movement, one of the panels in the wall slid aside, so as to show a little space, filled with shelves of papers.

"It was big enough to hold the priest," the Admiral said, "but I've filled it up with shelves now. This is where I keep my leases and some odds and ends of things, and all the account books of the Cringle estate; all the houses I own. They'll all be yours, one of these days. That is where you'll find them. Now I'll show you how to shut this thing. You press this, and it shuts tight."

It did shut, very tight, nor could I see or suspect a cupboard door when I examined the shut panel.

"That's one of my little secrets," the Admiral said. "It is one you've never heard word of, I'll be bound?"

His little sharp eyes were on my face, eager to see, if I had heard anything of the sort.

"Sir," I said, "I've never heard a word of any such hiding-place. I have been told that you keep £20,000 hidden in the house, but no one has mentioned a room like this."

"£20,000?" he said. "That was your half sort of step-brother, or whatever you may call him. He was here one time, asking if it were true. I gave him the end of a brace for his impertinence."

He led the way out of the powdering-room and sat himself down on the edge of his little cot-bed. Then he rose and looked if the double doors were still locked; he opened and relocked them, to make sure, and sat himself down again.

"It will all be yours, Ned," he said. "All that you saw and all that you see and will see. It will be yours and your heirs' for ever. They call me Crusty Cringle; I know it; Crusty old Cringle; but no one ever found me crusty to those I love. You'll see presently, whether I'm crusty."

"Sir," I said, "I have seen already, time and time again, that you aren't."

He got up from his seat. It struck me suddenly that he was extraordinarily frail. It was almost like his little soul coming towards me. He clapped me by the arm and patted my shoulder. "Ned, my lad," he said, "you tackled three for me. And I've never been fond of anyone as I've been fond of you; no, not for fifty years; more than fifty. The last man I took to, to like, was our friend that we were speaking of."

I was puzzled at this. We had been speaking of Dennis, but Dennis didn't date back so far, and wasn't exactly a friend. I must have looked puzzled, for he said: "I mean Keachy, boy; the Frenchman, Edmond Keachy. He was one I was fond of. And I've lied to the world about him, for over fifty years."

He sat down on his little cot-bed and began to cry. It was the most miserable moment I had ever had.

"Listen, Ned," he said, "I'll tell you. I've meant to tell you. You are the only one I can tell. When I went to Seize Pics that time, Keachy wasn't dying, as I gave out. He was alive and I let him get away."

"You mean, sir, that he escaped?" I said.

"No. I let him go. I disobeyed orders and betrayed my King, and deserved to be shot aboard the *Monarque*, like one I could name; a good deal more, by the Lord Harry."

"Sir," I said, "you must not talk of these things; they are upsetting you."

I was afraid that something had upset his reason and that he was mad; all this talk of my being his heir and this sudden burst of confidence, these things were surely old age's breaking-up of the order. I watched him carefully; he saw my look and judged my thought. He took control of himself and said:

"No, I'm not mad; but I've wanted to tell somebody for fifty years, and am not likely to find another to tell to. I had that little clue to Keachy's secret hiding cave, and I found him there, with two other men, one of them French. All three were slightly wounded.

"I ought to have seized Keachy and sent him up to Cabo to be tried, where he'd have been hanged, with a great show of law and no pretence of justice, on the words of slave traders. I did nothing of the kind."

"But why ever not, sir?" I asked. He was the last man I should have suspected of failing in duty. "Why did you not take him?"

"Well, for one thing, because he saved my life. I went up the track to his cave not thinking that he or anybody could be there. I went up alone. And the three were in ambush and had me covered. They could have shot me like a dog. I had no chance nor choice. Then Keachy, with the manners of a saint, told me that I had nothing to fear. 'Let us talk,' he said. He spoke a good English. He led me into the cave. It was a strange place, with a running brook at one end of it, and a marvellous view over the land and sea. As the carpenter had said, he had a tame king-snake there. He told me the most astounding thing; but the great thing about him was his charm. I've said he had the manners of a saint. I was bewitched by the fellow. There was he, wounded, with his hopes all knocked on the head, and myself with a ship of war below ready to take him to his enemies; he thought of my needing a cool drink. English enmity had ruined him; he said no word and showed no trace of all that. The man was lovely to look at, too. They say Alexander the Great was like that. I'm not disposed to like my fellow-man, by George, no, nor trust him; but that man I loved and trusted from the first glance. There were his paintings, too. He painted and made music and knew about the stars.

"I believed all he said to me. I'll tell you, Ned, what he said: you can believe or not. He had been a traveller far into the interior, where I suppose no other white had gone. He had come to some mountains which are in the legends. Old Brancker, who heard the tales, calls them the Ghost Mountains. In and about these mountains he found an almost white people, with stone houses, and straight hair and regular features. He thought they were descendants of some old colony of the Greeks. He had made friends with these people and learned their tongue. They had a great wealth, and needed certain things. Keachy

thought he could get these things for them from Europe.
You can get to the Coast from those mountains by one of
the rivers, though it takes some weeks to do it and, of
course, weeks longer to get back from the Coast against
the stream. He was going to make Seize Pics the port for
this white people. But it was necessary to keep the tribes
on the river quiet, if there were to be traffic to and fro.
That was why he tried to stop the slaving; and that, of
course, led to the end."

"By wealth," I said, "I suppose he meant that they had
gold mines?"

"No, Ned; I believe they had no gold, or not much. They
had emeralds."

"It is a strange tale," I said.

"Africa's a strange place."

"How had his enemies missed him in the fighting, do
you suppose?"

The Admiral shrugged his shoulders. "War's pretty
much a matter of fortune. Besides, the Cornudos were
busy plundering."

"Tell me," I said, being puzzled by the tale, which did
not seem to me to be one that would deceive a schoolboy,
let alone a shrewd sea-captain. "Tell me, sir, how could
Keachy escape? You say that the natives had turned
against him, his own friends were killed or scattered, and
you held the sea. He could not get away, and was quite
certain to be killed if he stayed where he was."

"He couldn't get away by sea," the Admiral agreed,
"and he'd have been killed if found. He told me that his
friends from the Mountains were even then coming down
the river in boats for him, to take him back to safety.

Africa isn't like England, where to-day is like yesterday, and to-morrow'll be the same. It's the unlikely thing that happens there. Imagine the craziest thing you can, and what'll happen'll be crazier. You look at me now as I looked at him then. He said to me: 'I tell the truth,' and I said: 'Of course.' "

"But do you think, sir, that he did get away?"

"I know that he did. I saw him start. Just as he had said, the boat came for him that evening. I saw her: I went into her and examined her. She was not a savage's canoe, but a carvel-built shell, polished with gum against the worm. The people in her were not darker than sunburned Englishmen; they were very fine fellows. They wore kits such as I never saw elsewhere, of unbleached linen with blue edgings. They wore soft twists of gold-leaf in their hair; they had spears unlike the savages, and their hair was straight. They took Keachy and his two friends into their boat, and then they rowed away; rowed, remember; the savages don't row; they paddle. They put poultices on to Keachy's wounds, and put the three of them prone in the stern sheets, and then away they rowed. I could have captured the lot of them and carried them to England; but I shook hands with them all and wished them well, and watched them go. They went round a bend out of sight, and that was the last that I saw of them; Edmond Quichet just lifting his hand to me.

"Just before he went into the boat, he said: 'All that there is in the cave is yours, Sir Cringle; yours and your heirs', if you care for it. It is worth a king's ransom, if you care to look; but I know you will not look.'

" 'No,' I said, 'you are right; I shall not look. I don't

mind being hung for you; and I dare say I shall be; but I won't be hanged for any king's ransom.'

"But all the same, I took the paintings and the books, and one or two hardwood boxes he had, which the ants don't touch.

"Well, I made up a tale, and wasn't hanged; I was promoted. But if you were to blab, Ned, I suppose I might be hanged, even now. If I wouldn't be hanged, I'd be broken and towed ashore on a grating."

"No, no, sir; never think of it," I said. I supposed that the tale was something like nightmare, and had no reality. "Did you ever hear of them, sir? Do you think he got away?"

"They just rowed away into Africa."

"Do you think they had a chance of getting away?"

"Yes, I do. I'm sure he got away. I've prayed and prayed for Edmond Quichet, and though I know he's not going to cross my path again, I've known he's well; even if he's dead, all's well with him."

"And what about the Matablancos, sir?"

"They went away to look for Marimba, which was a land their devil-doctors told them of, where they could get a lot of meat and women. I dare say they found it; for the stretch of the coast is less populous now, so sailors tell me. But war is likely to have done that for them. However, I've been talking and talking. I'll talk no more."

He rose from his seat, smeared his old eyes with the back of his hand, unlocked the doors, and led the way downstairs. In the sitting-room he was ill at ease. I could see that he regretted his confidence, for he kept repeating: "I told you that, as you are to be my heir. Some men might think that the men who made them heirs were just plaster saints. I wasn't. I let the fellow go, when I was sworn to take him. I'm glad I did."

I came away from Hannibal House then, and did not see the Admiral for some three weeks. As I expected, when I did see him, I found him prickly and vexed. Plainly he regretted that he had let me see under his armour. He showed me no more secret hiding-places and talked no more of the Sixteen Peaks, nor of Edmond Keachy. Instead of further confession, I found in him a certain foxy suspicion difficult to define; certainly, he was less charming to me after that long talk than before it.

His story puzzled me. I often thought of it. It was plain that Seize Pics existed, or had existed. Edmond Quichet had existed; there was his charming, thoughtful face in the drawing. I thought often of that face, and of the great peaks, red and grey, rising above the sea of green forest which stretched away into the continent. What had happened to Quichet in that carvel-built boat smeared with gum against the worm, with those Greeks, sitting well in order, rowing him to the Ghost Mountains? Had he got there? Had he found some other way of bringing to his Greeks those things which Europe might give them? And what was that king's ransom buried in the cave? Was it under the bed of the stream, like the bones of Domitian? Was it emeralds? What did a king's ransom of emeralds look like? And had Quichet taken away his pet king-snake? I should have liked to ask the Admiral all these things, but dared not. It was plain that those topics were not to be mentioned again. Still, I was welcomed at Hannibal House; all welcomed me there, when I could go there; I was Mr. Ned, the heir; and recognised as such. I saw Dennis, now and then, but we were not on even scowling terms; we crossed the road when we met. All reports of him were that he was mixing with a violent and disreputable company of sporting men, who would probably pluck him to the marrow of his bones before he was thirty.

It chanced that one of Dr. Copshrews's patients was a lord, who had once held a great position in the state. He had retired from public life, and had lately left his home in London for a new house in the country somewhere near to Greenwich. He fell ill there and wrote to Dr. Copshrews to come to see him. On our way there (I say "our," for Dr. Copshrews wished me to come too) we found the road busy with traffic, all coming from London. Dr. Copshrews's coachman, Maurice, told us that the people were all going to the fight; there was to be a fight, he said, between the black man, known as The Jouncer, and Tom Pugg, the British Hero. Dr. Copshrews compressed his lips and looked serious, for he did not like that kind of crowd, and shrank from being thought to belong to it. Presently, as we drove, we heard behind us a blowing of horns and a cheering. Dr. Copshrews sat still, but the driver, glancing back, drew close to the side of the road and pulled up.

"Why are you stopping, Maurice?" Dr. Copshrews asked.

"I think it will be one of them coming, Dr. Copshrews," Maurice said. "It might be best to let them get ahead."

He looked at the approaching carriage from his box. "Yes, sir," he said, "it's one of them. It's the black man, The Jouncer, sir."

"I wish he would get past, and all his followers, too," Dr. Copshrews said testily.

Almost immediately, with a great blowing of hunting-horns, half a dozen bucks came cantering past. They were the outriders of an open carriage, with four horses. A man on the box beside the driver, and a man on the step behind, blew coaching-horns. They were all decked out with scarlet ribbons and had a very gay appearance. In the carriage were four men. The two in the front seats were seconds and bottle-holders; the other two were Dennis and The Jouncer. Dennis, in the extreme of fashion, and smothered with scarlet rosettes, was looking very anxious. The Jouncer, a big, smiling, shiny black, was passing cheery remarks to the cheerers by the roadside. I had never seen a face quite like his, the big insolent, slobber mouth, a nose which had been badly broken, little scars over the eyebrows, and one exfoliated ear, such as is called a cauliflower ear. I picked up these details in an instant, and I saw, also, the enormous smiling vitality of the man, and his great teeth, white as ivory and big as dominoes.

"That's The Jouncer, sir," Maurice said, in deep respect.

"He looks a pretty ruffian," Dr. Copshrews said. "Is he going to win?"

"They say he's going to eat poor Pugg, sir," the driver answered.

"Well, as to that," my physician said, "there's no foretelling about war. His backer didn't look very happy about it. Who is the backer?"

"Young Mr. Rackage, the sporting gentleman, sir," the driver said.

But, by this time, the outriders following the triumphal chariot had cantered past, and we were free to go on.

Our patient was not in much need of physicians, but had snatched at a chance of talking about himself to sympathetic ears. He talked for a long time, and entertained us to a meal. As we crossed the heath upon our way home, we saw, as it were, a big black cloud of rascality break up from its mass and set in our direction. To our surprise, a yellow chariot came full tilt from the crowd with the driver bent down to avoid a hail of clods and stones. At the same time some men on horseback spurred out from the crowd and gave chase. The yellow chariot made for the London road just in front of us. A man in her, leaning out, swore at us to get out of their way; indeed, Maurice had to pull up a little to let them have the road, or they would have had us over. There were two men in the chariot; one was The Jouncer, the other, the one who had cursed us, was a flash white man, not Dennis; they looked anxious enough, and their driver, though getting the utmost from his horses, was scared white. As for the pursuers, they were out for blood. About half the crowd came surging in our direction.

"Whip up, Maurice. Do not let us be engulfed in this company," Dr. Copshrews said. "Get on, man; what are you stopping for?"

As it seemed an ugly crowd to be engulfed by, Maurice whipped up; we went on after the yellow chariot.

It had some little start and was going recklessly; but not without plan. A hundred yards ahead, at the crossroads, a cool-looking man was driving a dog-cart. As soon as ever the yellow chariot had passed, this man drove his

dog-cart across the road in front of us, completely blocking the passage. Maurice had to pull up, so had the horsemen who were pursuing. They cursed the dog-cart driver
for blocking the way; but he had climbed down and was
looking at his horse's hoof for a stone. It was a strange
scene; our carriage stopped; this pale, leary-looking man,
cool and insolent, holding up his horse's foot, and all about
us a fierce and swearing gang of horsemen. Dr. Copshrews turned to one of these men and said:

"May I ask, sir, the cause of your uneasiness?"

"Uneasiness?" the man said, swearing. "That damned
Jouncer sold the fight on us. That's what. Hey, sir, you,
sir. Pull your damned dog-cart out of the way."

"Never get excited," the dog-cart driver said. "What
... ever ... you do ... Nev—er get ex—cited."

I think the men would have laid him out with their
heavy whips, had not one of them, readier than the rest,
flung down, seized the dog-cart's horse, and thrust him to
one side. The cool driver was knocked over and rose up
less cool, but by that time the flood of the pursuit was past
him. Maurice touched up his horses, so that we, too,
scraped by.

"Sir," Dr. Copshrews said to the man, as we passed
him, "you deserve to be prosecuted for obstructing the
highway and conniving at an escape."

The man looked at Dr. Copshrews with a steady and
quite expressionless face. He did not speak, only stared.
Looking back at him I saw that he produced a toothpick,
climbed aboard his dog-cart, chewing the end of it, and
slowly drove on after us.

We did not get to London without hearing more about

it all. The Jouncer had sold the fight. After fighting with his usual skill and courage for six rounds, he had fallen seemingly senseless to a blow in the seventh. Pugg swore that he had not hit him over the heart; but there The Jouncer lay till Time had been called. Soon after that he had been up and away, into the yellow chariot waiting for him, with fifty furious backers at his heels ready for his blood. Some of these backers had assaulted Dennis, who was The Jouncer's main supporter; they said that Dennis had told him to lose. Before we reached our beds that night we heard that that at least was false. Dennis had backed The Jouncer heavily, and had lost a large sum; he had, moreover, lost his reputation in the sporting world, for having backed one who sold the fight. The newspapers next day were full of it. One that I read, was sarcastic about "Mr. R-c-g' who took such pride in going about among the wolves and had now been bitten." Another spoke of "Mr. R-c-g-, the Pl-ng-r, from whom the feathers were falling." A day or two later there was a paragraph to say that Dennis had been insulted in a tavern by one who had lost over The Jouncer, and had had to challenge the insulter to a duel. They met the next morning and exchanged shots, and Dennis had the luck to break his opponent's arm with a ball above the elbow. This did a little to reinstate him. The Admiral said: "He's headed for the Pit. Like all his kind, he'll go the faster the nearer he comes to the edge. He'll do a crazy thing next time." In this he was shrewd, for it was just what Dennis did do. An announcement appeared that he had backed himself to ride from London to Cambridge in five hours for two thousand guineas and a supper. He undertook to start from the "Hoop" in Holborn at noon, and be in the bar of the "Hoop," in Cambridge, at five. It is no light feat, for it is over fifty miles. He was to have no more than six horses. Allowing for possible bad going, delays by the way, such as the road being blocked by traffic, cattle, sheep, or even fallen trees, or by turnpike gates being closed or in the new mount not being ready at the changing places, and the accidents which might happen, through weather or harness, or horse's muscles or nerves, it was what the sportsmen called a close run home. The bet was unusual. It made a great stir. As the Admiral said: "He's chosen the one way he could have chosen to reinstate himself." Indeed, the general feeling was that Dennis had shown a plucky spirit; many who disliked him said that he had a good pluck and that they hoped he would win.

The ride came off in a day of drenching rain, with violent wind. It was said that more than half a million people were spread along the road to watch him pass. Many of them were in the road, blocking the road. Dennis had not thought of that. He had the utmost difficulty in getting out of London, and lost his match there. After the first stage sportsmen galloped ahead of him to clear the road, and it is said that he did well over some of the stages, but could not make up the time lost. It was five o'clock before he reached Royston; and in the last stage the roads were blocked again by sightseers. It was a heavy blow to him. The expenses of the ride had been heavy and the bet had to be paid. Word went about at once that he was on the rocks. A newspaper started a subscription for "Mr. Rackage, the true British sportsman, who lost his late match through the well-meaning curiosity of thousands who came to see

his feat and thereby made it impossible for him to do it."
Many thought that he had had bad luck, and were sorry
for him, but the subscription only brought in £1 17s. 6d.
As the Admiral said : "The nearer the brink, the faster
the stream. He's going down the cataract, and a good job
too."

These things made a great stir in London, and though
Dr. Copshrews was a strict man, not given to any sport,
and hating all of them, he read the accounts, and talked of
them with me. They seemed to have a dreadful fascination
for him. I was to know why, very soon.

Presently it drew to the end of September, with a cloud-
less, fine weather, the orchards full of fruit, and the country smiling; it had been a good harvest; and a healthy
summer. I knew that in a few days I should be free from
my articles and qualified to practise. Dr. Copshrews had
given one or two hints that perhaps he would take me as a
partner. The Admiral had told me that I was to be his heir.
I suppose that there was no young man in London with
better and brighter prospects; I was on the way to fortune, through my profession and through my destiny.
People were looking on me as a rising young man; I do not
doubt that I shared their opinion and was insufferable.

It is true Dr. Copshrews had not said much; but then
he was not a man of many words. I expected him to speak,
but he did not speak. At last, one day, he bade me dine
with him, and after dinner, when we were alone, I saw
that the vital moment had come.

"Ned, my lad," he began, "you are almost out of your
probation time, now. You are amply qualified. I would
like to talk to you seriously about your future. But in do-

ing that I shall have to tell you of my own affairs. I am sure that you are not indiscreet; but I wish you to promise me that what I tell you in confidence will go no further."

I gave the promise. I did not like this opening much, but it was his nature to be dry and rather solemn, more so than was necessary.

"I do not seek to know," he went on, looking mainly at his glass, but sometimes sharply into my face. "You may probably have heard that I have a son." I bowed my head! I had heard that; but had not seen the man, now, of course, nearly forty. "A son," Dr. Copshrews went on, "who has been of great cost to me in these last months."

"Sir," I said, "I have heard only something in general terms."

"Yes, yes," he said. "It is not likely that a misery will remain unknown." He left his seat, sighing. Presently he returned to it and sat there toying with his glass. At last, after a long pause, he said: "You have been here a long time now. Your father was a dear friend of mine, who put much business in my way, when that was a matter of moment to me. We have gone along very well together. You have done your work well; very well. I've nothing but praise for the way you have done your work. You have attended to your business."

"Sir," I said, "I am grateful to you for saying so. May I say that it has been a pleasure to work with and for you?"

"I'm happy to know that. I've tried to make it so. I am glad if I have succeeded," he said, smiling with his very sweet, rare smile.

"It is difficult for me to speak," he went on. "A year ago,

three months ago, no, last week, even, I was hoping to ask
you to be my partner, so that we might continue together.
I have not felt in that way to any other pupil who has been
with me; nor, in fact, to be quite honest, do I think that
any of that company has felt inclined to that extent towards myself. I could have asked you, as a favour to myself, to continue with me. But to tell the truth, Ned, I am
vexed with a rodent ulcer, which devours and devours. My
son is not all that I would desire. In fact, he has eaten me
like the locust and even now presses. In fact, Ned, my lad,
I need a large sum, to save him from disgrace."

Now, we who worked with Dr. Copshrews, had often
found him niggardly and careful. A young Irish medical
student had called him "as wee as a whelk." I had put it
down to a rigorous, thrifty upbringing, and had often
thought that with his practice he must have amassed and
put away a lot of money. I had always heard him talked of
as rich. I thought: "His credit must be good. Dozens of
men would lend him money enough. He is certain to repay,
and must have security to pledge."

He knew what was passing in my mind. "No, it isn't so,
Ned," he said. "I have been well to do. I have had property
and credit, both; but the one is gone and the other is
stretched to breaking-point. I have nothing but this fully-
mortgaged house, and an old man's practice. I will not tell
you the extent nor the pressure of my need; they are
great; they are, I may tell you, extreme. I know not where
to turn. I need two thousand pounds, and could not raise
two thousand pence, I am so deeply dipped. I can only sell
my practice, which would advertise what I must try to
hide, or a partnership. I can offer that to you for two thou-

sand pounds, if the payment can be made in a hurry, as my payment must be made."

"Sir," I said, "it is generous and kind of you to make the offer. Let me thank you for it. If my father had not done as he did in the last few months of his life, I could have taken it. But I do not think I can, now. I have but fourteen hundred pounds, at the very most, and cannot touch that; it is all lent upon a mortgage and cannot be brought in. It is security, of course; but I cannot make it more. I have no relatives of any sort. And I know no one from whom I could borrow the other six or seven hundred."

"Ned, my lad," he said, "it has been bruited abroad, that Admiral Cringle is making you his heir. You have never told me this. But I have heard it. Do not think that I have spied. A doctor has to know something of those who work with him. I have heard nothing but good of you. I have learned all about your saving of his life and how he esteems you. Now, I have heard something of the Admiral. He has the name of being a true friend and an honest man. Could you not go to him with this as a proposal? I offer you a partnership, which you know is worth the money. I could offer it to the medical world at large, instead of to you, but that again might advertise my need, which I do want to hide, nay, must hide. It would cause comment, if old Copshrews were to pass over Ned, who has been the prop of his practice for so long. You say that your fortune could secure, say, thirteen or fourteen hundred of the money. Could you not ask the Admiral to advance the two thousand pounds, against the mortgage of which you speak, and a charge upon the practice? It is not an unreasonable proposal. He would not stand to lose. Even if you died, he would have your money and a charge upon the practice, which would in a little while repay him to the full. If, as I am assured, he means you to inherit, it will not displease him to establish you in your profession. You are as a son to him; he will be glad to help his son into the saddle and set him riding forth."

I felt that that might be so, but somehow my heart misgave me. "Sir," I said, with some hesitation and misgiving, in my voice, "the Admiral has been very good to me ... but ..." Here I stopped, not seeing how to go on.

"I too have been good to you, Ned, or at least, not bad."

"That is true, sir," I said. "I know you have been good; very good. I cannot be grateful enough for your goodness. But the Admiral is not an easy man to deal with. He is crotchety and spiky. Sometimes he will fall foul of everybody for days together. He will take amiss the most innocent things one says, sometimes, and be savage about them for days."

"This is not quite the same as a chance remark," Dr. Copshrews said, "this is a matter of the deepest concern to you. Your future depends upon it. You have to discuss it with him, in any case. You will have to tell him of it. If he be your friend now, and your benefactor to be, he will expect you to treat him as such. It is my experience that the old may be testy about little things, but are glad of the deeper confidence of the young. I should be indignant with you, if I were in his place, and you did not come to me, and have it squarely out. There's nothing like frankness. With a sailor like that it's the only policy."

I saw that it was the only policy, and that the matter

had to be done. The sum of money demanded, though it seemed big to me, was not really big for the return offered. I was cheered also by the thought that the little fortune put away on a mortgage, and the charge upon the practice, would secure the Admiral against any loss. I was not asking him to venture money; he could hardly lose by me. Still, he was a crotchety old man. I knew that he hated anybody presuming on him or trying to presume; and that he had all sorts of queer old bachelor ways about money. He was, and had for years been, rather too fond of money. When he was in the mood, no one could be more generous or kind. When he was not in the mood, there was no one more crusty, more suspicious or more downright rude. In that crusty mood, moreover, he was miserly. One never knew how to get him into one mood, nor out of the other. He was just as prickly as a porcupine, and as touchy as an invalid, and with this prickliness and touchiness, there was, as I had seen, and as Will and his wife had told me, a stinginess which kept them, as Will said: "On the King's allowance," for sometimes a fortnight on end.

Still, it had to be done. My future did depend on it, and I shrank from letting the chance of the partnership go, for want of a little resolution. I, therefore, sent a message that evening, to ask the Admiral if he would see me on the second morning. I could not go on the morrow; the practice forbade.

After this conversation, Dr. Copshrews said to me:

"By the way, your Admiral was on the Guinea coast, was he not? Did he ever mention a place called Little Massa?"

I said: "Yes; it's one of the slave ports. Why?"

"There was a note in the newspapers," Dr. Copshrews said. "The Assizes are coming on, and a case is being brought against the captain of a slave ship for beating a man to death there."

"It sounds like a grim business," I said.

"It is," he answered. "A Captain Ashplant; I suppose a son of the pirate of that name. I doubt that that slave business is anything but crime and greed from first to last. But I doubt if any charge of the kind will prevail against the captain of a ship."

This was the first time that I had heard of Captain Ashplant, and the first time that I had heard or thought of that Autumn Assizes. Later, I was to know more of both.

Maurice took my note to Cholsington, and brought back the reply that night. The Admiral would be pleased to see me on the second morning, being the day of the October Hiring Fair in the village; he would expect me at eleven in the forenoon. I read the reply to Dr. Copshrews. Somehow, though it was polite, the note made me feel: "He suspects that you come for money." My heart, which had been dashed by the thought of applying to the Admiral, was now dashed down. I said to Dr. Copshrews:

"I must say, sir, that my heart sinks, when I think of what I have to ask of him."

"Oh no, no, Ned," he said. "You must not fear thus. It is a business matter. You are getting up into the world of affairs; the world is run by business arrangements of the sort. You must learn to plead for your own cause or be put upon. Do be sure, my lad, that I respect your modesty. Yet know that modesty must give way in a case like this. To set the right value on yourself is essential. Do not feel for one moment that you are asking an unusual favour of Admiral Cringle."

I did, though. I felt it all through that night and the more the next day. I wished that Dr. Copshrews would let me try my fortune with some business house or man of affairs, rather than ask the Admiral. But he asked me not to think of this. He said that possibly he could arrange it, thus, but only by making public, or at least communicating, matters which he wished to be secret. If I would try the Admiral first, then, if I failed, he would have to try the other way. I said to myself: "The Admiral will refuse, and what is more, will never forgive me for asking." I passed a very wretched day, trying to do my work, and at the same time going through speeches which might turn the Admiral to grant my request. The more I worked at the speeches the worse they seemed. I felt sure that he would swear at me for a cub and a sponger, and tell me to get out. He was not one to listen readily to a tale of woe. He had his own views about people in want, and a rough and ready way with them, which he called dropping a shot into their boat, to make them sheer off. The more I thought of it the less I liked it. And yet, from time to time, I told myself: "This is folly in you, Ned. He will be delighted to help you: he'll be charming about it." Then the thought recurred: "How many are charming when asked for money?"

The day passed in worry and perplexity. Now that I am older and have looked a little into my share of life, I feel that when the heart misgives beyond a certain point, it does so from a wise perception; it utters warning. I know now that I ought to have taken that warning, even if it meant the giving up the partnership. If I had taken the warning and not gone to Hannibal House how different my life would have been.

I slept abominably ill that night, with nightmares and terrors. A glorious, fine morning followed the night; it was a faultless October day, so mild, so still and fair, with blue sky and sunlight. I woke, or rose, rather, worrying over my mission, drank a couple of cups of tea, and set forth in misery. I had the dried-up feeling in the head that a sleepless night always gave me, as though there were no blood running into my brain; and as I went along towards the village my heart got lower and lower, and my mind more and more anxious. Presently I got down from the coach to walk the rest of the way, and soon came within hearing of the Fair. Like most fairs, it was loud with hurdy-gurdies, and the band, or Noise, as they called it, of the village. There was a continual banging of pistol shots at what were called the duelling booths, where one shot with pistols at jacks-in-boxes, which were supposed to represent your opponent in a duel. All the street of the village outside the church was crowded with the booths and the gaiety of the Fair. I have ever taken pleasure in gatherings of the sort in England; they are (or were then) the greatest of the yearly markets at which horses, cattle, sheep, pigs, poultry and pigeons were sold. I remember wishing that someone would offer me two thousand pounds down to act as a private physician to him for a term of years. I would have taken any offer to avoid going to beg from the Admiral.

The booths and shows of the Fair not only filled the village street, but pushed westward up the hill, away from it.

All those village fairs so near London attracted and still attract much rascality from London. Most of these visitors sold cheap jewellery, shoe-laces, buttons, etc., while they looked out for what they could seize. Throughout the area there was much noise. These rascals cried their wares above the clashing of the cheapjacks' dishes; the banging and popping of the shots, and the exhilarating bell-ringing, not only from the church ringing for its patron saint, but from the auctioneer's assistant, who rang a great peal with a hand-bell before any horse was trotted out to show his paces, or any beast put up for auction. Then, inside some of the booths, and outside others, there was rude music, designed to excite; men banged on drums, or blew upon pan-pipes. Besides these there were solitary musicians, of sorts. A one-legged sailor leaning on a crutch, played upon a whistle; a man in an almost worn-out red soldier's coat played "Jockies to the Fair" and similar tunes. Then there were the Irish harper and the Scottish piper, both followed by little gangs of boys imitating the noise they made. I will not say that the people looked as though they were enjoying it. The English do not show enjoyment readily. Still, some young men were yelling.

The place was crowded. The Hiring Fair was a general holiday; it was St. Marches' Day, the day of the dedication of the church, as well as the Fair of the year. Most people were in their Sunday clothes; and this fact (and the noise) had made all just a little excited. It was through such a scene of noise and bustle that I had to make my way. I must say that I shrank from it. It made me hate my mission even more bitterly.

It had happened a year before this that I had been to the Pie Fair, as they called it, beyond Islington, and had there seen a remarkable fair character, well known about London. There was a coloured print of her sometimes shown in print-shop windows. One or two poets had mentioned her in their poems. She went about from fair to fair, and as it chanced on that day of the Pie Fair, I had been of use to her. Her man, Joe, had had a bang over the head with a cudgel, and I had washed and stitched the wound. As I came into the Cholsington fair ground near the church, there was this woman's booth, roofed with green and white canvas, and all stuck about, as her way was, with big gaily-coloured paper flowers on wooden sticks. It looked as though she had a sort of garden in front of her stall: very bright and pretty it was. She sold all manner of fairings, ribbons, papers, pins, packages of needles, knives, scissors, razors, brushes, thimbles and combs, with packages of fruit and gingerbread for the children. Over her booth was the legend:

YOUR OLD FRIEND
JANE JOLLYCOK.

She was a Jolly Cock and well deserved the fame she had won; she remembered me at once.

"Hello, Doctor," she cried. "Welcome to the Fair. You must have a fairing for old sake's sake. No, no money between friends. You must take now some gingerbread. You, a doctor, don't need to be told the good there is in gingerbread. It comforts all the reins and all the veins."

She pressed upon me a gift of gingerbread, which is a

delicacy I abhor. I took it, and asked after Joe; but Joe was in trouble of another sort; that rough world of the fair often brought men into trouble, what with theft, fraud and assault and battery. We talked for a moment. She said Jollycok would be there presently, but he wasn't the man he had been; he had a tightness across his chest. All the time that she talked she had a roving eye all about her, and well she needed to have, for there were crooked fingers all round her. I asked about the tightness across the chest, and suggested one or two simple things that might give ease; then she said:

"But you, yourself, Doctor, don't look too well. You look all forlorn. I never saw you look like this before."

I said that I was feeling anxious about something that I had to do.

I remembered then that I ought to buy some little tokens for Will, Will's wife, and Polly; so I bought a little book of needles for Mrs. Will, a gay little bottle of brandy-balls for Polly, and then, looking about for something for Will, I saw nothing except a clasp-knife having at its back a bottle-screw.

Now I knew that Will, like all sailors, disliked clasp-knives and would never use one; so I said to Mrs. Jollycok ... but just as I was about to speak a wasp or two, disturbed from the sweetstuffs, buzzed into my face and made me start; I said to Mrs. Jollycok:

"I don't want a clasp-knife; it would shut up in the hand if one struck a good blow. Have you a strong knife, a sort of sheath-knife, not made to shut, that you could be sure of?"

She looked at me oddly, as I thought, cast an eye about

her stall, and bent to a package in one of her baskets.

"Yes," she said, rummaging, "I've got these two, but there's not much demand for these sort now."

She produced two knives, one a sort of carving-knife, the other a sheath-knife, with a leather belt attached to it. It was about nine inches long, over all. It was not quite brand-new. It looked as though Jollycok had used it on occasion, but it had something about it which I knew Will would like. Let into the handle, so that it could be opened and shut, was a small steel spike. The knife part of it was always a knife, but one end of it could become a marline-spike.

"That is the very thing," I said, and bought it and paid for it.

Something made me turn as she put it up for me. Just behind me was Mr. Henery, with both his snake's eyes watching my every movement. I thought that if hate could kill, such hate would kill me. I have often thought since then, that hate does kill, that it goes out of the mind against the enemy and rouses up evil against it, till it finds some hand that will take up some knife and do its horrid murder. Our eyes met. He gave no shadow of recognition. I'm sure that mine did not. Then he tossed his head with a savage gesture and moved on.

As I paid Jane Jollycok I noticed that she was looking at me very strangely. She was perplexed by me, and had some instinct that all was not well. All was very wrong; of that I felt sure. After I had passed away from the stall I felt that her eyes followed me.

I must say, that as I passed through that busy scene, my heart, which had been very low for the last two days, sank lower. I wished that I had not got to make this suggestion to the Admiral. I was young and strong; I ought to have been confident. I could hold my own with the men with whom I came into contact at my master's. I wasn't afraid of even the roughest patient in his most savage mood. I was not afraid of the madmen with whom I sometimes had to deal, nor even of the mad women; but I went through that Fair with my heart in my boots and at the point of tears. Of course, the fact was, I was not well. I had had a hard summer of it; I had been working too hard, reading till late, then being called to a patient, then, often, being called to another, so that for weeks I had had insufficient sleep and irregular food. Certainly, I was not myself. I may say, too, that I had been thinking more than a little of Patty Morsoe.

I have longed and longed since then to have that morning again.

If I could have it again, I should spend its early part in the surgery; then go my rounds in the city; then dine and discuss cases with Dr. Copshrews; then attend at the surgery again, and perhaps go out to Patty Morsoe's when the work was done, to hear her sing "When lovely Phyllis."

If I had spent the day thus, what would have happened, I wonder?

My hard heart was to be changed; and being so hard, hard measures were needed. What was coming to me came.

Presently, I was through the Fair, and walking towards the Admiral's house, with sad thoughts of my father and mother. I felt helpless, like a little child, and longed to be

again a child, having my life directed for me by someone
competent to do it. Then I turned along the grassy lane,
and presently there was Hannibal House, bright in the
sun, with white fan-tailed pigeons sidling and preening
on the roof, and a few golden apples still shining in the
topmost boughs of the old apple-tree. I remember with
great distinctness that, as I looked, one of these golden
apples fell, and, being wasp-ridden, broke in pieces at the
foot of the tree. I opened the gate and walked to the front
door and rang the bell.

I heard the bell jangle away somewhere to my right, in
the kitchen. Usually that well-drilled house leaped to any
signal. Usually, one or other of the three people who
served the Admiral saw any comer as he crossed the garden, and was at the door to open before he could ring. To-
day nobody answered my ring. I stood there underneath
the figure-head, shifting uneasily on the well-washed brick
of the walk. A Red Admiral butterfly settled and sunned
itself on the sill of a near-by window; a cruising wasp
came to examine the door and its fittings; it seemed to go
over it with great care, but saw or smelt nothing that it
wanted, for presently it moved off. There came no answer
to my ring. I knew well how angry the Admiral was if any
visitor rang a second time, and how much the three servants dreaded his quarter-deck manner. I would not ring a
second time, but walked round to the kitchen door. I
thought it possible that the Admiral might be ill. The
household might be attending to him in his bedroom. If
that were so, the man who rang a second time might just
as well jump overboard.

I walked round to the kitchen door, which was ajar. I called gently:

"Will? Is Will there? Are you there, Mrs. Will?... Or Polly?"

But there came no answer, only the slow tick-tock of the big kitchen clock made by Nicholas Culpepper, 1727. The kitchen fire was burning brightly; the little ginger cat was quietly asleep in the chair. I went into the kitchen, but nobody was there. I crossed the kitchen and looked into the long corridor which ran right along the house to the Admiral's study. The study door was shut, but the three doors on the left of the corridor were all opened and the light shone in. There was no sound in the whole house of anybody. I thought: "Could they have gone down to the Fair? But they would not leave the door open. I'll just go round the garden to the back," I said.

So I went. It was not a very prosperous garden at the back. A big yew-tree kept a darkness on that side. Beyond it were a few of the late flowers, such as sunflowers, and there, at the garden gate, with her back to the house, and her eyes on what little she could see of the Fair, was Polly.

The reason of her being there was plain enough. About a hundred yards from the gate on which she leaned was an opening through which she could see into the road. She could see a Punch and Judy show, surrounded by a crowd of little children. She couldn't see very much of the play, except the flash of the sticks with which the puppets knocked each other about, but she could hear the shrill crying or squealing of Punch, and the noise of the pan-pipes. There is something about Punch and Judy which is irresistible. I longed to be there just as much as she did. It seemed a wiser thing to be doing than this hateful task that I had undertaken, of coming to beg for money against my will. I called to her, "Polly . . . Polly," but she paid no heed. I had to go to her and speak at her elbow. She was very much startled. I said:

"I've tried to make myself heard, but nobody answered to me, so I came round to the back. Could I see the Admiral? Where is everybody?"

She said: "Oh, Lord, sir, Mr. Ned, I'm so surprised. Father and Mother are away this morning, as Mother's sister's being buried, away over at Redriff, and the Admiral's all alone in the house. Oh, I hope he's not heard the bell. I just peeped out to see the show; and he's not at all himself this morning. Oh, I do hope he hasn't heard the bell."

I noticed then that she wore black: still, that had not damped her zest for Punch and Judy.

We turned from the gate towards the house. My luck was out that day. From that point I was engulfed.

I said to Polly: "I bought you a little fairing on my way here, for I know that you like brandy-balls." And with that I handed over my package.

Everything that I did that day went amiss with me. I ought to have recognised the fact and passed the day in my bed. A man stays in bed when his health is out; he should stay in bed when his luck is out. But my luck was out, and I didn't. I looked up, and there was the Admiral watching us from the door.

Whenever he was not himself, or feeling that old bruise in his knee, or any of the other twinges which afflicted him, he used to pass the day by the fire, with his feet in an old pair of red slippers, and himself in a plum-coloured dressing-gown, wrapped round with an old blue and green rug, which old Will, who knew the symptoms, always called the "Danger Signal." "He's hoisted the Blue and Green this morning," were his words. Whenever he did hoist the Blue and Green he was like an old bear with a sore head. And there it was hoisted. He looked at me with grim disfavour.

"What are you doing out there, child?" he said to Polly. "The bell's been ringing off its wires."

Polly turned as white as a ghost.

"Oh, I do beg pardon, please, sir," she said.

Polly was a very pretty girl, and she looked so miserable that no man on earth could have blamed her very much. She knew, too, that the way to the Admiral's favour was to confess the fault at once. She looked as desolate as a half-drowned kitten. She was genuinely grieved at having done wrong. And out came a tear or two, real tears. She was like Beauty in Distress.

"Sir," she said, "I'm very, very, very sorry. I went to see the Punch and Judy."

"Well, go in," the Admiral said, testily, but not unkindly; and Polly went in, feeling pretty sure that the matter was ended.

I came up to the Admiral to greet him, but I got no greeting from him. It was one of his bilious days.

"Was it you who rang then?" he said.

I said: "Yes, it was, sir. I came to discuss a matter of business with you."

"Come in, then," he said, and led the way.

He was a shocking figure of fun. He had not shaved; there was a hard white stubble on his chin. He wore no coat. The buckles at the knees of his breeches were loose. He had no stockings; his bare feet were thrust into these old red slippers; "Moorish slippers," he said they were; and there he was, wrapped in his Danger Signal, with his eyes red with inflammation and with anger. I should have done well to get out of it, while there was time.

"I'm sorry to see this," he said, when we reached the study. "Polly is a good girl, and I'm not going to have her made a fool of by you or anyone."

I said that that was quite the last thing I'd thought of.

"Don't tell me," he said. "I know what young men are; I've been one myself. And Polly's a pretty girl that any young man would seduce, if he had half a chance. I don't like it at all; the way you got round to the back there, taking her from her duty and giving her your gifts."

"It was only a packet of brandy-balls," I said.

"Brandy-balls will work as well with the poor as emerald balls with the great," he growled. "I don't like it and I won't have it."

"I don't like to be misunderstood," I said, "nor misjudged, and I won't have that."

Usually he liked to be stood up to. He did not like it this morning, but looked at me with a sinister lip and said nothing. Presently he said:

"Did you know that Will and his wife were out of the way?"

"Polly has just told me, sir," I said.

He glowered at me, but said nothing. He was determined not to give me any chance. In the silence the noise of the Fair rang out suddenly.

"There's a lot of noise," he said, testily. "There seems the devil of a lot of noise. Can one of the government be being hanged?"

I said: "No, sir; it is the Hiring Fair; all the village is crowded."

"Ah, yes," he said. "They told me. That precious step-brother of yours, or whatever you call him, that Dennis fellow, was in here this morning. He said there was a fair. He asked me to come to a Main of Cocks at Roger's Ring. Like his damned insolence, to ask me to come to his low dens."

Then there was another silence; the morning didn't seem to be going too happily.

"Sir," I said, "I am afraid your knee is paining you; if you'd let me have a look at it I'm sure I could make it easier for you."

"Neither you nor any other doctor will look at my knee," he said. "Who told you that it was paining me? Has that girl, Polly, been talking nonsense?"

"Nothing of the kind, sir," I said. "I'm a doctor, and I can see that you aren't well."

"Doctor, are you?" he said. "How many have you killed since you were here last?"

"Oh, the usual score," I said.

"Well, when I want to die," he said, "I'll manage it my-self, without calling you in to help me to the tomb. I wish to God you'd shut that door when you come in; it's blow-ing half a gale of a draught right down my neck."

It was true; nothing that I did that day was done rightly. I had not shut the door; there was a draught. I rose and shut the door and apologised. There was another silence.

Then he said: "You said you wanted to speak to me. What d'you want to speak about?"

"Sir," I said, "I feel that this isn't the right occasion. I don't think you wish to hear me."

"God, boy," he said, "you've come here and rung the bell off its wires; I caught you trying to seduce Polly in the back there; and your excuse was that you wanted to talk to me; now you say you don't want to talk to me. You *had* come to seduce Polly."

"Sir," I said, "I'll go. You ought not to accuse me thus. You've done nothing but accuse me since we met. I will not submit to it any more."

This put him, unfortunately, into a flaming rage.

"Sit down," he said. "Give me a plain answer. What d'you come here for?"

"Sir," I said, "I came to ask for money."

"Oh," he said, "so now we come to it."

He twitched the Danger Signal rug more tightly about him and glowered at the window; his lips moved as though he were swearing; once or twice he licked them. I suppose all his organs were as much out of gear as mine. He seemed to be gathering material for a new explosion, which presently came.

"While I'm on the subject of Polly," the Admiral went on, "let me warn you that there's a young man after her here who will make an honest woman of her. It's young Jack, the baker's son."

I said : "I'm very glad to hear it, sir. I give you my word
I've no more thought of Polly than I would have thought
of my own sister. You've misunderstood me, sir."

"It's not so easy to misunderstand a thing like human
nature," the Admiral said. "Nature's ways are fairly
plain."

We remained silent for perhaps half a minute after
this. He was testy, angry and malevolent. I suppose that
really he was angry with me because I had made him unjust. I had more than ever the feeling that I ought not to
have come out that day, but having come I knew that I
could not go, no, though every moment that I stayed made
the matter worse. There we were, silent ; he, savage and
red-eyed, and myself feeling that whatever I did or said
was wrong.

"You say you've come specially to see me, and about
money, of all things in the world," the Admiral said at
last. "What is it you want? Or was that excuse made up
on the moment?"

"Sir," I said, "I have really come about money."

"What money?" he said.

This wasn't a very helpful beginning.

"What money d'you come to me about?"

I then explained the situation : how I had a prospect of
obtaining a partnership on very favourable terms, if I
could get the money at once ; that I had often felt his kindness to myself, and had, therefore, come to him, rather
than to any lawyer or money-lender ; that it was a large
sum, but that I could give security for seven-tenths of it,
and could make sure that the remaining six hundred
pounds could be repaid in full within three years out of

the receipts of the practice, and could, in any case, be fully
secured by the practice, with interest. I felt as I explained
these last points, that they seemed very unlikely to persuade or convince. Who could tell that I should live for
three years? Dr. Copshrews's assistant was exposed to
every noisome infection then raging in the City of London. He might die or fall ill within a month of starting
practice; then where would the six hundred pounds be?
The Admiral kept his red eyes fixed upon me, and I knew
that these thoughts passed through his mind as they
passed through mine.

"What makes you think that I've got any money," he
said, "or that I should want to lend money?"

I said: "Sir, I don't know anything about it. I come
to you as the only friend I have, now that my father's
dead."

I thought for a moment that he was going to relent and
be kind; then I saw the wayward devil in him determine
to be nasty.

"I've not got any money," he growled, "and I don't lend
money, even if I had it to lend. That's a fool's game that
I've got out of at my age, thank you. I wouldn't lend the
price of a plug of tobacco to the Queen of Sheba. You want
two thousand pounds, which a Commodore would hardly
get in three years."

His voice had risen considerably as he spoke; he himself had risen; had taken the poker and banged at the
coals in the grate. There was a little silence, during which
I distinctly heard footsteps outside the door. I knew that
Polly was listening there to what was going on.

"Very well, sir," I said, "I am very sorry to have troubled you. I dare say that some lawyer or banker will let me have the money."

"What the devil led you to suppose that I would lend you two thousand pounds?" the Admiral said.

"I supposed nothing of the sort, sir," I said. "I came to you as my one friend, to ask you if you would. You won't so I'll go."

"Who said I won't," the Admiral said. "What the devil d'you mean, you young jackanapes, putting words into my mouth like that? By God, you young cubs, if you'd knocked around at sea a little you might have manners."

When the Admiral was rude it was usually best to be ruder: I promptly was: the words were there: out they hopped.

"Sir," I said, "you lead me to doubt that."

"You'd better get out of here before I do you an injury," the Admiral said.

At this, the footsteps, quite certainly the footsteps of two people, slid away into a little room outside the sitting-room, in which unwanted books lay. There was a door in this little room, by which one could reach the garden. I did not want to betray Polly, who had certainly been listening at the keyhole; I knew very well that if the Admiral caught her at any trick of that sort he would make her jump out of her skin. I walked slowly to the door, after he had told me to get out, and at the door I turned and said:

"Sir, I should like to shake hands with you."

"Would you?" he said.

"You've told me to get out," I replied, "and I'm going, and shall not feel like coming back."

"Well, stay away, then," he said. "Send Polly to me."

"I'm not your servant," I replied. "You'd better ring for her. I might seduce her."

At that I walked out and closed the door behind me, and being hot with temper it occurred to me that it would vex him to the quick if I walked through the kitchen as though to find Polly. That was in my mind, but it was also in my mind that I had still in my pocket my little gifts for Will and his wife. As I went to the kitchen I hoped that the Admiral would call me back. He did not.

The kitchen door was open. I called: "Polly . . . Polly," but nobody was there. I stepped in. The little cat was on the seat, as before, and the clock was ticking. I was sick at heart at the mess I had made of things. I had had the folly of trying to do business on a day when I ought to have been in bed. Now I had spoiled the business and broken with my best friend.

I looked about for something on which to write that these gifts were for Will and his wife. There were no writing materials there that I could see. Then I spied the slate on which the Admiral was used to write his orders for the day. It had a little damp sponge tied to it with a string. A slate-pencil was attached to another string. I took this slate from the wall and wrote on it: "Gifts from the October Fair, for Mr. and Mrs. Will Coxwain, from E.M." I laid the gifts on the slate on the table. I suppose this took me about one minute to do; then I went out by the open back door. There was no sign of Polly. I called her: "Polly . . . Polly, there?" but she was away somewhere, either with Jack, the baker's son, or peering again at the Punch and Judy. "God help you if the Admiral catches you," I muttered.

I thought to myself: "Well, now I leave this house for ever," and walked out. I longed to get my back turned upon the place. I was hot with rage. I said that the Admiral had been an old bear, but then, I knew, too, that I had been a young ass. My first impulse was the very wise one to go back to the inn, take horse, and return to my work in the City. Then I thought: "No, I am too savage; I couldn't see patients like this. I'll walk for a little and try to cool down and get the thing clear."

I walked away from the village and the Fair, but in that state of madness I did not find walking any help. I had breakfasted very early. I felt that I ought to eat, so I went to the inn, "The Three Toms," which lay roughly in the direction in which I was walking. The landlady knew me. She looked at me curiously, as if she wondered at my being there and wondered, too, at the odd look on my face. Like all the people of the district, she knew that I was the young doctor whom the Admiral was going to leave all his money to. I said that I'd be glad to have some food.

She asked, Would I join the Ordinary, which was set for dinner in the room off the bar? There was a piece of beef and a cheese set out. I sat down, but I found I could not eat: I was too full of trouble. I heard the landlady saying to somebody in the bar: "That young doctor and the Admiral must have fallen out, or why would he come dining here? Something's up." One man, I suppose some sort of farmer or gardener, said that these young fellows often didn't know which side their bread was buttered.

I could not stay in the inn toying at this food, tormented by the comment and sick at heart at the mess that I had made of things. I paid my score and went out. I had some thought of going down to the river to fish. I wish that I had done so, but instead of doing that I wandered aimlessly about the fields, and then turned back towards the village with some half-made plan of asking for a reconciliation. I was on my way back towards the house when a villainous young man, with a downward and deadly look, slouched out of the hedge to me, to ask if I would give him a penny to buy a bit of bread, with some story of having walked from Stamford looking for employment. I had learned from Dr. Copshrews never to refuse to listen to a tale of distress, but always to try to get at the truth and to avoid giving to the undeserving. I knew that this man was a rogue; his face was a danger signal; but I kept him in talk for a minute, and found his answers to my questions very unsatisfactory. While we were talking in the footpath there, two men (both bailiffs of near-by farms) came past me on their way to the Fair. They seemed surprised that I should be deep in talk with a knave of the kind; after they had passed they looked back. I had now caught my knave in a lie and left him.

Unfortunately, my talk with him had unsettled my purpose again. I moved down towards the river, but did not go to "The Angler's Arms"; instead, I went on to another inn called "The Beggar's Bush." There was a green space in front of this inn. Somebody was playing a fiddle in the door and on the green space was a knot of about a dozen men, women and children about a gipsy woman, who was telling fortunes. She was telling the fortune of a lean, brown-faced man in a way which made him angry, though everybody else laughed. As I came up he wrenched his hand away from her and went off. She was a big, strong creature, with a face of a dark, scarlet-brown, and glossy black hair, covered with bright-coloured silks. She had big silver rings on her fingers, and had a lot of gold bracelets on each wrist. I had always heard that the gipsies turn all their gold into ornaments, so that they can carry their fortunes with them. She looked in the height of savage power and health. Her eyes were black, fierce and bright, and as the man wrenched away she turned these eyes on me, and gave me a very queer look. I had never seen her before, nor she me, but she said at once to me:

"I've only one thing to say to you, brother. You get away and hide, or the nets will be over you, and you'll be like a calf in the cart."

"What nets are these?" I said, "and why should I hide?"

She looked at me again in a very strange way and she said: "Did I say, 'Hide' and 'Nets'? Well, if I did say 'Hide' and 'Nets,' I said the truth; and you'll give me a sixpence for the truth, won't you, dearie?"

The people laughed at this, but I pulled out my sixpence.

"I'll gladly give you sixpence," I said, "and I hope you'll drink my health with it."

She took the sixpence and again looked at me strangely. "No," she said, "I won't drink your health, for there's no health coming to you for a long time; and I won't take your sixpence, for you'll need it sorely before this day is past."

At this she gave the sixpence back to me, and you may laugh, but I must say I felt my blood run cold.

I say that you may laugh: it was no laughing matter to me; there was something in the woman's manner that was terrifying; I was aghast, too, suddenly, at the feeling of the people round me. I felt upset, and know that I must have looked upset; and as this prophetess prophesied evil to me I felt the company looking at me as though I had done a murder and was now to be discovered. I tried to put a good face on it; I took the sixpence back, and said:

"Will you not tell me why I shall need it before to-day is past?"

She shook her head slowly. I thought there was a kind of pity in her fierce face.

"There's little joy coming to you, son," she said.

A couple of men who were there began to mock, saying: "What's he been doing, lady?"

"You leave the kid alone," she said. "I want a drink to clear my throat."

She turned back to the inn and I moved away from that place, feeling the eyes of all the people intent on my back as I went.

I must say I loathed that afternoon, although so much of it was beautiful. Bright, sunny autumn was everywhere. I walked through some apple orchards, where men were crushing apples for cider. They were merry at their work, and on in front of me I could hear the murmur of the Fair; but my heart was sick with misery and foreboding, with a knowledge of failure and a fear of evil coming. And as a doctor I said:

"Very likely this is the beginning of being ill. This may not be real; it may be all hallucination."

I went on towards the Admiral's house, being determined to ask his pardon, and put an end at least to some of my misery. Just as I came into the last of the fields which shut me from the grassy lane, I saw two little old men, twin brothers, carpenters, coming through the gate towards me. Somehow, I did not want to greet anybody in my then mood. The shrinking was so strong, that I turned away from them, and this, after they had recognised me. They said later (and truthfully) that I was trying to avoid them.

After they had passed I left that field and went straight on towards the Admiral's house. In front of me and away to my right hand, was all the noise of the Fair, now at its loudest. I suppose that it was then a quarter to four in the afternoon.

I headed straight past the kitchen garden for the kitchen door. I entered the little blue gate, went along the cobbled path, and there had a sudden surprise. At that point there was a gate leading into the flower garden. This gate was open, which seemed to me odd, for it was usually always latched, to keep the hens out of the flower-beds. Three hens were routing in the flower-beds at that moment. I thought: "Well, this house is all topsy-turvy, like everything else this afternoon. If the Admiral sees this, Polly will be blown from a gun." It occurred to me that if the Admiral saw me, that might be my fate, too.

The kitchen door was shut. I tapped upon it gently, but heard no noise within, and nobody opened to me. I gently

pressed the latch and opened, expecting to find the door
on a chain. It opened easily, and I thought at once: "The
Coxwains are back," so I went in. Nobody was there and
Will's stick was not in its long basket near the door. The
little cat was gone, and I noticed that the knife which I
had left for Will was gone from the slate, and my inscrip-
tion on the slate had been rubbed out. "So Will is back,"
I thought; and at that moment I felt sure that I heard a
light footstep moving in the Admiral's room.

The Admiral's room was not quite overhead where I
was; it was a little farther along the upper storey; but as
often happens in old houses, the noise of footsteps upstairs is very plainly audible below. I thought: "Depend
upon it, the old man is feeling ill, and is up there with
Will, being put to bed."

There were no signs of Mrs. Will or Polly. "They will
be changing their dresses upstairs," I thought. I sat on
the edge of the kitchen table, wondering what I had better
do next. If I ventured to go upstairs, into the Admiral's
bedroom, before I had made my peace with him, I should
have my head bitten off for my impertinence. That would
not do. "Will and Mrs. Will must be back," I thought, "because my knife has gone. They are all upstairs. One of
them will be down in a minute, then I will send a message
and ask if he will see me."

So I sat where I was, swinging my leg in time to the
pendulum of the clock, waiting for someone to come down,
or come in. I heard no noise up above, after those first footsteps. The clock ticked, and the fire in the kitchen grate
settled a little from time to time; and then I thought that
I heard a footstep or a noise of someone moving at the end

of the corridor near the Admiral's sitting-room door. "Well, perhaps the Admiral is there," I thought. "I had better go along and speak to him there. He cannot blow off my head worse than he's already blown it. But I'll wait a while still." So I waited a good while, and then, as I had had enough of waiting, and no one came, I rose up, and looked out along the corridor to the sitting-room at the end.

It was all just as it had been when I had left it, except that the Admiral's sitting-room door was now open and letting some light into the corridor. I walked boldly along the corridor, knowing that the Admiral resented any quiet step.

Now, I have said that the whole front of the house looked out upon the garden, and that the doors in the corridor were open. As I went past the open door of the Admiral's little study I glanced towards the light. I think, in nearly every case, a man will instinctively look into an open door; I did. I saw the window, and as I passed, I saw someone who was passing through the garden gate, disappear behind the gate pinnacle and the brick wall. I did but get the glimpse; I couldn't see more than that somebody went out. I cannot say that I saw more than, perhaps, just the flicker of a coat-skirt and a moving leg. I could not tell the colour of the man's breeches, or stockings or shoes; I only knew the fact that a man had gone out.

Just beyond the study was the passage which led to the front door. Now, the front door was open, and at that sight I paused. I had been startled to see the hens among the flower-beds: now I was amazed. I well knew that the

Admiral was as fussy as an old maid on the point of the front door being kept shut. I stepped to it and shut it, then walked to the open sitting-room door, tapped at it, and having no answer, went in. As I expected, the room was empty. The fire had died down, but was not out; the blue and green rug lay on his chair. One thing I noticed: a decanter of port always stood beside his chair; it had been there that morning, full; now the stopper was out of it, lying on the floor, and somebody had drunken a good half of the decanter, more than half, two-thirds. I thought: "Well, he has taken such a swingeing dose that he hasn't been able to put back the stopper." Then I thought: "Could that have been the Admiral whom I saw going out at the gate? If he had drunken two-thirds of a decanter, he, being usually abstemious, would be much the worse for it, and might well have gone out, leaving the doors open. Then, if he had gone out, not feeling well, and primed thus with good wine, he might well collapse on the road, soon after reaching the fresh air."

At this point the clock in the Admiral's room gave its sudden warning for the hour and struck its silvery chime. I was scared by the sudden noise. It was four o'clock; and now for the first time I was alarmed about him. I thought at once: "When I was in the kitchen I heard somebody upstairs in the bedroom; they must all be there. The poor old man may well have had a stroke and been carried up to bed. If Dr. Gubbins has been in the doctor may have had the port; or Will may have spilled it, trying to restore him. I'll make sure." Going to the foot of the stairs, I stood to listen, but hearing nothing, called: "Will ... Mrs. Will ... Polly ..." and had no answer at all.

This scared me; the house seemed deserted. In my scare the words of the gipsy fortune-teller came back to me: "You get away and hide, or the nets will be over you, and you'll be like a calf in a cart."

I said to myself: "I must find out what is happening. If he is all alone he may be ill and in need. What if he has had a stroke upstairs, and is lying there dying?" I went up the stairs three steps at a time, with my ears cocked for some sound which didn't come. At the top of the stairs the banister-head was the figure-head of a little ship, *The Fortune of the Sea.* The Admiral had come by it in one of his cruises against the pirates, and had kept it ever since. It represented half a mermaid, holding a seaman's shoe. Well, I stood at the top of the stair, with my left hand on the head of this mermaid, listening.

I was in an empty corridor in a silent house; the Admiral's door was closed, a couple of late flies moved in a kind of dance near the window. I called in a loud voice: "Are you there, Admiral Cringle? I am Ned." There was no reply.

You may remember that the Admiral's door was double. I knew that if the inner door were closed, he would not hear a knock upon the outer. I did not knock, therefore, but just turned the handle boldly, and found the door not locked and the inner door not closed. I stood between the doors and called: "I am Ned, Admiral Cringle. May I come in and make it up?"

From that point I could just see his bed; he was not in his bed. Craning forward a little I called again: "Admiral ...may I come in?"

Now as I craned forward, I saw that the door of the

powdering-chamber was open and that a candle burned
there. A man's foot, with a red Moorish slipper half off it,
could be seen on the floor in the doorway. I darted in towards it at once. I knew from the slipper and the pathetic
old man's foot, that the figure was the Admiral. There was
no doubt of it. He lay face downwards, with his feet near
the door and his head towards the secret cupboard. I knelt
and called: "Admiral; Admiral," but I knew from the
way he lay that he was dead. I caught at his left wrist for
the pulse, which had stopped. Then I noticed or reflected
that a candle was burning in a sconce on the floor beyond
him; it had been burning for some time, for the air of the
room was heavy with candle-smell. I lifted the Admiral's
body a little and saw that he was lying in blood, that he
had had a heavy blow on the brow, and that a knife had
been thrust into his neck. It was my knife, the one that I
had bought for Will that morning. As I lifted him up I
saw that his right hand, which was crumpled under him,
clutched a candle-sconce; the grease of the candle had
smeared his coat as he had fallen on it. Close by the head
was something which looked like a snake. It was a black
silk stocking, into the toe of which something hard, round
and heavy had been shaken. "That is the slungshot which
did the deed," I said. I was weeping by this time. "Lord,
Lord," I said, "what can I do? He is dead. He has been
murdered."

I ran to the bedroom, snatched the two candlesticks,
and lit their candles at the stump burning in the sconce.
I saw then, that the little cupboard had been broken open;
papers from it had been pulled out and now lay scattered
on the floor.

Though I was shocked and shaken (or perhaps because I was knocked out of my usual senses into a clear perception) I saw how the thing had happened. Someone chose this Fair Day, with Will at the funeral, to come to rob. The Admiral may have heard some noise and started to come up to examine with a lighted candle, or may have wanted something from the cupboard. The thief heard him coming, lay in wait for him at the door and struck him down with his slungshot just as he entered. Then, to make sure, he thrust my knife into him after he had fallen to the floor. The thief probably came into the house by the kitchen door and took my knife from the table, just a few minutes before I did. Those may have been his steps that I heard. It was he whom I saw leaving the gate. I saw the murderer, that must have been he. What was he like? Alas, I could find no answer to that question. I had seen him flit out of sight, and could swear only to his being a man in dress and walk. I could swear, too, that when I saw him he was moving to the left. It was not much to go upon.

I knelt there by the body, wondering what on earth I had better do. I was not afraid of the sight of death; I had seen it too often in its grimmest forms, to be shocked by that. But I knew now how fond I was of this old man, and how kind he had been to me. It was an anguish to see him thus, and to know that he had parted from me in anger and now lay murdered. I remember thinking that three candles were said to be unlucky. "It's an unlucky day for me," I said. I took the three candles into the bedroom and blew them out. I thought: "I must rouse the neighbourhood. John Lambert, the constable, will be in

the Fair somewhere. The Rector may be at home. But Sir
Charles Coggs, the Coroner, or a magistrate, those are the
people to go to first."

It happened that Sir Charles Coggs, who was one of
the Coroners of the county, lived only five or six hundred
yards from Hannibal House, in a mansion surrounded by
elms. I had once watched the rooks in the rookery there.
I had once given evidence before him in a Coroner's Court.
"He is the man," I thought. "Oh, if only Will were here,
or one of them. That the house should be empty thus . . .

"Well, the sooner I get the Coroner advised the better,"
I thought. "He will be the man to advise Sir John, and to
call the magistrates." Sir John, I may say, was then in
charge of the thief-takers in London; I thought of him
from the first, but judged that the Coroner and justices
would be the ones to set him to the work.

I left those rooms of death calling : "Will, Will," in the
hope that he would answer. I ran down the backstairs and
out at the kitchen door. I did not bother about my hat; I
set off running across the fields up the slope towards Sir
Charles's house. Hurrying thus, hatless and hot, I must
have looked distracted; and my hands and white stockings were all smeared with the poor Admiral's blood,
though I did not know this : I had not noticed it.

I was running towards Sir Charles Coggs's house thus,
and had gone perhaps a hundred yards, when I came
straight upon those two bailiffs who had passed me in the
fields some little while before. They had last seen me talking with a young thief or footpad, seemingly planning a
crime; now I came upon them white-faced, hatless, sweat-

ing, wild and smeared with blood. What could they think of it?

"God bless us, Dr. Mansell," they said, "what is it? What's the matter?"

I said: "Is Sir Charles Coggs at home, do you know? I must get a magistrate; the Admiral's been killed."

"Killed?" they said. "What d'you mean, killed?"

"Murdered," I said.

"Murdered?" they cried.

One of these men was called Bert, the other Jack. Horror came into their faces. They were slow to speak; they looked at each other; they looked at me. I was quite out of breath; I panted.

"Why," said Jack, "I believe Sir Charles is at home, come to think of it."

"Well, I must tell him," I said. "But wait just a second. I'm out of breath."

From that point I could see the kitchen door of Hannibal House. As I looked I saw three figures in black move, with a fourth figure, from the back gate towards that door. These were Will, Mrs. Will and Polly, I did not doubt, with Jack, the baker's boy.

"See there," I said, pointing, "there are Will and his wife. Do run and tell them. They've been away at a funeral. Run, tell them. The Admiral's in the bedroom. Don't let them find him." They turned to the house, but hesitated. "Run, run," I said. "I'm going on to call Sir Charles." They set off at this, and I started off again. An instant later the man Bert was running with me; Jack was running fast towards Hannibal House.

"I can take 'ee the short cut," Bert said. "There's a gap at the back."

Jack was now shouting to the Coxwains, and glancing back I was thankful to see them stop; they had not yet entered the house.

Bert was not quick-witted. He said: "That's Will Coxwain by the door there. He hasn't been murdered."

"No, no," I said. "Will was away at a funeral."

"Ah," he said. "But you say the poor Admiral has been murdered?"

"Yes. But come on, now; we must tell Sir Charles."

"Yes," he said. "But who is that there at the house with Will?" There were two or three others with the Coxwain party.

I said: "They must be friends. Come on now."

He followed on and showed me a gap to the left which cut off a lot from our run. As we took it I saw that Jack had reached the party of people near the house; after that I passed out of sight.

"If you please, sir," Bert said, "whoever's gone to kill the Admiral?"

"God knows," I said. "I suppose some scoundrel from the Fair, who knew that the house was empty but for the girl."

"She wouldn't have done it," Bert said, "not Polly wouldn't."

"Of course not," I said. "Some scoundrel did it for money."

"And how was he murdered, sir?" Bert asked.

"Clubbed on the head and stabbed," I said.

We came upon a group of half a dozen bound to the Fair.

"Whatever's the hurry, Bert?" they asked.

"Admiral Cringle's been murdered," I said. "We're running to tell Sir Charles."

Half of them followed us, the rest ran on towards Hannibal House. Some others joined us and caught the news almost like breathing.

One said: "You'll never get in by the gates. Sir Charles has locked his gates because of the Fair. You'll get in by Tom's cottage, there."

We hurried on to Tom's cottage, and through Tom's little garden into Sir Charles's grounds. I know that Mrs. Tom came out of her door, to ask what was the matter. They told her it was young Dr. Mansell, and the poor old Admiral had been murdered. She leaped to the conclusion that I had killed him. She cried: "Oh, look at the blood all over him," and swooned away. We did not stop, but hurried on. It was when we were knocking at Sir Charles's back door, waiting for someone to open to us, that I became aware that the horror on the faces of those near me was horror at myself. I have no doubt that I attracted attention. I was ill, I was haggard from grief and worry, and much out of breath from my run, and while we waited on the steps I noticed these men creeping round to have a good view of me and muttering among themselves.

Presently, an unbuttoned, drowsy footman, who had been having an afternoon nap, opened the door to us, plainly much surprised to see anybody there at such a time on such a day. I said that I wished to see Sir Charles at once because Admiral Cringle had been murdered. Being stupid from sleep, and I dare say still a little drunk, he caused me to repeat this, but having grasped the fact that somebody was dead, he knew well what he had to do. When there was a dead body to enquire about, Sir Charles moved swiftly and had well taught his servants to be swift.

He said: "Come in then, sir. Please come in at once. Perhaps you wouldn't mind waiting for a moment in the tenant room?"

I told Bert to come in with me; we followed the footman along a cold, dark corridor to the study or office, in which the steward received the rents. Here he left us, saying that he would tell Sir Charles at once and send Mr. Thomas, the clerk, to me. He then left us in the tenant room.

It was a dark little place: the fire had not been lighted; all the woodwork was painted lead-colour; the once black curtains had faded to the colour of rust; there were rows of undusted books on two of the walls; two blunderbusses, both black with grime, hung on hooks over the mantel. I asked Bert if he had ever seen Sir Charles at a case? Bert said yes, he had given evidence before him about poor old Dick Tollinger, who'd got into the way of eating metal, and had at last ate fourteen pounds down at the blacksmith's, mostly nails and that, for fear his innards were softening, and so had died. "Some of us thought Old Dick had kill hisself," Bert said, "but Sir Charles said, no, we wasn't to say that, he said. He said we were to say, he wasn't right in his head. A fine, big man, Sir Charles."

Certainly Sir Charles was a fine, big man. When I had given evidence before him I had seen that, and had ad-

mired his power. I had been told that he had made much
money in contracts for army clothing, and that he had
traded to sea with this money, with great success in the
Eastern trade. My memory showed him to me as a big,
portly man of seventy, rather pompous in appearance,
and with much decision and authority in all his acts and
deeds, as well as uncommon shrewdness in business matters. He dressed with great splendour, even for those ex-
travagant times. He had a rosy, somewhat plump face,
insolent, keen eyes, a mouth that was both hard and loose
at the same time, with great dark shaggy eyebrows. He
was said to care much for drink (much, even for that
drunken day), but he never lost his head for business,
even after three bottles.

We waited for some time in that little room, and I
thought: "Sir Charles has been asleep after his wine and
has needed a spill of cold water and some touches to his
dress." The first few minutes were quiet enough, then the
house seemed to waken and people passed about, now
along the corridor, now up or down stairs, always in slip-
pered feet I thought. No message came from Sir Charles,
but there sounded suddenly far within the great barrack
of a house a peal from a violently plucked bell, which rang
and tottered and jangled for a full half-minute. There
came the sounds of people hurrying and of the front door
being unbarred and opened. It all seemed to me a sign
that Sir Charles was making his presence felt. If he had
drunken his third bottle of port only an hour before, he
could hardly be ready for action immediately; a certain
preparation might be needed; and the preparation might
be angry. But the jangle did not bring Sir Charles. We

waited what seemed a long time; though all time seems long to one frantic for action. Then, without any sound of footstep as a prelude, there came a tap at the door. I said: "Come in," and Thomas, Sir Charles's clerk, came in. I had seen him in the village sometimes. He was a shrewd, wizen-faced little man, very observant, who played the flute in the church choir, and had an intense love of the theatre. He said at once: "Why, they don't seem to have given you much light. Wait just a moment, till I bring a candle." I think he went down a passage to the kitchen. He returned in a moment with a lit taper in a brass bedroom candlestick; with this light he lit the two candles on the mantelpiece. Once again we had the three unlucky candles, two of them high up, one of them on the table, all making darkness visible and the gloom more marked.

"There, sir; that's better," Thomas said. "Sir Charles asks me to apologise for the delay. He was not quite prepared to receive visitors when you arrived. He asks me to ask you a few questions, while he dresses, if you will be so very kind; it will save time later, if you have no objection, sir?"

"No objection at all," I said. "But it is important that I should get back at once to Hannibal House."

"We shall be going there at once, sir," he said. "Will you please be seated at the table?" He offered me a chair.

"No, I'll stand, thanks," I said, "but do you sit."

He sat at the table, put down his tablets, fixed me with his gentle but very shrewd, observant eye, and began:

"The things Sir Charles specially asks are: You are Dr. Mansell? Christian name?"

"Edward Mansell; and not yet quite a doctor."

"He understands, sir, that the late Admiral spoke of making you his heir?"

"Yes."

"Do you know, sir, if he made dispositions to that effect?"

"No. I've no means of knowing."

"Still, you saved his life, I believe, sir; it might be said, that you were on very friendly terms with him?"

"Yes," I said. "But there are points about my relationship which I would prefer to tell Sir Charles in person."

"Yes, sir," he said thoughtfully, making a note on his tablets. "When did you last see the Admiral alive?"

"Somewhere about half-past eleven this morning. It may have been a few minutes before that time, but about then."

"Was he then well, sir?"

"Not ill; but irritable, from his knee: out of humour."

"Sir Charles would like to know, sir, if you parted from him on friendly terms this morning?"

"Not exactly," I said. "That is one of the points about which I wish to speak to Sir Charles."

"Did the Admiral expect you this afternoon, sir, when you went and found him dead?"

"We had no appointment together; but he may have thought that I would come, because he knew that I was fond of him."

He jotted something on his tablets, looked earnestly at me, and said: "How did the Admiral meet his death, in your opinion?"

"From the appearance of the body, and of the room, I

am sure, that he surprised a robber who was pillaging his strong-room, or secret cupboard. The robber stunned him, knocking him down, and then stabbed him through the neck. I was in the house, I do believe, almost at the moment of the crime, and half saw a man, whom I believe to be the murderer, slipping out of the garden. It is most important that Sir Charles should come at once. We may be able to trace that man."

"Could you describe the man at all, sir?"

"I wish I could. I half saw him through the window. I had a glimpse only of a man whisking out of sight. It was certainly a man, and not a very burly man."

"I see, sir," Thomas said. "I thank you very much, sir. I'll go with these notes to Sir Charles. He will be down in a very few moments now, sir."

He left with a peculiar look of interest and horror, which made me uneasy. When he had gone, Bert said that there was one sign that never failed to tell the murderer. If he came near the murdered body, the wounds would all break out a-bleeding, ay, even if the body was buried. "Blood speaks," Bert said. "You can't silence the blood."

I said that murder is so shocking a thing, that all Nature tries to punish it, and in time does.

"Ay, murder will out," Bert said; "after thirty year sometimes. In my aunt's cottage now, they did use to hear a child crying on the stair, every night. And they found a child's bones hidden there under the stair. The woman who lived there before had killed the poor little thing and hid it there."

"Was anything done about it?" I asked.

"Yes; she was put in question for it. It was the blood

speaking till somebody heard. Murder will out; always it will, when the blood speaks."

I heard people moving about the house, and doors shutting; there was a bustle in the house, even though Sir Charles delayed. I could not sit. I went to the shelves and pulled down some of the books. They were mostly sermons, books of devotion, practices of piety, and comments on the books of the New Testament. They seemed to have belonged to one Eliza Coggs about the year 1710. At the far end of the room were some lighter volumes. One of these was a copy of Gay's *Fables* inscribed to Chas. Coggs many years before in a bold beautiful hand, with the couplet:

> "These *Tales* I hope the *Child* will love,
> The *Morals* too the *Man* approve."

I did not know, that that Child, now grown to a Man, was even at that time hearing from Will Coxwain in an inner room of that house, a theory of the crime which was to tumble me to trouble. I went from book to book, shivering, fidgeting and vexed, while the patient Bert sat and wondered. I was chafing at Sir Charles's delay, and wondering at it, for here was his near neighbour murdered, and all things seemed to cry for speed. This did not seem like the Sir Charles whom I had seen in the Court some months before; he had caused things to be done then. At last, going to the door, I found Thomas returning. I said:

"Will you tell Sir Charles, that I shall get back to Hannibal House and wait there till he comes? My place is there, and all my story can be told there."

"Ah, but wait, doctor, wait," Thomas said. "The horses are just coming round. We can all go together. There are the horses."

"I don't need horses," I said.

As I spoke, I heard the sound of wheels and horsehoofs on the stones of the drive on the other side of the house. Thomas held up his hand for silence; we heard doors open, and the portly voice of Sir Charles saying: "See that they come on with Thomas," as he passed out of doors.

Horses and wheels moved away immediately, and Thomas said: "The carriage is there at the door now; will you come then?" He picked up the candlestick from the table and led the way into the hall and along it to the front door, where an old, rather bent, grim man stood with a blunderbuss. He showed me a waiting carriage, and asked me to go into it. I said that I would wait for Sir Charles.

"He has gone on in the phaeton," Thomas said. "He'll be there before us."

I saw the phaeton at that moment going out of the front gate, and revised my judgment that Sir Charles had been slow. I got into the carriage, Thomas told Bert to get up beside the driver; he himself sat beside me; the old man with the blunderbuss climbed up on the step at the back. The coachman clicked up the horses, and away we went down the hill to the gate, into the road and so by the roundabout way to Hannibal House.

As we started, Thomas said: "You understand, doctor, that Sir Charles has his way of procedure. He keeps the blanks of his summonses all ready. He kept you waiting just now only so that he could fill in a twenty or so and send them out by his men. He'll have his jury at the house almost by the time we get there. He'll hold the inquest at once. He is always one to act promptly. And he always holds in making no enquiry save at the inquest, when he can make it upon oath."

I was startled to find that Sir Charles had been moving with such energy, when I had thought him slow. I revised my judgment still further. I said : "I am glad to think that there will be no delay." It seemed to me, none the less, that there had been much delay. It would soon be dark; the murderer was not yet pursued. In my shaken state I was all for bloodhounds, and a hue and cry after that half-seen figure who had slipped out of sight from me.

After this we said very little to each other. Indeed, I had a heart so full of misery that I had no power to talk. As we came to the front of Hannibal House I thought of that day, about a year before, when the Admiral had driven with me by that same track from the Manor. I remembered, too, how he had stood at that point waving a welcome to me, only a few weeks before. My heart smote me with anguish for him, and with rage against his unknown slayer. It was sunset now and a glow of light was on the house. Just such a glow had lit up the picture of the Sixteen Peaks when I had first stayed there.

The gates were locked, but a couple of hundred people were there in front of the house, peering through the gates or railings trying to get a better view. John Lambert, the constable, was inside the gates with his men. The carriage or phaeton which had brought Sir Charles was pulled up a little way ahead. Some little lads, friends of the coachman, had clambered up the steps to the driver's seat to

have a look at the house. Climbers were at every point of
vantage; every tree bore one or two. A Fair came once a
year, but who could tell when there would be another murder? There had been nothing like this in the parish for
perhaps a century. The crowd gave way as our carriage
drove up. Thomas said to me: "We'd better be quick inside, when Lambert unlocks for us." Lambert unlocked as
we drew up and I slipped into the garden with the two
others. The grim man with the blunderbuss came in after
us, and Lambert thrust back the pressers-in and relocked
the gates. Quick as I was to slip through and reach the
house, I heard what the people said. These were the words
I heard: "What? Which one? The one with no hat, the
young one? Lord, the blood's all over him still. He did it
for his money." It was absurd enough to smile at, but with
it came a serpent noise of hissing, and a dog noise of
growl, and these were caused by me. I knew now that some
of them believed that I had killed the Admiral.

As we drew near to the door Will opened it and came
outside it. He was changed indeed from the Will I had
known; his face was white and sunken with grief, and
stern with anger.

"Will," I said, and held out my hand, "this is a sad
day."

He gave me a look which went through me like a knife,
and shrank back from me.

"Enough of that," he said.

"Will," I said, "don't be absurd."

"I have a message," he answered rudely. He spoke in a
low voice to Thomas, that we were to go into the little
study and wait there. We went to the study door.

I said : "I will go to where Sir Charles is at once."

"No, no," Thomas said. "No, no, doctor. Sir Charles has much to do yet; he will not be ready yet awhile. If you will take a seat and a book, he will call you as soon as he is ready."

There were many people in the corridor, and a noise of men moving upstairs.

"This is all rubbish," I said. "I am going to see Sir Charles." I pushed past him and asked a man : "Where is Sir Charles Coggs?"

The man said : "Upstairs, sir, with the body. No one is to go up, sir. If you will be so kind as to wait in the room yonder, he will be down presently; he knows you are here, sir."

It would have been unseemly to insist. I went into the little study and Bert followed. Thomas said : "I have to see to the court-room. Will you please excuse me a moment?" On this, he slipped from the room into the corridor. Bert held a chair and asked if I would sit down. I said : "No, thank you. I'd rather stand." It struck me suddenly, that I had acted foolishly and impulsively in running to Sir Charles's. I ought to have waited for Will, and then sent him with a letter. However, by this time, I had come to know, that everything that I did or did not do on that fatal day, would be wrong utterly and irretrievably.

The study was a bald little room. I saw that a good many men had been trampling about in it recently: for the floor, usually spotless, was marked and muddied with feet. The shutters had been closed, and suddenly I noticed that there were three candles burning; one in a sconce on the table; two in the candlesticks on the mantel. The three candles for bad luck seemed to be everywhere that day. I was not a superstitious man; all my life I had been among doctors, who set themselves to know and to prove, who will try to combat ignorance and dispel fantasy wherever they meet them. But this third appearance of the three candles struck me to the heart. I remembered the words of the gipsy, that I should be tangled in the cords like a calf in a cart. They burned ominously to me.

I went to the mantelpiece, and blew out one of the candles, and stood there watching the ember in the wick smoulder, smoke, brighten and then die. I noticed, then, a little point about the mantel which was unusual.

I have mentioned that on shelves and brackets in some of the rooms there were little garlands of shot, painted red, as ornaments or curiosities. Usually there were two such little pyramids of little cannon-balls on the study mantel. Now as I stood by the candle, I saw that one of these pyramids was defective; it had three fewer little cannon-balls than the other. This I could not account for. Usually they were exactly symmetrical; Will had great pride in their symmetry. Then I remembered the hard round weights shaken down into the stocking upstairs. The murderer must have been in that room; he must have taken the shot for his weapon from that pile. His shoes must have left some mark upon the floor there; possibly even now they were there. I took the lighted candle and examined the floor. There were a good many footprints all about; all the men now in the house had been shown into that room on their first coming to the house. While I was still peering at the marks, with both candles on the floor, much to the amazement of Bert, the door

opened and the Rector of St. Marches Church came in. At
the same moment, I heard a clatter of many feet, and a
murmur of many voices coming down the stairs.

The Rector said: "They have now viewed the body and
are settling to their places in the dining-room. As soon
as they are quiet, we will go there, shall we?"

I said that I longed for the enquiry to begin; so much
time had been wasted already. He looked at me curiously,
and said with great sadness that St. Marches' Day had
never before brought such an event to Cholsington. "I
have often," he said, "I have often read the words: 'In the
midst of life we are in death'; but I have never thought
until now, that in the midst of the deeds of life we should
be amidst the deeds of death. It is a sad, sad, sad day."

By this time, the feet and voices had moved to the
dining-room and had fallen still. The old grim man with
the blunderbuss opened the door and said: "The Court is
set, if you please."

"Shall we come then?" the Rector said.

"Yes, indeed," I said, "let us come."

I stood up, and motioned the Rector to go first; he
wished me to go first, but I said: "The Church leads," and
on that, he led the way. Bert wondered what he should do.
I told him that he would have to come to the Court too,
in case they enquired about the time of the finding of the
body; he followed me. I told the old man with the blunderbuss to blow out the candles. He scowled at me and muttered something, but blew them out and clumped down
the passage after us. The company in the dining-room had
fallen still; I could see that some people were sitting in
the kitchen; they, too, were still. The Rector and I both

trod quietly in that house of death. This old man with the gun came after us noisily. He might have been Death with his Scythe clanking all his bones.

The dining-room was lit with a great many candles as well as by a bright fire. The shutters had been closed and the curtains drawn. The table was pulled towards the windows. Sir Charles sat in the middle of it, with his back to the windows. To the right of him sat two justices of the peace who lived in the parish; one was a Mr. Ryme, the other was a Mr. Suker or Soker. Both these men had writing materials before them. To the left sat Dr. Gubbins, the Admiral's doctor, the only physician in the parish, and Thomas the clerk ready to take down depositions. Opposite Sir Charles, in chairs taken from all the rooms in the house, and now ranged along the wall, sat a jury of householders. At the end of the room, Mrs. Will, Polly and a girl sat weeping. Another woman there was Mrs. Henery. About half a dozen men stood between the jury and the women. These, I supposed, were witnesses. Henery was among them. I wondered what brought the Henerys there. The table was bright with candles. I noticed particularly Sir Charles's dominant head and sharp eye. I should have said that on the table, on two big flat blue and white dishes, were the slung-shot and the sheath-knife.

All eyes turned upon me as I entered; I bowed to Sir Charles, who gave me a nod and waved to me to be seated at the table-end, near Dr. Gubbins. The Rector sat beside me. The jury had been sworn. Sir Charles was not one to lose time, I found. The door closed behind us. The old man with the blunderbuss remained outside, as a guard upon the Court in session.

Sir Charles lolled back in his chair and said that he had come to enquire into the death of Admiral Cringle, whose body they had now all viewed. They would examine witnesses upon oath to decide how the deceased came by his death and whether by accident, by felo de se, by manslaughter or by murder, and whether anybody had been guilty of causing the death, and if so, what person, and whether he had fled. He spoke with easy force, rolling his great eyes from face to face in the jury. He was a man of great splendour. He wore scarlet, heavily splashed at the cuffs and collar with gold lace; he had a fine ruffled shirt, across the chest of which some thin gold chains hung, bearing his quizzing glasses and the little ivory tablets on which he made notes. He ended by thanking all there for having come so promptly to his calls.

He ceased his prelude, signalled to Thomas, who rose, called Dr. Emanuel Gubbins, and swore him to tell the truth.

Gubbins was an oldish man who could never have been very young. He was rather a healer than a physician. It was said of him, that he could never cure anybody, but that he had a wonderful power of persuading people to get well. He was very strangely perceptive of the patient's ailment. It was as though his soul was sensitive to the exact location of the trouble. He was loved by all his patients, except perhaps some impatient young men who thought his methods antique.

He said that he had examined and identified the body

of Admiral Cringle, who had been his patient for many
years. The Admiral had been stricken on the head, between three and four inches above the left eye, by a blunt
instrument. He had been stricken with much force, for
the bone of the skull was fractured for about one inch.
The blow must have stunned but had probably not killed
him. The cause of death was a knife wound in the throat.
Someone had driven a sheath-knife, the knife now on the
table, a knife having a blade five and one half inches long,
into the Admiral's neck from behind. This thrust had been
delivered after the Admiral had fallen to the floor. He
judged that the Admiral had entered the powdering-room
carrying a candle, had been instantly smitten senseless
and had then been stabbed in the neck. Neither wound
could have been self-inflicted. The slight marks on the face
and hands had probably been made in falling. As to the
bruise and fracture of the skull, it had been made by some
such weapon as the slung-shot now on the table, which
bore upon it some of the Admiral's hairs. The slung-shot,
he added, contained three small balls or grapes of iron
each weighing half a pound. He had not examined the
other vital organs of the deceased. He was satisfied of the
cause of death. He had no doubt that the candle carried by
the deceased had been burning at the time of the fall. The
deceased had fallen on it and had put it out; his coat was
slightly singed and smutted where it had pressed upon the
hot candle-end.

Mr. Ryme, the justice, asked if the Admiral had suffered from a weak heart, and had died from some shock
to that. Gubbins said: "No, his heart was sound; he was
a hale old man, but beginning to feel age in some of his

joints. He had been murdered. He had walked into the powdering-room, had been suddenly stricken, and then fatally stabbed."

Sir Charles said that they had all viewed the body and had now heard the medical evidence; he took it that they would agree that the Admiral had been murdered; it was no case of accident or misfortune; no case of manslaughter, but one of murder. With some little mutter of: "Yes, I agree," they consented. Sir Charles said that in all cases of murder they had to examine into the case to try to find the murderer, and whether he had fled. He wished to examine first, who, as far as they could tell, had last seen him alive, who, if anyone, had been seen near the house at that time with motive or opportunity, and who had found the body. He thought, and perhaps they would agree, that the crime had been done by a robber disturbed in the breaking open and robbing a secret cupboard in the room above them. That cupboard had been wrenched open by savage force and its contents, or some of them, hastily pulled out and scattered, by someone who disregarded papers, even papers of value, in his search among the cupboard's contents. What was the robber searching for? It is to be presumed that he was searching for things of value. As he neglected papers of value, probably he was looking for money, for plate or for jewels. It is a matter of common gossip in the district that the Admiral kept a large sum of money hidden in the house. Usually the house contained within it three servants, and had an extra guard in the person of the gardener. On this day by an unhappy chance the gardener had a holiday, because of the Fair, and the two elder servants had gone to a funeral at some little distance. The gardener, being a bell-ringer, had passed his day with the other bell-ringers, either ringing the parish bells or attending the parish feast, which had been interrupted by the news of the crime. He and the other servants would give evidence.

The gardener was soon done with; he had not seen the Admiral since the evening of the day before, and had been all day long with his mates, either in or near the parish church. Will, who came next, told how he and his wife had had to attend a funeral, and had said that they would be back at St. Marches Church by the carrier's van from London that stopped at the Church at four. They had asked the Admiral if Polly might come to meet them at this van, and the Admiral had given leave. He added that Polly had not been left alone in the house with the Admiral. A girl friend, Kirrie Trinsicker, had passed the day with her and that, so far as he could tell, they must have been the last, except the murderer, to see the Admiral alive. Here Will, whose hands were clenched, turned a deadly look upon me. He then added that his girl was much upset and though she would always tell the truth, he hoped the Court would let her mother be with her. Sir Charles said, of course. Polly was called.

Mrs. Will, looking like a Female Death in her mourning gown, brought the two girls forward; they were given seats and a pot of smelling salts. Kirrie Trinsicker sat nearer me, Polly on the far side of her mother. In my visits to the Admiral I had seen Kirrie several times about the kitchen; she was one of Polly's friends. She was a good, steady, shrewd, silent girl, with a round bullet-head covered with a mop of pretty hair; she was much more sure of herself than Polly.

Polly was a very pretty girl with unusual features, which are ever much marked in women; her eyebrows were darker than her hair, which was golden, and her eyes were dark. I have always thought that fair women lose their looks at once in a time of stress, while dark women may become better looking; this may be all prejudice. Certainly Polly had lost her looks; she was all blubbered and swollen, with black pouches under her eyes; she had a spasmodic sobbing which sometimes threatened to pass out of control into hysterics. She said that she had been left in the house at half-past ten that morning, when her parents set out, that she had been alone in the house until Mr. Mansell came at eleven. Soon after this Kirrie had come in and had been "in and about" ever since. She went on to say that she had served the Admiral with his meal at noon; he had been pernickety and had asked for this and that, had then asked for a boiled egg and had refused it when it came. He had gone down into the cellar later, for brandy, had opened a bottle and had drunken some of it. She had made him some tea; but he had refused that, as only fit for petticoats. At about twenty minutes to four she had asked the Admiral if she might slip down into the village to meet her parents at the Church, where the van from London stopped. He had been sitting in his chair at a table dressed in his dressing-gown, polishing the glasses of a telescope with a piece of soft silk rag. "He often took his telescopes to pieces and cleaned his glasses," she added. He had told her, yes, to go down and come back at once, for he expected Mr. Mansell. Here she gave me a ghastly look and broke down.

I must say that my heart leaped when I heard that the old man had been expecting me. He had known then, that I should return to seek a reconcilement. But an instant later I saw all eyes turn upon me, and felt all hearts turn against me; my heart turned a little sick for a moment; for no man is such a good dog that he can bear the pack against him. But I remember thinking, in spite of all this: "she hasn't been quite strictly truthful; I know this Polly; she did not leave the house at twenty to four; no, she was off to the Fair before half-past three."

Sir Charles waited a little till she had recovered somewhat, and then asked if she had ever seen the knife or the red grapes or shot of iron now lying on the plates on the table. This question laid her low.

When she could speak at all, she said: "Yes; the shot are like the ones in some of the rooms. The knife is the one left by Mr. Mansell for my father. He put it with a writing on the slate on the kitchen table this morning."

"Did you see him put it there?"

"No," she said, "I was out of the kitchen then, sir; but I saw it when I came in and read the message. It was lying on the slate when I left the house this afternoon to meet the van, of that I am certain."

"Was it there when you returned?"

"No, sir. And the writing was rubbed out."

"When did you see it again?"

"When Father and the Doctor brought it down, sir."

"You were present when Mr. Mansell called upon the Admiral this morning?"

"Yes, sir."

"You heard something of their conversation together? What did you hear?"

This was too much for her for a time; at last she said: "I heard Mr. Mansell say: 'I come to you as the only friend I have,' and the Admiral said: 'You want two thousand pounds. What the devil led you to suppose I would lend you two thousand pounds?' "

There was something of a titter at this. The Admiral's testiness was well-known. Polly got some support from the mirth; she needed it.

"Was that all that was said?"

"No, sir. The Admiral said: 'You'd better get out of here before I do you an injury.' "

"Where were you when this was said?"

"Just outside the door, sir."

"What were you doing there?"

No answer.

"You were listening at the keyhole, eh?"

No answer.

"Answer. You were eaves-dropping?"

"Yes, sir."

"Were you alone?"

"No, sir."

"Who was with you?"

"Jack Pannifer, the baker's son."

"And what happened after that?"

"Mr. Mansell said he would go and would not feel like coming back, and the Admiral said: 'Stay away then.' Then Mr. Mansell walked out and so along to the kitchen and left the house."

"Yet when you went to meet your father, the Admiral told you to come back soon because he expected Mr. Mansell, since he expected him to return. Did you not hear him make some appointment to return?"

"No, sir."

"The last words were: 'Stay away,' you did not expect him to return?"

"No, sir."

"Why then, did the Admiral expect him?"

"I don't know, sir."

This ended the examination of Polly, who collapsed into her mother's arms and stayed there. Jack Pannifer was then called.

He was one of the village lads whom I had seen about the house from time to time. I remember him vaguely, still, as having curly hair and a somewhat merry manner. He was a good, clever lad. He was one of Polly's admirers, as the Admiral had said. His evidence was much the same as Polly's, but as he was more of a person than Polly, he made much more of the quarrel between the Admiral and myself. He said that he had been in the kitchen delivering bread, when he had heard such a noise of angry speech from the Admiral's room, that he had said: "Is that anyone going for the Admiral?" and at once both had crept along the corridor to hear. "I wasn't going to let the Admiral be set upon." He was truthful, but he had a dramatic sense, and certainly made the most of the quarrel. He said, too, that Polly had urged him to come back to the kitchen, "But I wouldn't let her go, nor go myself. I said, 'If there's violence being done, or going to be done, I must be here to stop it.' So I kept inside the little room there till Mr. Mansell had left."

Two of the jurors asked about the quarrel. One asked if it were about money? He said: "Yes; Dr. Mansell asked for two thousand pounds." The other asked:

"Was Dr. Mansell angry at being refused?"

He said, yes, he should say it sounded so.

After some more questions, now forgotten, he went on to say that he had returned with the Coxwains at a little after four, had been with Will at the discovery of the body, and had then run for Dr. Gubbins.

"Yes, I know," Sir Charles said, and allowed him to stand down.

Kirrie Trinsicker was called next. She was clearer-headed and more strictly truthful than Polly. She said that when she reached the house at about half-past eleven, she saw the knife lying on the slate with the message, "Gifts from the October Fair for Mr. and Mrs. Will Coxwain, from E.M." She said that the knife and message were both gone when she returned with the Coxwains at some time after four. She was sure that the knife on the table was the one that had lain on the slate, or one exactly like it. She said that she had heard that Mr. Mansell and the Admiral had had a dreadful quarrel about money. The Admiral had been cross all day, and at three went down into the cellar for some brandy. At a quarter past three by their kitchen clock she went with Polly to ask if they might slip down to the church to meet the van. The Admiral was then in his coat; he had taken off his dressing-gown and was cleaning parts of a telescope. He was very cross, and asked: "What d'ye want now, girl? To go to the church? Yes, go, for God's sake, and leave me in peace. But mind you come back soon, for I'm expecting Mr. Mansell." They had then set forth, over the fields, to the church, to meet the van.

"Did you lock the door when you went . . . the kitchen door?"

"No, sir."

"Why not?"

"The Admiral told Polly not, sir."

"She asked him if she should then?"

"Yes, sir. Just before she left him, she asked should we lock it? He said: 'Lock it? What for, lock it? Leave it and leave me.' "

One of the jurymen asked if it had not seemed rash to her to leave the door unlocked on a fair day, when the district was full of strangers, many of them disreputable?

"No, sir," she said, "he said Mr. Mansell was coming; we thought Mr. Mansell would be there. The front door and gate were locked, and we saw nobody about. We looked out for Mr. Mansell; but did not see him. So we did what we were told."

They had no more questions to put to her. Sir Charles said that as far as he could gather these two girls were the last mortals to see the Admiral alive. When they had left the house between a quarter past three and twenty to four, he was alive, well, busily engaged and expecting Mr. Mansell. When Mr. Mansell found him, perhaps within half an hour of their leaving the house he was dead, by the act of some felon. They would now hear Mr. Edward Mansell. I was thankful that my chance had come at last. "Now for it," I thought. I rose and took the oath. As I rose I perceived by that extra sense which often comes to us, that the company there had shrewd suspicion that I was the murderer.

I felt that nothing but the strictest possible truth could persuade. I told why I had asked to see the Admiral; I explained that though I needed the lump sum of two thousand pounds for the purchase of a partnership, all but six hundred pounds of it would be fully secured by a charge on my estate, and the six hundred pounds would be secured by the partnership itself. I explained that the Admiral had told his household that I was to be his heir, because I had once scared some footpads from him. I had gone to him as to my only intimate friend, and as the man likeliest to help me, though I had had thoughts of applying to a banker in the City. I said that the Admiral was often testy and irritable, that he had been unusually vexed that morning and that we had quarrelled. I had left the house in a rage ...

Here I was asked, had I had any arrangement or appointment to return to see the Admiral at half-past three or so?

I said : "No, none. Our parting this morning was angry. We meant never to see each other again."

A juror said : "Yet the Admiral said plainly that he expected you."

"Possibly," I said. "We were much attached to each other. We were really friends however much we wrangled. He knew that I should want to make friends. He knew that I should be as much upset by our quarrel as he was. I am glad to think that he knew I should return."

"But at half-past eleven you meant never to return?"

"A cross mood doesn't last an hour. I could not have slept without making an effort at reconciliation."

"So you returned to the house to end the quarrel? How did you enter the house?"

"By the kitchen door."

"Why?"

"Because I expected to find the Coxwain family returned. I wished to ask them to ask the Admiral to see me."

"Why did you not go to the front door in the usual way?"

"I approached the house from the fields. The kitchen door was nearer."

"Had you ever entered by the kitchen door in other visits?"

"No. Never. I did not enter this afternoon till I had knocked. As no one opened I looked in and then went in."

"Now it has been said that you left this knife with which the Admiral was killed as a present for Will Coxwain. Was it where you left it when you entered the kitchen?"

"No. It was not. I noticed that at once. And the writing on the slate had been erased. I judged from that that the Coxwains had returned."

I told my tale as you have heard it already; how I half saw some man leaving the garden; and how I found the Admiral dead, among the scattered papers from the cupboard.

Sir Charles then asked me if I knew of the cupboard or hiding-place in the powdering-room. I said: "Yes," and described how the Admiral had shown me the way to open it, and how he had told me that it contained leases and accounts of his property. They then asked if I knew of gold hidden in the house. I said that it was often said in the district that he had twenty thousand pounds hidden in the house; that he had once almost admitted that there was some, somewhere; but that I did not know where it was.

One of the jurymen asked why I had left the body lying on the floor when I had found it; why had I not at least laid it on the bed? I replied, that having some medical knowledge, I had seen that the Admiral had been killed, and felt that it might help the investigation if I left the body exactly as I had found it; men might judge from it how the crime had been committed. He asked why I had not at least covered the face? I said that in the shock of finding a friend and benefactor murdered, my first thought had been to rouse the district and bring in the magistrates. I had rushed out to do that. I said, too, that I had hoped that hue and cry might be raised after that man who had left the garden.

"Yes," Sir Charles said. "Now to go back to this knife. Will you look on it and say if it be the one that you bought for Coxwain here?"

"It is very like it," I said.

"Take it in your hands and see."

"There is no need," I answered. "I cannot swear to it. It is as like to my knife as a pea to a pea. It is most unlikely that there would be two knives of this unusual kind in Cholsington."

"We can prove the knife, as it happens," Sir Charles said. "Call Mrs. Jollycok."

The words: "Mrs. Jollycok, there," was passed along the passage. She presently appeared, rather white and frightened, and curtsied to the gentry. She was then sworn and asked if she recognised the knife. She said she did, but would like to look at it close to be certain. She then said that it was marked with her mark. It was the knife she had sold that morning to young Dr. Mansell. On being asked if it were not a very unusual knife for a young doctor to buy, she said that she had been puzzled, no, she said, she'd been upset, and on being asked why she said: "He acted so queer while he was buying it, that I felt he meant no good to somebody. I was in two minds about letting him have it, and directly I heard the poor gentleman had been killed, I said, 'That was my knife did it, depend upon it.'"

Sir Charles said that her feelings were not evidence; but she had now uttered them and that with such deep feeling, that they told as evidence.

Sir Charles said that there was still another witness as to the knife. "Call the man Henery."

A voice answered: "Here, sir," and Mr. Henery came forward, neat, reserved, hatchet-faced, with his fingers pressed together in front of him, and those eyes pale and wide apart which had never looked upon me, save with hatred.

"Swear Mr. Henery," Sir Charles said. Then, on his being sworn, he added: "You wish to give evidence about the purchase of this knife from Mrs. Jollycok?"

Mr. Henery bowed his head a little, and very gravely said: "Yes, sir."

"Tell your story," Sir Charles said.

"Sir Charles and gentlemen," Henery began, "I was in the Fair this morning at a little before eleven, as a spectator. Being near Mrs. Jollycok's stall, I noticed the young Mr. Mansell, whom I knew by sight, examining a knife. He was behaving so strangely that I could not help noticing him."

"In what way, strangely?" Sir Charles asked.

"Ay, let us know that, please; it is important," another man said.

"I can only say, sir, that he looked desperate," Henery said. "He looked, if I might put it so, as though something would have to give way before him."

"I do not know what sort of a look that may be," the Rector said. "We are not enquiring into looks. He was examining a knife, you say, and behaving strangely. Tell us of his behaviour."

"Sir," Henery said, "he did not seem at ease; he was nervous. He kept looking over his shoulder, and then knitting up his brows, as though making up his mind. Then he refused some clasp-knives; he said: 'No, they might shut up on the hand if you struck a good blow with them.' He said he wanted 'a strong knife of the sheath kind, that you could be sure of.' "

"Does that agree with your memory, Mrs. Jollycok?" Mr. Ryme asked.

"Yes, sir," she said. "Those words were used. After he had bought the knife, I said to the gentleman, 'I hope he needs it for no bad purpose.' I was half afraid to let him have it; he said he wanted it for a gift."

"May I continue, sir?" Henery asked.

"Certainly," Coggs said. "Have you more to tell?"

"Yes, sir; I have, sir; about the return of Mr. Mansell to Hannibal House this afternoon."

"Did you see him return, then?"

"Yes, sir."

"When?"

"At a little before four; perhaps a quarter to four, sir."

"Tell me what you saw."

"I saw Mr. Mansell come up towards the house from the fields in a very suspicious manner."

"In what way, suspicious?"

"Sir, he crept up, and stopped to listen. Then he peered over the wall to see if he could see anyone."

"How was this suspicious?"

"Sir, it was not straightforward. He showed that he did not wish to be seen. He seemed to be spying out the land."

"Where were you when you saw him?"

"In the lane, sir, not fifty yards from where we are now."

"Did you call his attention to show that he was seen?"

"No, sir."

"Why not?"

"Well, sir ..."

"Why not? You were spying out the land. You didn't want to be seen, perhaps?"

"Sir, we were watching ..."

"I don't doubt it," Sir Charles said, with contempt. "I ask, why you didn't interfere? You say, you had seen him buy a knife in a suspicious manner, then come to a house in a suspicious manner, yet you didn't call out, nor tell anyone, nor do anything."

"No, sir. We were waiting to see ..."

"How long did you watch? And what did you see?"

"Just the minute or half-minute that he was there, sir, till he went to the door and went in."

"Were you alone?"

"No, sir; Mrs. Henery was with me."

"Did he knock on the door?"

"Yes, sir."

"What were you doing there, you two, so near to the house?"

"We were on our way, sir, to read the Bible to old Mrs. Iffleys at four o'clock."

"That is true, Sir Charles," the Rector said. "I saw them at old Mrs. Iffleys' at a few minutes before four. They read the Bible to her twice a week."

"But come, now," Sir Charles said, "what did you think he was doing or going to do, coming slinking up to the house, as you say he did?"

"Saving the company's presence, sir, we thought he had a girl from the Fair in one of the outhouses, and was going to join her there."

"Did you see any girl?"

"No, sir."

"Did you think he had bought the knife for the girl?"

"We didn't know, sir."

"And he didn't go to the outhouse?"

"Not as we saw, sir."

"You are prejudiced against Mr. Mansell."

"No, sir."

"You helped to throw him out of your master's house only a year ago. The Admiral told me so himself."

"Sir, Mr. Rackage, my master, ordered me to see Mr.

Mansell's things removed, as he was not to continue among us. I owe an obedience to my master."

"When you saw that Mr. Mansell did not go to any girl or outhouse, but into the house, you felt that your suspicions were unjust, did you?"

"No, sir."

"Why not?"

"Sir . . ."

"I ask you why not? You had seen that they were false. Why didn't you see that they were unjust?"

"If you please, sir . . ."

"Why didn't you go to the house to see what this suspicious man was going to do there? Plainly, you had had to admit that you were wrong about him. You were foiled of the bit of scandal you hoped to publish."

"We supposed that it was all right, sir, and had, in any case, to go on."

Sir Charles scowled at him and shrugged his shoulders. "I don't think you need pay much attention to a prejudiced witness, gentlemen," he said. "But I've not done with you yet . . ."

He had a grim, bullying manner when he was against anyone. He now leaned forward over the table, and shot out his threatening lip in a very ominous way. "Hark you to me, you, Henery," he said. "Where were you and your wife when you saw this Mr. Mansell approach this house? Come you out with the jury and show us the exact spot."

This going and coming took some little time. I went with them, and was startled to find that it was dark now. I was startled, too, to see how all shrank from me, except that grim man with the blunderbuss. When we had all gathered again in the room, Sir Charles said:

"Don't stand down, you, Henery. Now, gentlemen, you have seen the lane which runs along the front of the house. These Henerys, by their own showing, were near the house in that lane almost at the time of the crime. Now, you, Henery; but wait one moment; we need the other. Come you out, Mrs. Henery, you, too, and be sworn."

Mrs. Henery came out to be sworn, too, and a frightened woman she was.

Sir Charles glowered at them, and had them both white before him, licking their lips, and everybody against them. Sir Charles had some prejudice against Henery; I do not know what it was; but I think that Henery may have cheated him in some way during Dennis's minority. Part of the Rackage estate was a small brick field where they made a cheap yellow brick, of which Sir Charles was sometimes a buyer. Perhaps Henery, as man in charge, had given Sir Charles short measure or bad quality, in some delivery of brick. Sir Charles was a vindictive man, who never forgot one who had once had a little the better of him. He watched the two wretches in front of him, and relished their misery. He had been drinking hard that afternoon; some of the cruelty in him was no doubt due to his wine. It is a grim thing to say, but I know that I felt relief when the pack there gathered changed their quarry and turned from me against the Henerys.

"Now then, you Henerys," Sir Charles said, "on your peril and by your soul's salvation, you made up this tale of Mr. Mansell to put the scent from yourselves."

"No, sir."

"When did you come to that place in the lane this afternoon?"

"Just when we saw Mr. Mansell, sir."

"Where were you coming from?"

"The Manor House, sir."

"When did you leave the Manor House?"

"Just three minutes before, sir; perhaps four or five minutes."

"What time would that be?"

"A few minutes after half-past three, sir."

A voice from among the men seated at the end of the room said: "May I be sworn, sir, please?" The man who spoke was the young man, Joe Stevens, employed at the Manor.

"What d'ye mean by interrupting?" Sir Charles asked. "Swear him."

Joe was sworn and Sir Charles then asked: "Now you are sworn. What is it?"

"Sir, I can tell the time Mr. Henery left the Manor House; it was twenty minutes to four. I timed it by the stable clock, sir, as he went out, he and Mrs. Henery."

"What made you time it? Did he tell you to time it?"

"No, sir. I knew he was going to Mrs. Iffleys, and I thought he'd left it later than usual. Generally he starts at the half-hour."

Sir Charles sank back in his chair, still glowering at the Henerys. He reflected, no doubt, that these Henerys were telling the truth. He turned to Joe Stevens.

"Did you go with them along the lane at all?"

"No, sir."

"You saw them start?"

"Yes, sir."

"Was anyone with them?"

"No, sir."

"Did you see anyone else in the lane at the time?"

"No, sir."

Sir Charles told him to stand down, and turned again to the Henerys.

"Listen, you Henerys," he said. "When you were in the lane near this house this afternoon, it was broad clear daylight. Did you see anybody in or near this house's grounds, coming to or going from this house; anybody at all?"

"No, sir," they both said. "No one but Mr. Mansell."

"After you had gone on from the house, did you glance back?"

"Yes, sir."

"Why?"

"To see if we could see Mr. Mansell, sir."

"Did you see him?"

"No, sir."

"Did you see anybody?"

"No, sir."

"Was anybody following you in the lane?"

"Nobody, sir."

"Or going away from you in the lane?"

"We saw nobody, sir. Everybody would have been at the Fair."

He reflected a little, spoke in French with Mr. Ryme, and told the Henerys to stand down. After this he asked me to stand up again. He said that he wanted to know one or two little things which perhaps I could clear up. I said I would tell him all that I could.

"You are positive that you had no engagement to return to this house after leaving it in indignation this morning?"

"Positive."

"Although the Admiral expected you?"

"He expected me only because he knew that I should seek a reconcilement. We had no engagement together. We parted angrily; crossly would be a better word."

"You had meant not to see him again?"

"That was the mood of the moment. People soon regret crossness."

"If you were not going to see him again, why did you remain in the parish? Why did you not return to London, to your work?"

"I was unsettled by the quarrel and wished to compose myself."

"It is said that you were seen talking to a scoundrelly-looking ruffian in the fields here. Who was that?"

"I do not know. A man begged from me; he told me a story, which I exposed. I took him to be one of the many rogues who frequent the fairs near London."

"Was he the man whom you say you saw leaving this house?"

"I cannot tell. As I said, I did not properly and clearly see that figure."

"Having composed yourself, you sent no message to the Admiral, asking him to see you?"

"No."

"You did not send this beggar-man to him with a message?"

"Of course not."

"Nor anyone else?"

"No. I sent no message."

"Yet you have heard the Admiral expected you. How could he have expected you without some message from you?"

"Sir, I have answered that. From his knowledge of my affection for him. These girls were with him all the day. They know that no message from me was sent or given to the Admiral between my leaving the house and their going down to meet the van."

"As you value your salvation, now, answer me this. When you arranged by letter to see the Admiral to-day, was it arranged that you should see him in the morning, then leave him, but return later in the afternoon?"

"No. I had no engagement to return; none."

"Yet you did return, just as he expected."

"I am thankful to think that he knew that I should seek a reconcilement. I grieve that it was never made."

"When you had composed your mind, after walking in the fields, had you resolved what you would do for this two thousand pounds which you need?"

"Yes. I planned to ride home by the house of a friend of my father, to ask him to advance me the money against my own estate and the partnership itself; it is not an unusual nor an unfair business proposal. If my father's friend could not arrange the advance, doubtless some banker would do so, on payment of some sum for the use of the money."

"Yet you knew that the Admiral had, or was said to have, a vast sum actually in the house here?"

"I have heard the rumours; no more than that."

"You said that the Admiral almost admitted the rumour."

"I think he loved to hear the rumour."

"When you returned you meant to ask him for the money?"

"I meant to seek reconcilement. If he had lent the money after reconcilement, why, well. But my purpose in coming the second time was to make friends. I did not wish to let the sun go down upon my wrath. You have heard a witness say that I approached the house in a suspicious way. I say 'rubbish.' I stopped to listen if I could hear Mrs. Coxwain's voice. Usually, when she is in the house, she sings. I wished to ask her to go to the Admiral and ask him to see me."

"Did you really expect her to sing, immediately on her return from a funeral?"

"Yes; she sings hymns and psalms. As I did not hear voices I looked over the wall to see if I could see anyone. As I went on I saw that someone had gone to or from the kitchen door only a little while before me, and had left the little gate open; the hens were in the flower garden."

"How can you tell that it was only a little while before?"

"Because only three hens had gone in, and not much of the beds had yet been scratched."

At this, Polly and Kirrie Trinsicker were asked if the little gate had been closed when they had set forth to meet the van. They said that it had been closed. They were certain of it, as the Admiral was so particular. I went on to say that I had no doubt that the murderer had left the gate open, had entered the kitchen, taken my knife, gone to the cupboard, and there been surprised. It was he whom I had seen leaving the house, after doing his deed of blood.

All this time I had felt the passion of those about me swaying up against me like a wave or flooding a little away from me. As I made these points I knew that some there began to think better of me. They began to believe in this half-seen shadowy figure, who had left the gate open just before I appeared.

Sir Charles said: "As a medical man, how long, in your opinion, had the Admiral been dead when you found the body?"

"I do not pretend to say, Sir Charles. It must have been between ten and twenty minutes. The girls left the house at about half-past three. The Henerys saw me enter at about a quarter to four. It must have been within that quarter of an hour that he was killed."

"I put it to you, that you had determined to break open the cupboard, in the hope of finding some of this twenty thousand pounds."

"Sir Charles," I said, "you talk offensive rubbish. I saw the cupboard opened, not very long ago, and knew that it contained no money, but leases and papers. I was also shown how to open and close the cupboard. You saw for yourself that it was burst open."

"It was wrenched open by the spike on the knife with which the Admiral was stabbed; the knife which you bought this morning. If you had taken up the knife when I bade you just now, you would have seen, that a bit of painted splinter from the cupboard has been shut into the knife, as the robber closed the spike after using it."

"I do not doubt it," I said.

"Will you take up the knife and look?"

"Certainly," I said. I did so. I knew that all thought that I was the murderer, and that the knife would drip blood at my touch. I saw a spasm of horror pass over the faces watching me. "Yes," I said, examining the splinter caught there, "I do not doubt that this is some of the cupboard. But I still do not see why any man should break open a cupboard when he knows the very simple catch that opens it."

"You admit that you knew that the cupboard was there?"

"Certainly."

"I put it to you, that you went there, tried the catch, failed to open it, and then wrenched it open at once."

"I spurn any such suggestion," I said angrily. "Even if I were a thief, why should I? The catch opens easily. If you will go upstairs you can prove that."

"The catch is now broken," Sir Charles said. "You knew that the cupboard is in that spot, and that it contains valuables. Who else knew, or knows?"

"Probably nobody. The Admiral was a secret man."

"You admit, then, that the man who went there this afternoon knew that it was there?"

"No. I admit no such thing. But it is surely the likeliest place in the house. Where else would a hiding-place be? Anyone can see that there is room for a hiding-place in the thickness of the wall there. And where would the Admiral secrete his treasures, save near his bedroom?"

"You did not tell anybody that you had seen the cupboard?"

"Of course not."

"It was not a part of your talk with the beggar-man in the fields this afternoon?"

"Certainly not. Why should it have been?"

"It should not have been," he said, "but men in need of money will sometimes enlist strange allies."

"I am not in need of money," I said. "I never have been. This chance of a partnership is a fair one, not an overwhelming opportunity. I can well afford to let it go and try for something else. Besides, as I have told you, and as you must know, from your knowledge of affairs, many people would lend me the money."

"They would not," he retorted. "You are still a minor."

At that I felt that all the feelings in my favour (and some still lingered) ebbed right away from me.

"I shall not long be a minor," I said.

"Perhaps," he answered, meaningly. There was a pause for a moment, while the Rector whispered something to him.

"Tell me, Mr. Mansell," Sir Charles went on, dropping from his bullying way into one of persuasion, "as a medical man, do you think with Dr. Gubbins here, that the Admiral had been stunned by a blow, before being stabbed?"

"Undoubtedly. He was stunned, and fell forward unconscious. His skull was fractured over the left eye."

"Would that have caused death?"

"Probably not. It would have caused a complete unconsciousness for perhaps some minutes."

"During which he was fatally stabbed?"

"Yes."

"What caused the fracture?"

"I should say the slung-shot lying on the floor near the body. The fracture of the bone seemed just such an one as the slung-shot must have made."

"Would much force have been needed for the blow?"

"It was, no doubt, a violent blow."

"You see the shot or grapes of iron on the plate here?"

"Yes."

"Have you seen them before?"

"I do not know. They are like the grape-shot arranged as ornaments in some of the rooms here. In the little study where I waited a few minutes back, several shot are missing from one of the piles. It struck me that these shot may have come from there. They are in use in all ships, the Admiral said, but these ones are painted red, and probably were picked up in the house."

"You see the stocking into which the shot were shaken as a weapon?"

"Yes."

"Have you seen it before?"

"I take it that it is the one found near the body."

"It is that one. Have you seen it before?"

"Certainly. I saw it near the body, when I found it."

"Yes; but before that?"

"I think not."

"Yet it is your stocking."

"No."

"I say, it *is* your stocking, plainly marked with your name. Take it up and look at it."

I did not believe him; I stepped to the table, reached for

the stocking and looked at it. It was a black silk stocking of no great fineness; there were thousands such in London City daily. I turned to the open end and looked inside. There, sewn on a little tape, was my name embroidered, "Edward Mansell"; it was quite true; it *was* my stocking. I was dumbfounded, and my face must have shown it. I felt the nets come over me and pluck themselves tight.

"Well," Sir Charles said, looking at me with some triumph. "It is your stocking, I suppose?"

"It seems to be," I said. "It is marked like all my stockings. The pair that I wear is marked with just such a tape."

"How did it come to be in the room upstairs?"

"The murderer took it there," I said.

"How did he come by it?"

"I do not know," I said. Indeed, I was so startled by this last fact, that my wits were all astray. After what seemed a long time I collected my thoughts a little, and said: "I have several times slept in this house, and in another house in this parish. I have had stockings like these for the last three or four years. I may well have left a stocking or a pair of stockings at one or other place. I do not remember losing any, but I may have done so. I'm afraid I'm not so careful of my clothes as I might be."

"It will be easy to prove if you have left stockings in either house," Sir Charles said. "The servants of both households are here."

I stood down, while the Coxwains, the Henerys, Joe and Tryphena all swore that I had never left a stocking behind me at any of my visits at either house.

Presently, they had done. Sir Charles said that all had

now heard the evidence, and knew perhaps as much as ever would be known of the comings and goings and doings and undoings at Hannibal House that afternoon. He would now clear the court, so that the jury might deliberate in private. The witnesses would wait in the kitchen; he and the justices would go along the passage, and Mr. Mansell would come with them, perhaps. Here Mr. Ryme whispered something to him, and he hastily said: "Ah, yes; perhaps, then, you ... Rector," and whispered something to the Rector. We all stood, as Sir Charles left the court, with the justices. The Rector said to me: "Let us go into this little study, shall we?" and led me back to the little room where I had waited before. The constable, John Lambert, brought us one candle, and the man with the blunderbuss stood outside the door.

The Rector's first act was to take the candle from the table and light the two candles on the mantelpiece. Those three candles were to light me to my ruin, it seemed. Somebody tapped at the door, I went to it, and though the Rector tried to get there first, I opened. Dennis stood there.

"I say," he said, "I'm sorry it has come to this."

I looked him in the face without replying, and brazen as he was, he didn't like my gaze and couldn't bear it, but slunk away. The old man with his gun and John Lambert with his truncheon both standing just outside the door were the witnesses of this scene.

After he had gone, the Rector tried to make conversation. Had the Admiral any relatives? I said, I believed none; for his brothers had died young and unmarried, and his sisters had died childless. He had been alone in the world for years. There was a cruel constraint upon us. He thought that I had just murdered my benefactor, and was still all smeared with his blood. I thought that he was probably there to exhort me to confess and did not like to begin. I gave him no incentive to begin, and I expect that he felt that if he did begin he might be murdered too. I knew that in the room on one side of me Sir Charles would be drinking the Admiral's brandy, and saying that he had got at the truth of it, while in the room on the other side of me the jury was debating, if it was Wilful Murder, by young Mr. Mansell. I know I thought: "The murder was done just before I reached the house. If I had been just two minutes sooner, I'd have caught the murderer, with his deed undone." I thought, too, of my stocking. "I'm caught in the net, indeed," I muttered.

"What is that?" the Rector asked.

"Oh nothing," I said. "I was talking to myself."

I know that the Rector asked me how constant I had been in my attendance at church. I said that no doctor could attend church very regularly, and that often I was called away during the service. I pointed out to him, how some of the shot were gone from the garland on the mantel.

After this our conversation lapsed again.

Presently the dining-room door opened, and somebody spoke. I heard a light footstep pass through the Admiral's sitting-room, and a minute later I heard Sir Charles say: "Well, ask the Rector to take Mr. Mansell in."

The light footsteps came to the door of the little study; Thomas opened the door and said: "If you would come, please, Rector and Mr. Mansell." So we rose up and followed him to the dining-room, where some of the wit-

nesses had now re-assembled, and the jury had taken their
seats. They had replenished the fires since I was there
last, and had brought in more candles, so that the room
was now very bright. Presently, Sir Charles and the two
justices, who had been refreshing themselves in the sitting-room with the Admiral's brandy, now came in and
took their seats. We all rose as they passed, and then settled down again. I did not need any telling that all there
were against me; that was quite perfectly plain.

A great man, who was then living, had said a year or
two before, that when a man is going to be hanged it concentrates his faculties wonderfully. I say that that is not
so; it annuls his faculties; but I know that it develops in
him an unusual sense of what others think and feel.

"Gentlemen," Sir Charles said, "have you considered
your verdict?"

The foreman, who was a rosy-faced man, with a wide
mouth and very good teeth, otherwise quite unknown to
me, said that they had. Sir Charles asked what their verdict was. The foreman said that they found that Admiral
Topsle Cringle had been wilfully murdered, and though
they did not charge me with the crime, there were circum-
stances which justified my being attached and put upon
my trial. Sir Charles said that he couldn't accept a verdict
like that. Did they find it Wilful Murder against me, or
did they not? The foreman looked at his jurymen; there
was a little half-minute's whispering and muttering;
then the foreman said: "Yes, Sir Charles, we find it Wilful Murder against Mr. Mansell."

After this there was a sort of gasp of relief from all the
witnesses; then there was silence, while Thomas wrote the

findings of the Court. It took him some little time, and in the silence the pen scratched and scratched on the paper, like a mouse gnawing through something, or trying to gnaw through and never getting through. At last he had done with the writing, and sprinkled it with the sand from the sand-box on the table. As I was very near to him, I saw his writing, and remember it to this day. I should recognise it anywhere. It was neat and rather pointed, not very good, not good enough for a clerk, I thought; it wasn't clear enough, it wasn't bold enough. When he had finished I saw that Sir Charles was busy writing. When he had finished, he turned to me and said: "Since this Court has found a verdict of Wilful Murder against you, it is my duty to see you committed to safe keeping, in order to your trial, where you will have every opportunity of defending yourself according to the law. You will be delivered from this to the custody of the Sheriff or his officers."

Thomas brought some paper or papers for Sir Charles to sign and for Mr. Ryme to witness. The Rector leaned over to me and said:

"You will understand that this is only a Coroner's Inquest? The law allows you still two chances of showing your innocence: the Grand Inquest, and the Petty Jury. I, of course, foresaw this verdict, and I have taken steps to procure a coach to be ready for your conveyance."

He waited till Sir Charles had finished writing, then whispered to him. Sir Charles consulted with the other two justices. I think that they were debating whether I ought not to be bound, but the Rector clinched the matter (and I must say that I have been grateful to him ever since), by saying:

"I feel that it is my duty to go with him. Perhaps in that case you could spare him the indignity."

Sir Charles said: "Very good, Rector, if you care to take the risk; but my own duty is clear: I shall take what precautions are usual. Where is Lambert?"

"Here, sir," Lambert said.

"Listen now, Lambert," Sir Charles said, "you will take this man here to Newgate, deliver him there and take receipt for him. The Rector here has ordered a coach, which is now all ready at 'The Three Toms,' and the Rector has very kindly consented to drive with you. You will have Spilltimber on the step behind with his gun; you will ride inside the coach with my pistols, and young Spilltimber is to go on the box with the driver. You will slip out the back way, and so avoid any unpleasantness. I gather the people in front are waiting to tear him in pieces."

The Rector turned to me: "Shall we come along, then, Mr. Mansell?"

Just outside the door was Will, removing a tray of soiled glasses from the sitting-room.

"Will," I said, "you surely don't think for a moment that I could have killed him?"

There was a deadly look on Will's face: he made a noise like a cat spitting. "Don't you speak to me," he said, and moved on, trembling.

The grim man with the blunderbuss, Old Spilltimber, and his even grimmer son, Young Spilltimber, with a musketoon, closed in behind us; and so we set forth, through the little room near the sitting-room, out to the garden at the back of the house, and so away. Soon we were in the fields, Lambert and the Rector saying nothing, the Spilltimbers talking about when the case would come on.

"The Assizes are on now," Old Spilltimber said, "but they only hear murder cases at the end, on the Friday or on the Saturday, so that them as is condemned has all the Sunday to repent afore they go out on Monday."

By the forethought of the Rector we found the hackney-coach in the road near the field path; we did not go to the inn, where people would have stared, and recognised me. I was put into the coach almost at the very spot where the three men had attacked the Admiral. Here was the result of my running up, then, to "save the Admiral's life." We made a good load for the horse, and went slowly, sometimes at a jog-trot, sometimes at a walk, by various lanes and darknesses, past some lighted places, through crowds and noises, and so at long last to Newgate.

It was late at night when we reached the door of the prison. A lamp, with dirty glasses, burned over the entrance. Half a dozen people hung about the door, and as our coach stopped, more gathered. Old Spilltimber knocked; with a click and clang the door opened, showing a lighted court within, and men who jangled with keys and held lanterns. Young Spilltimber stood guard. As if by magic more people gathered. I saw pale peering faces. John Lambert and the Rector helped me out. I heard the people saying: "What's he done? He looks a bad 'un. You'll be out on Monday, you will. What's he in for, soldier?" I heard Young Spilltimber say: "Murder," and on that the door clanged and the lock clicked. I was a prisoner.

Just inside the doors was a sort of den or snuggery for

the warders "on the door," as it was called. The Rector
pushed into this to try to arrange something for my comfort. John Lambert had to go in, too, to sign my order and
to obtain a receipt for me. While he did this, two prison
officials held me and talked about a prisoner whose case
had just that moment ended at the Old Bailey. He had not
been tried, but the case had been dismissed, because the
evidence had not appeared. I found that they were pleased
about this, because money was flowing. One warder said:
"Not one man appeared against him for all their talk;
not one. That was management, if you like."

The man who was making out the receipt in the snuggery, looked up and said: "He'll be good for glasses round
and a bit more. Cut up warm, he will."

The other man, at my side, said: "It'll have cost 'em all
of a hundred quid to get 'em out of the way."

"All of that," his friend said, "but that's management."

I heard horses moving in the street outside and somebody called to the man who had driven me to pull up further, so as to leave room. There came a running of people,
too. It was all just outside the great iron doors. I could
hear it all, but saw nothing. People were pressing round
the doors just outside. They were all free. I, who was just
inside, was a prisoner. You cannot guess what a difference
that made.

"Ah now," one of my warders said, "here he comes. Get
ready the discharge, Al."

I thought it a good omen, that just as I arrived someone
should be released. I did not worry too much at the
thought, that this man was released unjustly, through
"management." I was imprisoned unjustly, through mis-

management, or through Destiny, which at that time, and for long afterwards, I believed to be the same thing.

In the inner darkness of the prison there was a turbulent yelling and cheering. Presently some lanterns came across the court to us. A party of men drew near. They were talking loudly and excitedly among themselves. The people in the street took up the noise. Al, who had now made out the receipt, pushed out of his snuggery with the Rector and Lambert.

"Here's one of our guests going out," he said. "You two gents had better go out with him. Ah, here he comes, the Captain. Well, Captain, I'm glad to see you weathered the storm."

My two guards tightened their hold upon me and moved me a little to one side. I must say, that that grip upon me showed how very tight the nets upon me were. I was not easily going to wriggle clear.

Lambert wished me "a good delivery"; the Rector said he was sure that no innocent man need ever fear. He was a good, kind man, he was very good to me that night, but kindness is not always wise.

These little farewells kept my eyes from the newcomers. When the Rector and Lambert had left me, I saw that the two leaders were a sort of head turnkey (a pale, fat man, with a bunch of keys and a corrupt smile), and his guest, a grim-looking man, white-faced, with a yellow tinge on him and savage rolling eyes.

"This way, Captain Ashplant, if you please," the turnkey was saying. "Step this way. Your coach is at the gate, all ready. Way, gents all, for Captain Paul Ashplant."

I knew, then, who this was. This was the Captain Ashplant, charged with murder on the high seas, whose case Dr. Copshrews had talked of with me.

A burly bully of a man, who was in the party, called to Al: "Well, old man; they couldn't bring the charge when all was said." The two shook hands, and I heard the clink of coin in the handshake.

Al said: "I'm much obliged to you, I'm sure, sir, for all your kindness. But where was the evidence?"

"Why," said the bully, "they are on their way. They'll be in London by to-night's coach."

The two laughed together. Then there was a shaking of hands and a giving of largesse to the crowd of gaolers expecting it. The chief turnkey received something handsome from both men.

"I thank you, gentlemen," he said. "Really, I must say, I've never had such gents as you, nor been so sorry to lose a gent."

One of the turnkeys opened the wicket-door, to let the two pass out. It opened with an oily click and closed with a steely snap and jangle. As they went there was a cry from the people waiting: "Three cheers for Captain Ashplant and British commerce." It was not much of a cheer. I suppose that a dozen poor men had been given a pint of ale apiece for it. Then I heard the coach drive off and knew that the Rector and Lambert had already gone, and that I was in Newgate, charged with murder, and not very likely to escape.

The Rector had told the turnkeys that I was to be gently used and that I could afford to pay for luxuries. They came round me, now, to find what money they could get from me, for what they called garnish. My first thought was to find one who would take a message at once to Dr. Copshrews, who was so near to me, within a quarter-mile as I judged. But on searching my pockets I found that they had been picked; all my money was gone. It may have been done at the prison door, even as I crossed from the coach to the prison: I had no money left on me; none.

Now at that time and for long afterwards, the gaolers lived by what they could make out of prisoners. Any prisoner with money fared well; a penniless prisoner fared hardly. I came in for grumbling and abuse: "They expected a gentleman to pay his way"; "By right they ought to put fifty pounds' weight of irons on me": "Garnish is the Rule of the House. A gent is expected to pay his lodging inside the House as out of it." All the band expected something from me, while, as for taking a letter half a mile, or less, at that hour of the night, why, I could not expect a man who had been working hard all day, so they put it, to be out of pocket by it. The chief gaoler said that he'd a very good mind to put me in on the Poor Side; but on being assured that I certainly had money or should be able to raise some, he relented, though with a surliness and a grudging. He said that he did not like doing it, and might lose by it, but would take my word that I could pay for a room, and would see about finding a messenger. He took me to a mean little room, in which a dirty bed and a small square wooden table were the only furnishings. This he said would be only three guineas by the week or part of a week, but as the Assizes were on, it would not be wanted long. He said that letterpaper and candles came expensive, but that a gentleman like me would not expect a poor man to be out of pocket by them. His charges for letterpaper, one rather grimy sheet, came to a shilling, but this included the use of the pen and ink; and for candle, one candle in a battered tin sconce, he charged another shilling. Sitting on the bed I wrote a letter to Dr. Copshrews, describing my misfortune, and asking him to have the great kindness to come to me to advise and to help. I gave the letter to the gaoler, and besought him to find someone to take the note at once and wait for an answer. I said that it was not only important to myself, but to sick people, since the doctor who employed me was now left without a helper. I added that it was not far to go; one could get there and back in ten minutes, and that as soon as I had money, I would pay ten shillings for the delivery of the letter, if it were taken and delivered that very instant.

"Well, for ten shillings, then, it shall be done," the man said.

"And wait for an answer," I insisted.

The man took the letter and said: "It is not usual for prisoners to have letters taken without a sixpence paid for a pot to the taker. Have you ne'er a sixpence about you?"

I repeated that all my money was gone. He shrugged his shoulders, took the pen and ink, and locked me into my prison. I then remembered the gipsy woman's words, how I would need a sixpence sorely before that day was past.

I sat on the dirty bed, watching the dirty candle and praying that Dr. Copshrews would be there soon. Whenever I was not hoping for him to come, I was thinking that it was all a dream, and that I should soon wake up; then after a minute I would know that it was not a dream, but very real, and that I was in deadly danger, for if those who knew me thought me guilty, how could strangers think me innocent? I was not only in the nets like the calf, but drawing very near to the slaughter-house.

I remembered grim Old Spilltimber's words: "They try 'em on Friday or Saturday, so as they can have Sunday to repent; then on Monday they goes out of it."

I told myself not to hope; never to dare to hope; to do anything but hope, lest the fact drive me frantic. But I was innocent, and I was very young; hope did and would spring up. Then despair would spring up and fight with the hope in me and strangle it. What with terror, despair and hope, I hardly once thought of the old friend whose blood was now dry on my stockings.

Still Dr. Copshrews did not come, although it was now an hour since the letter went. "He must be out on a case," I thought: "some woman has fallen in labour." I wondered which woman it could be. At last the candle was quite burned out; the wick fell forward in the puddle of grease, flickered, and stank and went out, leaving me in the dark, in my cell, sitting on the dirty bed, under a sort of glimmer from a window not made to open, high up in the cell wall, waiting still for Dr. Copshrews, who did not come. Nor was it strange that he did not come, for the bearer of the note had thrust it under the door of his house and had then come away. Dr. Copshrews did not have it till the morning.

I will pass over some of the next days, but not the parts relating to Dr. Copshrews. I had always been told that misfortune will show how lonely every human soul is; how few care twopence for the grief or pain of others. I had not believed the stories; I had thought them the work of cynics. I had thought myself well-liked, respected, even honoured. I had thought that the many who knew me would know that I was incapable of murder, that I could not be a murderer. I was grimly taught the truth. The word went round that I was committed for murder; the word went with it that the case looked very black against me. At once I found myself alone. "I was in prison and ye visited me not." "Ye" were no doubt sorry for me, and perhaps felt that I had not done it, and were willing to bet that I should be found not guilty, still, prison is prison, there is no smoke without a fire. If I had not done it, still I stood to profit by it, and after all, providence that regards the sparrow, protects the innocent, if he be innocent. "No, it would never do to visit that young man, besides, I never really liked him," etc., etc. I was alone in Newgate, save for Dr. Copshrews.

He was there, with money, raiment, food, wine, and a heart full of comfort and help within twenty minutes of his receiving my letter. He had been up half the night, doing the work that I should have done, but no weariness was allowed to stand in his way, when there was good to be done. He told me to be of good cheer, that the case was preposterous, and that not an instant should be lost. He knew a good deal about the prison; he had treated some of the gaolers or their families in former years; he had me lodged in a better room at once, and gave directions for my meals to be sent to me from a tavern near-by. He told me that he would at once cause his lawyers to fee counsel. As a result, a Mr. Parchemin and a Mr. Puisne were with me before noon to settle my defence.

Dr. Copshrews had left me happy, confident that my innocence could be easily made clear, and sure that I should be out of prison within a few days. In any case, his belief in me and abundant charity and goodness had been of the greatest cheer. Mr. Parchemin, who was a lively, cheery man, with much solid sense, was a patient of Dr. Copshrews; I had met him once or twice, and had helped to set his arm, broken in a fall from a horse, about eighteen months before. He, I felt, believed in my innocence, and was as cheery and merry as I had known him in the past. Mr. Puisne, however, if he believed in me, and I do not think he did, had a critical manner, which damped the cheer left by his friend. At the trial he did better than I had hoped; he did his best; in the interval before the trial he gave me some sorrowful hours, of the blackest despair.

You will think that I was weak to despair, that religion should have given me hope, and the consciousness of innocence, firmness. Well, you try being in Newgate on a murder charge, and see if you have hope or firmness. You may think that a man has but to speak out from his soul, to show that he is not a murderer. I spoke out all I could, but they believed that I was a murderer and went about to prove it. You say that this kind of thing concentrates a man's faculties. Does it? I found that it flattened out all my faculties under a blackness of fear and misery. Then, prison itself is a weight the more, whatever you may have on your soul; you are there in the net, with the lost and the despairing; and the depth of their loss and their despair you cannot know till you have felt. In a prison, you cannot choose but feel. You see men in the yard, and know, from their look alone, that "They are to be out of it on Monday." You see faces in the chapel, and know, from their look, that they see only the one thing always flying nearer on the awful hours.

Of all the fearful places man had made for man, I know none more awful than a Christian prison. I have seen some of what the savage does: give me the savage, every time. He kills in three days at the most, however cruelly. He knows no better, and loves to have your skull on his wall or as a border to his little garden; but the Christian white man, who believes in love, and in doing to others what he would that they should do unto him: "An ounce of civet, good apothecary."

The days passed, and although Dr. Copshrews did his best, and urged his friends to their best, I dared not hope.

One of the worst things in those few, awful days, was my overhearing two gaolers discussing Dr. Copshrews, and wondering whether he ought not to be charged as an accessory before the fact. I cannot tell you how this shocked and terrified me. As far as I can now tell, it was only the natural working of the prison mind that suggested this to those two men; there was never any thought of it in the minds of the authorities.

I was not so torn with grief for myself that I could not feel for Dr. Copshrews. I was made happy by him one evening, I think the third of my imprisonment, by his telling me that he had settled his son's difficulties, and now felt sure that the same power which had saved him would save me.

The Grand Inquest found a true bill against me; and

the Assizes found room for me at the end of the week, when the murder cases came on for hearing.

Newgate at Assizes time was at its most dreadful. There were twenty-nine men and women in the prison that Assizes, waiting trial upon capital charges of one kind and another, and of these few had any hope. The mornings were the worst time, for then there was the solemnity of the Judge's coming to Court, with trumpets and crying, the wail of the poor women being taken, the stir and swearing of the gaolers, and the shouts and oaths of the prisoners damning fate and trying to cheer those going to trial. I had seen hospitals in times of epidemic with many dying, but some there had hope of cure, and were cured. In Newgate the expectation was of death; none hoped; none admitted the possibility of hope. They talked of only one remedy for death, a little gold in the palms of the witnesses that they might not swear home to the facts; no other drug was reckoned good. Many had drink and were jaunty, but as the day of trial neared even the boldest looked sick, their eyes wandered, their cheeks took the corpse-look that you only really see in a prison when the Assizes are on, and the hangman hopeful.

Dr. Copshrews gathered a dozen witnesses to bear evidence to my character. It was one of the only happinesses remaining to me, to know that some of those to whom I had ministered in the practice believed in my innocence and were ready to speak for me.

When the morning came, I was taken to the hideous, stinking and dirty Court, where the sweet herbs only made more noisome the stench of the prisoners' bodies. I

stood in the dock and held up my hand in the foul air and
pled Not Guilty to the charge; then I listened to the clear,
finicky legal voices, and watched the jury grow white,
headachy and sick from the foul air. The Judge sat up
above in his box; he was a stern and glorious-looking man,
with the eyes of a hawk.

You will have heard prosecutions calling for blood, and
defences showing the iniquity and the imbecility of even
suspicion against such a paragon of virtue as the client in
the dock. I will spare you all that. The Judge made notes
and presently spoke with great clearness.

He said that there were two things always to be considered in any question of crime; motive and opportunity.
People had said, or tried to prove, that no motive in this
case existed, or that the character of the accused was such
that no motive could have weighed. That was not so. Quite
clearly a very strong motive existed. He did not speak of
the proven need of a large sum of money or security for
the money, but of the quarrel between the accused and the
deceased. The defence had tried to make it appear that
this quarrel had been nothing more than the testiness of
an old man to one in the position of a son. He did not take
this view. Plainly the quarrel had been a real and final
dispute, such as might never be healed. Had it been a family wrangle or the usual petty testiness of age, the accused would hardly have left the house in a distracted and
despairing condition. The evidence that he had done so
was overwhelming. He had been seen by half a dozen people in different walks of life. All spoke of distraction, his
whiteness, his ghastliness, and look of desperation; and
why not? This quarrel must not only have dashed the

young man's immediate hopes, but all prospect of the promised inheritance. "Nor," he said, "is that all. I cannot doubt, and you cannot doubt, from the evidence, that the quarrel was accompanied by insult. You Gentlemen of the Jury may not know, as a frequenter of these courts knows, the terrible power of injured vanity as a cause of crime. From the evidence we cannot doubt that the old man in his rage was outrageous, and cried aloud things which stabbed the young man to the heart and sent him out white with mortification. Let those who doubt that need of money provided a motive for the crime, remember that in such insult there remained abundant motive to any quick-tempered young man.

"Now," he said, "we come to the second important point; that of opportunity. Granted (and it is a big assumption) that the young man came to the house without motive (or overwhelming motive) for the crime, and knowing nothing of any opportunity for committing a crime, he left the house after the quarrel and the insult with a motive and knowing that he had an opportunity. He knew when he left the house that the Coxwains were not there, and would not be there until after four o'clock. He probably knew (I do not press this point) that the Admiral would be alone in the house between half-past three and a quarter-past four. All these things made for the accused an opportunity, which is the second great cause of crime.

"Now the evidence has shown how the accused left the house, and how he passed the afternoon slinking about, talking with disreputable persons, muttering to himself and looking desperate. Very shortly before the crime he was seen by two very important, clear-headed witnesses drawing near to the deserted house in a suspicious manner. I have said 'deserted house,' because as those witnesses have said, the Fair had drawn the population away from that part of the parish. He and no other, was seen drawing near to the house, peering and listening to discover if anyone were near.

"Counsel has said that guilt goes boldly about its work. That may be true of hardened guilt, but the young in deed is like Macbeth, he hesitates, he shrinks, he is for casting aside the temptation, and shakes like the trembling of his own heart. Those witnesses took a charitable view of this suspicious behaviour; they thought that it was due to some irregularity of passion, thinking that some woman of ill-fame was waiting for him in the outhouse. That was not so. His quarry whatever it was, his purpose whatever it may have been, lay within the house. And it is significant that in the kitchen to which he entered, lay the weapon that was to open the cupboard and destroy the victim. Within a few feet of that room lay the shot which provided an immediate weapon when shaken into the stocking found beside the victim. The stocking admittedly is the property of the accused. How came it there?

"Now you must not pay too great attention to the presence of the stocking. What man, young or old, can say where his stockings are at any given moment? A man's stockings are at the mercy of the laundress and her assistants; they may be sent to the wrong house, they are easily stolen and as easily mislaid. The accused has for the last three years used stockings of this colour, make and mark; and declares, through his Counsel, that he may conceivably have left such stockings in two houses in the parish in which the murder was committed, both in the Admiral's house and in the Manor house, in which his father once lived. Still, it is strange that the stocking used should belong to the man who had the obvious motives for the crime.

"Now what was the crime? The crime as planned (not the crime that we are trying) was one of robbery. The criminal, as no one can doubt, meant to rob the secret cupboard of the Admiral, who was famed all over the parish as having within his house a fabulous sum of gold. The accused has claimed that he knew the secret of the cupboard and had no need of any wrench to open it. He has told us, through his Counsel, that he had seen the cupboard open, and knew that it contained only papers. He had been told that they were papers. Granted that he had been told so, granted that he knew the secret spring, you may remember the Scottish expression: 'Ise mak siccar' —'I will make sure.' Money or jewels might well lie among the papers. If the spring had been changed or supplemented since the initiation, a wrench would be necessary. It is significant also, that the thief, whoever he was, went straight to the cupboard; he knew where to go; he tried no other place, but burst in the vital place at once. It is certain that while he was busy with the spoil the Admiral interrupted him; the Admiral came in upon him holding a candle, so that the thief, surprised, had to strike at once with the prepared bludgeon and knock the old man sense-less. So much is certain. The Admiral was stricken on the temple and stunned, so that he fell and singed his clothing and smeared it with the grease of the candle he carried.

Many might think that a criminal would be content with
his opponent senseless on the floor and the booty in his
grasp; but you must at this point remember that the blow
upon the temple was not a fatal blow; it had stunned, but
stunning was not enough. The criminal had to go farther.
He had to 'mak siccar.' In the instant of the interruption,
can one doubt that the criminal had been recognised and
knew that he had been recognised? He knew that to the
crime of theft he must now add the crime of murder. The
Admiral had seen who he was and knew who he was. If the
Admiral lived he would denounce him and bring him to
the gallows. To prevent that the Admiral must die. To
consummate the frightful deed was but the work of a moment; all could have been done in thirty seconds; and no
doubt was so done. Whether booty was then taken and hidden, no one has yet determined.

"You have heard the evidence as to what happened next.
The accused was the first to find the body, the first to give
the alarm; you have heard how he claims to have seen one
whom he takes to have been the murderer, escaping by the
front of the house. You have heard all the points made for
and against him, and it is for you to decide whether he be
or be not guilty of the charge brought. No other human
being was seen near the house. No other eye saw this figure or supposed figure, who disappeared round the corner.
The accused had, though I did not stress this, a motive for
the robbery, he had certainly a treble motive for the murder; he had also the special knowledge which the criminal
displayed, and the special opportunity which the criminal
took.

"I said: 'a treble motive for the murder.' He was the Admiral's heir. After the quarrel he knew that the inheritance would not be his. But if the Admiral were to die before he had altered his will, how then?

"You now know," he added, "as much of the fact of this crime as will, in all probability, be revealed to man before the final revelation. The accused must be guilty or innocent. You have heard all the evidence for and against. You know what degree of credence can be given to what has been adduced and testified. You are now to decide according to the evidence. If you think that the evidence is insufficient, your duty is clear: you are to find the prisoner Not Guilty. If you think that there is even a grave doubt of guilt, the prisoner is entitled to the benefit of that doubt. It is for you to decide. I now dismiss you to your deliberations."

He rose, and everybody present rose with a noise of scuffle and ceremony and the ushers clearing the way.

I was taken down to a dark room where some turnkeys sat in guard of some of the capital cases who were waiting to hear sentence after being cast. These poor wretches sat white and sick and stunned, except one middle-aged man who looked at them with contempt, and a young woman who sobbed.

The turnkeys were talking among themselves of the case of Captain Ashplant. One among them was saying:

"Say what you like, he's a real gent, Captain Ashplant, as well as a supporter of Commerce. The evidence was all sailors. He just contrived they shouldn't reach London till after the case was called. They didn't appear so he was discharged. You can't help admiring a chap like that."

"No," said the other, admiringly, "but it must have cost 'em a pretty penny, first and last."

"Yes," the other said, "but there's money in that trade. Who've you got there, boys?"

"It's that murder case of the Admiral," one of my guards said.

They looked at me with interest, as a flower that gave credit to the Newgate garden. As they stared, one man asked how the case had gone.

"Oh, fine," my keepers said; but I noticed that one of them touched his throat with his finger, and winked. At this, all stared at me the more, as a flower more than ever worth having.

"Ah," one man said at last, "another Monday Morning. Well, one never knows."

My Counsel came in here and had me moved to another room.

I had no doubt whatever, that after the summing-up, the jury would find me guilty. I had no hope left. My only hope was that I might still wake up and find it all a dream; but I had so often hoped that and been disappointed. My Counsel, who looked exhausted by his efforts, said that Dr. Copshrews would be with us in a moment. I could see that he thought that my case was hopeless, so I did not ask about it. I could tell a man's mind then without asking, nor was I ever wrong. He had spoken with great clearness and conscientiousness for me; I thanked him for all his efforts. Dr. Copshrews came in then, looking very grave. He said : "I had not thought it possible that a Judge could sum up with prejudice."

We were there, I suppose, for half an hour or so while

the jury deliberated. They were very kind to be there at all, trying to comfort me, and I was sorry for them. Nothing that they could say could comfort, but I was thankful for their presence. I have thought of it with gratitude every day since then, and pray that some of my thoughts of them may have brought blessing to them.

Well, presently we were summoned back to the Court to hear the end of it. I remember thinking that the Court looked like a part of Hell, where all were sad and sick and hopeless, with unforgiven sin and perverted hearts and everlasting punishment. "I have now died and gone down into Hell," I thought; "this is it." Then I remembered that in the tales Christ had once come to harrow Hell, and would come again with fury against stony hearts and mercy for the wretched. However, it was not Christ who came in to the crying of the Judges; it was the Judge, hawk-like and proud, looking liker Lucifer than ever. All stood till he had seated himself. My Counsel who was near me, whispered: "I am afraid it's gone against you; but be of cheer still." The Clerk called to the Foreman of the jury, to ask if they had considered their verdict and were agreed. The Foreman said that they had, and were; and on being asked, declared that they found the prisoner Guilty.

The Judge made some remarks about my youth, about the sacredness of the healing profession, and the violence of the passions which had led me to this unfortunate position. He told me not to expect any least remission of the punishment rightly decreed for my heinous crime, and advised me to use the few hours of life still remaining to me in preparation for my end.

There was some delay then, for it was the custom to pass all the sentences of death together at the end of the Assizes; the Court waited while the other unfortunates were brought in. Usually they tried to finish the cases on the Friday, but it had been a heavy list and here it was late on the Saturday. As Monday morning would see us all out of it, we had very few hours of life remaining.

As I came last, I was alone in the dock when it fell to my turn. The Judge said that in view of my previous good character and youth, and the dignity of my profession, I should be spared two of the usual accompaniments of my punishment. I should not be publicly dissected nor hanged in chains upon the scene of my atrocious crime. I was to look for no further mercy from man, and was advised to seek it elsewhere before it was too late. I was then sentenced to be hanged, and removed at once to the Ironing Room to have fifty pounds' weight of shackles put upon me. After this I was taken to one of the cells in the Condemned Hold, where my cell companion was the defiant man whom I had seen when the jury deliberated. He was already secured to a ring in the floor in one corner. The gaolers soon had me shackled to a ring in the corner opposite.

"Ha," he said to me. "We're both for the cold-meat cart on Monday. Got any blunt?"

I said that I had some money.

"Well," he said, "a newcomer here stands treat the same as everywhere else."

I said that I would stand treat and asked the gaoler to bring a can of something, which he presently did. We then drank and talked a little. He knew all about my case from the common talk in the prison. I knew nothing about his. He had broken open a house, he said, and had hit the owner a little too hard, and only regretted that he'd not done the same by the witnesses, as that would have made them less talkative. "Still, they've got me," he said, "and that's that."

At this point the gaoler, who had been sharing our liquor, took away the empty cans and left us to ourselves. When the door had clanged behind him, the fellow said:

"It's said all through the quad that you got a bag of diamonds."

I said that that was false.

"There's no sense in mock modesty here," he said. "If I'd a bag of diamonds, I wouldn't be here. If you've got the blunt and could give me the office of it where it is, I could put you into the way of getting it to one or two who might make our sentences transportation. Even now they could, short as the time is."

I told him again that the tale was false, that I had very little money, and that I was as hopeless as himself.

"Well," he said, "it's a bastard being in quad with no blunt so, my joker, you and I will wear the King's Necktie. Well, a short life and a merry one, and I'll take some of it in sleep."

And with that he turned over on his straw mat.

I was thankful when he slept and stretched myself on my own straw mat, which was by no means a bed of roses.

It had lain on that stone floor, which was noisome with the compost of vice, filth, poverty and misery, for perhaps as much as three years, during all which time it had been pressed by dirty and condemned bodies in the interval be-

tween sentence and Tyburn. It was nothing but a long sack
which had once been filled with straw. The straw was now
broken to short ends, so that it resembled a black, damp,
verminous bag of bad chaff. Lying on this while the vermin
began upon me, I began to distinguish the nature of the
Hold. The floor was hard flagstone, damp, filthy and stinking. The stone walls were panelled over with thick board
to the roof, which seemed to be vaulted, with small stones.
There was one window high up, over the door. It was
glazed with thick yellow glass. It was not made to open,
nor could man look through it, even if he could ever climb
to it. It was barred across with thick iron cross-bars. The
door was of great thickness, plated and barred with iron.
I had noticed that when they opened and shut it, two turnkeys had to heave together to swing it back or to.

Even so the turnkeys had not trusted the Hold to keep
its visitors. We were in our chains; mine weighed fifty
pounds, but I had seen that my comrade's were at least
twice the weight of mine. Heavy chains linked my ankles
and light chains ran from them to my wrists. These the
turnkeys had called my garlands. The big iron rings in the
floor of the Hold they called Irons. The Irons were sol-
dered deep into the stone of the floor; they were heavy
enough to keep the victim from moving easily; they held
him by both ankles. The thick planks on the walls were
studded with big, hand-forged nails, so thickly that in no
place could one have laid a hand without touching the
iron head of a nail, but there was no point nor sharp thing
anywhere in all the surface of the wall. Those who beat
the nails in, had beaten the edges flat in the interest of
true religion; it had been feared that some unhappy

wretch, finding an edge upon a nail-head, might have contrived to scrape open a vein with it and so cheat Justice of its victim.

I had heard, and had read that one or two prisoners even in the Holds, had contrived escapes. When I had seen this Hold I knew that none could escape save by the help of someone in the prison. Even then, the escaper must have great strength, agility, luck and tools, as well as the skill to use them. My days in prison, loathing food, had taken much strength from me; the Hold was pitch dark now; and I had no tool, not even a pin or a toothpick.

I asked my companion presently when he woke, if there were any chance of our escaping, since some had escaped.

"No," he said, "not without you've got a girl who's the turnkey's darling, and has a pot of blunt to boot. If she'll slip you some files, a jemmy or two, and some of these lock-pickers, I don't say. Have you got those?"

I said : "No."

"Well, my lovey-dovey," he said, "I reckon you'll have to stay till Monday."

I had resigned myself to a long, long night of misery, when the locks were turned and the door was opened. The chaplain was admitted to us. He had a battle-lantern with him, a ship's lamp with a strong reflector, which gave many times more light than the turnkeys' usual lanterns. He put this upon the floor and began his ministrations to us. He was a good, devout man who did bring comfort to many poor souls there. To my companion he brought some chewing tobacco, and to me some sugar candy. Perhaps people cannot guess what cheer a little present may bring in a place like the Hold. He offered spiritual comfort, too;

but my companion was not one to receive it. He had lived in violence and defiance and meant to die so. I myself was not one to receive it either, in that mood of mine. But let it not be thought that I have anything but praise for the sweetness and patience of his devotion. He gave all the charity of his nature through all the years of his manhood to the friendless, the mad and the lost, to whom his gentleness was often the first ever shown, and his comfort always the last ever given.

Dr. Copshrews was the one light to me in those hours. In the forty hours left to him he tried to stir a petition for me, he tried to urge a re-trial, he tried to obtain a mitigation of sentence. When he knew that there was no hope, he said : "Be sure that I will not rest, till I have seen you justified." My goods, as I knew, were confiscate to the Crown ; I had only my body left to me. I remember his saying to me : "Be sure that I will see that bestowed."

You will think all this a little matter. It was everything to me who had nothing left, save that man's good thought of me. I knew, too, and have discovered since then, how men cast it in his teeth, that he visited Newgate to see his past apprentice who had foully murdered his benefactor.

At three that next afternoon the door of the Hold was opened. The turnkeys stood there, calling my name. I thought : "It is the chaplain again. Why cannot he leave me alone, to die at least in quiet." But it was not the chaplain, it was Dennis, very raffish and loud but a shade ill at ease.

"Well," he said, "and how are you? I'm sorry to see you here. By gad, they don't give you much of a place to roost in."

I said : "No."

I had hated Dennis pretty badly always I suppose, but worse then than ever.

"Well," he said, "it won't be for long, I suppose. It's to-morrow you go out, I think?"

As he knew, I didn't answer.

"There's one thing I came to ask," he said. "You can tell me or not, just as you like. You may know where the Admiral stored his gold. Eh? He told you, didn't he?"

"I know nothing of any gold," I said.

I felt that he looked at me curiously. The keeper had allowed him a candle; he could see my face as I could see his.

"We know the gold is somewhere," he said.

"Who are 'we'?" I asked.

"The people who remain," he said, "who are likely to be interested."

I did not answer this; we remained silent for a while. He said that the place was pretty poisonous and that he wasn't going to stay. I said that the chances were that he would come back, and stay.

"You think so?" he said. "I think you're wrong. Well, if the bird won't sing, it won't. And to-morrow it won't be able to sing. So you won't tell me where the gold is? You might tell a fellow. It is not possible for it to do you any good, but if you would tell me I could do you a lot of good, even now."

"What good?" I asked. "What good can you do me, beyond leaving me alone?"

"Why," he said, "if you tell me where the gold is, and it is known to be a big sum, much could be done. I could oil the palms of three or four so that there would be a reprieve."

"No, you could not," I said. "This is Sunday afternoon; you would not have time. Even if you had half the gold in Christendom, you could not on a Sunday get at the people; nor could they, nor would they get at the King."

"Even if what you say were true," he said, "you forget that there are other ways. A few hundreds of guineas in the hands of the warders, less than that, one hundred, we should have an escape; that could be arranged. Life is sweet. It would only cost a hundred guineas. And this gentleman, your companion, might be glad to add his words to mine. I'm asking this man to tell me where the gold is so that I may buy your escape," he said, raising his voice, and turning to my companion. "Since he doesn't seem inclined to deal perhaps you can persuade him."

I saw my companion turn his eyes on Dennis; he had a real wolf look, hungry and fierce; he looked hard at Dennis, then he looked hard at me. He did not speak. He seemed to have made up his mind about the case.

Dennis spoke again. "See here now, Ned," he said, "we never quite hit it off, I know, but bygones are bygones. Hannibal House is coming into the market of course. The Crown is selling. I'm going to put in for it, to find what it contains. If you'll tell me where the gold is so that I shan't have to pull the whole place down, why, I can do something for you that will save you even yet."

"Can you save my friend, too?" I asked, indicating my companion.

He looked at me with a sudden quickening of greed. I

was sure that he would tell any lie in order to have the secret.

"Yes," he said, at last, "I can do as much for your friend."

"What is it, then? Show," my companion said.

The door, which had been ajar, was pushed open and then closed; a turnkey who had been listening there, had now entered. Dennis pulled out his purse and showed the man some guineas.

"See, warder," he said, "you spoke of being able to do something for my friend. Perhaps you could do as much for the other?"

"What can you do?" I asked.

The turnkey looked with some alarm at my companion; and then said, yes, he could do much, and could do it for both of us.

"Show, then," my companion said.

The turnkey said that he had a thing which had been used several times with gents, yes, and ladies; a silver tube, which went into the windpipe and saved you from being choked. He had the tubes and could slip us one each, yes, and see them fixed for us. Then, if we would pass the word to our friends, we could be taken to a place near-by, where they could restore breathing and open a vein and there we should be, free men. "Of course," he added, turning to my companion, "the gentleman will do the handsome thing by you and set you up in life."

My companion looked at the two of them with bitter mock. "Don't try to come any of that guff here," he said. "I'm too old a bird. Many a poor Joe has given his last

tosser to stick your silver straw in his gullet, and what
one has ever been saved by it, I ask you?"

"Lots have been saved by it," the turnkey said, "and all
would be, only they struggle."

"Ah, they struggle, do they?" said my companion. "Listen you to me, now. I've been among smashers and bow
men all my days. I've been near to being nobbled half a
hundred times, and I've known scores paid for this silver
pipe, as you call it, a bit of chemist's copper pipe, if you
ask me. It never saved a man yet and never will save. But
I'll bet it's as good as fifty guineas a year to each of you
turnkeys; that tube which saves men's lives. But you've
come to the wrong shop here."

He leaned back on his pallet with his head against the
wall and looked at the two of them. "I don't which of you
two lice I like least," he said. "Well, I'm going to God to-
morrow, they tell me. I'll tell Him some truths about you,
I promise you. You're Mr. Dennis Rackage, who sold that
fight of The Jouncer's. By God, I'll do you an injury yet."

He leaped up with a sudden shock and clank which
made them both leap back, though they must have known
that the man was ironed fast and could not possibly reach
them. They moved back to the door and for a few seconds
did not speak. However, Dennis was greedy for gold; it
was his ruling passion; and he began again on a different
tack.

"It's very hard," he said, "to come down here at some
risk and trouble to try to help you, and then be misunderstood and not answered. In any case I shall have the gold,
if I have to pull down the house piecemeal. You might just
as well tell me what you know."

"Don't be too sure that it is in the house," I said; and I said this with malice, for if the house were a large place to search through, the gardens and outhouses were larger.

"Get out," my companion said. "Get out."

"I'm getting out," said Dennis. "I've given you your chance. Well, I won't waste good breath on you in this stinking den. As for you, Ned, you were always a poor stick, and now that you've come a mucker, you're a poorer one than ever. You and your mate there will sing smaller to-morrow when the cart is at the door."

And at that he took a pinch of snuff with great insolence, and left the cell.

"Don't you mind 'em," the turnkey said to him, "don't you mind 'em, sir. They'll come round before to-morrow. They'll be glad enough to hear from you, when it's time to start."

He went out, and with a great heave clanged the door to and locked it.

"Ah," my companion said, "they've got the greed of the grave, them turnkeys, and that bright lad was the one who sold The Jouncer's fight, and I'm sad I couldn't smash his face in. But as I'm not going to rejoice again, I'm going to rejoice to-night so soon as ever my man brings the brandy; and if you take my advice, you'll do the same."

The chaplain visited all of us later that evening, to fit us, as he said, for our journey; but we asked him to leave us and try to console the poor woman at the end of the row of cells; when he had gone the brandy came, for which all in the Hold were thankful. After the brandy, though we had only a few hours left, we all slept heavily, as condemned men often will.

I was wakened by the turnkey who had brought Dennis there the night before. He produced a bit of paper and a chalk, and said that he came from the gentleman (meaning Dennis), and that if I would just note on the bit of paper the whereabouts of I knew what, why, the man in the cart with me would slit my pinions with a pen-knife just as we passed Turnstile, and I could leap down and be in the fields and away. I could not fail to get away. It was plainly false, so I laughed in his face. I knew that this proposal was one more of Dennis's lies. There would be no knife to slit my pinions, no chance of escape at Turnstile. The dog was a dirty dog to me the end.

But now, from the stir in the filthy den it was plain that it was time. We were taken out to have our irons knocked off and ropes put on us instead. The State had never cared for its children so tenderly before, but now it gave a cart, a chaplain, armed guards on horseback, and foot guards to clear the mob from the gates. I will not tell of all this.

As we passed the Turnstile I saw that it was all blocked by a hoarding, so that no man could have darted through it. That had been a lie the more from one or other of them. I was glad that my days in prison had at least made me quick to detect falsehood.

It is two or three miles, as I suppose, to Tyburn from Newgate. It was the custom to stop at the "George," on the way, to drink the strong drink left by some charitable soul as a comfort to those about to be killed. Some poor souls were too sick to drink, others feared to stupefy themselves just before appearing before their Maker, but the carts always stopped, and all feared to lessen the delay, for a story went about that in the past a man had refused to stop, had

gone on and been hanged, so that he was out of the world
before his reprieve came; had he but stopped as usual he
would have had this, and been set free. We drank our
drams and went on; the delays brought no reprieves to us.

As there were no reprieves there were executions, all of
them reported on by the chaplain, and commented on in
broadsheets in which you may read the full story of how
that hardened young villain, Edward Mansell, refusing
the pious ministrations of the Ordinary, died unrepent-
ant, with the blood of his benefactor on his hands. They
were sold for a penny or a halfpenny during that week;
they are scarce now, but may still be had round the Dog-
geries; they take a stern, moral view of me.

One of them has a woodcut portrait of me. When I was
looking through these broadsheets I found that this portrait had figured, two years before, as Jonas Sickface the
Child Murderer, and figured again some years later as
Arch the Poisoner.

I died denying Providence. If Providence could watch
unmoved the misery of a boy unjustly hanged I reckoned
that I would have none of it. I died hating men, loathing
life, longing to be quit of it for ever, yet in terror of what
might be to come. If you think that you would have died
in nobler temper, do try it.

Somebody, some medical writer, whose name has gone
from me, once wrote that to be born may be as painful as
to die. It may be so. Dying I found unendurable, and then
suddenly very pleasant. Being born again was torment of
a very terrible kind.

I know that there was a succession of waves of red fire,

each painful, which came along my brain and seemed to break behind my eyes; then there were stabbings and confusions and red-hot gimlets in all my veins and at my extremities. In all this I had a confused sense that I was still I and that probably I was dead. There was a good deal of confused pain, a knowledge of this fire on my brain, and a sense of fire and of shadow passing and surging. It may be that I struggled and moaned; I had a sense of great struggling and moaning and being unable to get any farther. I know that I was somehow aware of terrific shadows passing and moving, but the pain of looking at them was too great. After an eternity of all this I knew that I was in Hell. I knew that I had been judged, although I could not remember being before the Judge, and that now I was with the damned in Hell, to burn and be tormented for ever and for ever and for ever. I did not know how anybody could endure any such torment for even a half-hour; and at that the horror, as I suppose, became unendurable and I swooned.

Presently it seemed to me that the pain was less and that certain things were more distinct. But they were not yet clear and I had ever a horror of the thing not quite clear. I was in a bad dream in which things happened over which I had no control. There were again great shooting shadows and big figures moving. It was hot and I was helpless, tied, as I supposed, and I was being moved from side to side in a rhythm. Again I knew that I was in Hell. People were right, after all; there was a Hell. In spite of all the misery that they inflicted on each other and themselves, Hell was waiting for them at the end. This was it, exactly as the books said, hot, thirsty, agonising and continued. But this was only the beginning of it: they were only just beginning on me. And why were they so down on me? What had I done to deserve all this? Why had I not been told?

It struck me soon that Hell was strangely silent, there were slight noises, but not the yelling, shrieking, howling and devilry which Newgate had led me to expect; nor was there the hammering and clanking of chains, metals and so forth. It struck me that perhaps the devils made life easier for themselves by destroying the vocal cords of their victims. It seemed a sensible act. Yelling would be a relief to the victim and a great annoyance to the devils in charge of the case. My own throat was very painful, so painful that I was sure that my own vocal cords had been torn out. From time to time an appalling face drew near and then receded. He came near again and spoke: "He's come back," and a voice nearer to me said: "It looks like it." "So the devils talk English," I thought; but then I reflected that of course an English soul would have an English devil. He would know so much more subtly what would torment an English soul. I tried to move myself but felt myself controlled and being swayed from side to side, as before, and a hand came along my bare ribs and touched me up and down as though palping for a nice place to stick the claws into. I remembered all that I had read and seen imaged of Hell. The worst scenes known to me were some of female devils or harpies, who had less mercy than the male devils, so my informants had always said. I concluded that the female devils would be let loose presently. Then I reflected that I did not know how long I had been there, nor how the time was passing; it was passing slowly, but however slowly it might be passing, it was not going to pass: it would never pass, but go on and on and on. However much I might be destroyed I never should be destroyed, there would ever be something to torment and to suffer. But at this point the appalling face with the great eyes drew near to me. It was that of an old rosy devil, bald as a vulture, with no vestige of hair on the skull except the white bushy eyebrows above the great burning eyes. The face glared down close to mine, so that I could see the coarse wiry hair of the brows and the yellow gleam in the eyes. I smelt a smell of pouncet, and saw the trace of sweet snuff at his nostrils.

"He'll do," he said in his stern voice, "but keep on with the breathing. We'll get the heart later."

I remembered to have read that devils tore people's hearts right out with tongs. That was what they were to do later, get my heart. Of course they had torn out my vocal cords, and I had swooned from the agony and the shock. Now, although my throat was in pain they were getting me ready to pluck out my heart; very likely the fire which caused the shadows above me was being kept in to heat the tongs or pincers. "We'll get the heart later." What would they do with the heart? Blister it, I supposed, and then put it back so that it might be torn out again, then again, then again. And why? What had I done that was so atrocious, that I had deserved all this? What wild, awful and unpardonable crime had I contrived to do? Was it pride? I had as I thought been but ordinarily wicked. Yet here I was in Hell, even after a frightful punishment in life. Somebody had once said that some church or religion had the theory that those who were much punished for their sins during their lives on earth were less punished after their deaths. It did not seem correct somehow. I had been punished with man's extremest penalty, for a sin that I had never committed, yet here I was in Hell suffering the torments of the damned and about to have an even fuller measure. Presently the appalling bald head looked closely down on me again.

"I expect he's feeling the torments of the damned," he said; "red-hot spikes and trickles in every vein. But he understands, I see. Hurting you, are we?"

I tried to say: "Yes, most damnably," but my voice was not under control; I said some rubbish.

The devil knitted his brows and said: "I would give him a dram, Jordan."

"Perhaps it might be well," the other devil said.

He had been rolling me from side to side, this devil named Jordan. It seemed an odd name for a devil, the name of a river in Palestine, but Hell was probably an odd place, and inhabited by a lot of fallen angels among others. Jordan may once have been a rather special angel. His rolling of me stopped and presently he brought me a little brandy in a glass and held up my head while I drank. It was kindly and skilfully done, and the brandy was new life to me. In a few seconds of rapture I knew that this was not Hell, but a room with a fire, a long room, well lit by the fire and by candles, as well as by sunlight. I was on a table under restraint, for a bandage held me to the table. There was a picture on the wall over the fireplace. The hairless, awful face craned forward at me and spoke.

"You're back again," he said. "I don't suppose you are thanking us at the moment. How is it now with you?"

Though he looked very awful without any hair but these extraordinary eyebrows, he spoke with kindness. I tried to answer, but could only gurgle, myself being not quite returned and my throat, for a very good reason, being out of order. I perceived that the other devil, Jordan, was sitting at my side; he had been rolling me about.

"His breathing's all right now," he said. "He is going to live. I'll let up on the rolling. Now I'll take his heart." I made an effort at this; he restrained me. "Quietly does it," he said. "No strains yet, lad."

The older devil with the eyebrows said: "Well, since the worst is past, I'll dress."

I saw him move to the wall, take a wig from the peg, and adjust it upon his bald crown. It cast a shadow on the ceiling exactly like Satan putting on a horned crown.

There came a tap at the door; the man Jordan went to the door and asked: "Yes, who is it?"

A voice, which seemed somehow familiar, said: "It is all right."

Jordan unlocked the door and let in Dr. Copshrews.

"He's round; he'll do, Father," Jordan said.

Dr. Copshrews came quickly to me, looked at me, took my pulse, went to the old devil and said something of heartfelt thanks, then came again to me, and said:

"Ned, my dear boy; don't try to talk. You're round. Be easy in your mind, now."

By this time the old devil, for so I call him, had finished his dressing and washing. I recognised him now. He was Sir ———, the famous surgeon. I had seen him three times doing his famous operation, still known as ———'s Section. I will not mention his name. He came up again to look at me in his shrewd, medical way.

"Well, we've got you round," he said. "You must take it easy for some days. You may trust us. We believe in you. I knew your father. It was I started him on those precious kidneys he was so fond of. Think of nothing but rest. He'll do now, Copshrews."

I gurgled something about wanting to know where I was. As I was probably unintelligible, he guessed my meaning, as wanting to know where I was.

"You're in my house," he said, "and here you'll stay a while. Rest easy."

He said something to Dr. Copshrews about my being better in bed in the dark. They shifted me to a bed; then he took away the candles and drew the curtains; then all three of them left me.

I was in a comfortable bed, but in a good deal of pain. I had been washed and now smelt of a solution of vinegar. I was in soft, clean linen and a fire was burning near me. I know that the thought came to me that I had been sick to death of some fever and had dreamed all the horror in my sickness; that now I was in my right mind, and would perhaps find the Admiral alive still, and all the horror just a nightmare shattered by waking. I suppose that I slept for many, many hours and wakened to a new world.

It was latish the next day when Dr. Copshrews next came to me. He told me that Sir ———, as an old friend of my father, had suggested that he should try to restore me, after the Law had done with me. It was well-known among doctors that the supposedly hanged were quite frequently restored on the dissecting table. Sir —— and he had resolved to try it in my case. They were sure of my innocence; they were sure that in time they would prove it. Jordan Copshrews, the son, the reprobate, usually called Dick, who had some medical knowledge was their accomplice. He had brought my body at speed from Tyburn to the surgeon's house in the Fields and there, after a long tussle, they had brought me back from wherever I had been. He added: "I did not mention this plan of mine to you, for it is wrong to raise false hopes; and I had feared that the sentence might make it impossible. So far all has gone well. You need have no fear. You have been born again."

Something in his face or voice gave me my sick man's certainty, that all was not quite well.

"There is some fear," I said. "What is it? Am I to be taken back? I'd rather you cut my throat at once."

"No, no," he said. "There is no fear of that; none."

"Ah, but there is," I said. "I know very well that my sentence was that I be hanged till I be dead. I am not dead as it seems, therefore my sentence is not carried out. You haven't been in Newgate as I have; they talk of these things there; hardly of any other thing. As a convicted murderer I am without hope of pardon. If they find me alive they'll hang me again. I know that there have been men and women restored from the gallows who have been pardoned, but never murderers. It was to stop murderers from being saved thus that they caused them to be dissected publicly. I only escaped that by a bare chance. But I'll not go back to Newgate alive; never."

"Gently, gently," he said. "We all think that you are safe."

"How can I be?" I asked. "And you cannot be. You and your son and Sir —— are liable to be hanged for aiding a condemned felon. You'll all be hanged if you're caught."

"Then we shall need a Staffordshire gallows," he said gently. "Three men in the one knot."

"Tell me," I said, "there's danger. What is wrong? Let me know the worst."

"I do not know that anything is wrong," he said, "but that pernicious man, Dennis Rackage, has been to me asking to see your body."

"Whatever for?"

"I do not know."

"What did you tell him?"

"I told him that you were buried yesterday, in St. Giles's."

"But that is false."

"I am not without guile of a sort, Ned, or forethought perhaps," he answered. "I expected and feared I might have to bury you. I expected also to have difficulty with the clergy. I prepared for both troubles. And I thought it prudent to have a body. You know very well that we doctors can always get a body. I found a clergyman willing to make an exception in your case and to bury 'you' in consecrated ground. Consequently 'you' were buried yesterday."

I was not relieved by this. I was now terrified. Of course Dennis suspected; he could not possibly fail to suspect, that the doctors might have conspired to save me. He believed that I had done the murder, had found and had hid-

den the Admiral's treasure. Naturally, he supposed that
on a word from me, the doctors would save me, that I
should retrieve the treasure and share it with them. Now
he was prying round to make sure that I was dead. He had
wished to see my body. If he hinted his suspicion to a magistrate, the grave would be opened and the fraud shown.
He would get some reward for that perhaps, or be able
to get hush-money from Dr. Copshrews. Half of this was
mad enough, no doubt, but you spend a while in Newgate
and take the Tyburn ride, and see how sane you will be.

Dr. Copshrews saw my terror. "Be of good cheer, Ned,"
he said. "The grave is watched by the watchers, to keep it
from the resurrection men. It will have a stone slab
marked 'E.M.' on it to-night, as well as iron railings round
it."

"I don't fear the resurrection men," I said, "I fear the
magistrates."

"What can the magistrates do?" he asked. "They may
order the grave to be opened and may see it opened. What
then? 'You' have been buried in quick-lime. No man will
be able to swear to you."

This was a great relief to me; but men who go to Newgate hear much of the tiny chances which betray them
thither. I was not freed from my fears.

"Who is in this house?" I asked. "Who knows of my
presence here?"

"Sir ———, my son, myself and you," he answered.
"This is a lonely house to which Sir ——— comes for Sun-
days and holidays. No one save we four knows that you
are here. No one can suspect. You were not seen to enter
nor is anyone likely to look for you."

"The sooner I get out of England the better," I said, "if you can help me."

"We will talk of that when you are quieter," he said, and made me swallow a sleeping-draught.

Presently, when I was quieter, Sir —————— and Dr. Copshrews came to my bedside to talk of my future, which was not rosy when examined. I could not stay in England without fear of discovery. I could not very safely go to Scotland or Ireland. I had no name. I had no possessions. All my belongings, all my money on mortgage, and all the Admiral's property which had been left to me, had been seized by the Crown, even to the knife, value two shillings, which did the deed. I had no past, and therefore no profession. I was just a neck condemned to be strangled, and certain to be strangled if caught.

They thought that my only chance was to get to some new country, where I could practise medicine without much (or indeed any) enquiry into my qualifications. Even there, they judged that I ought to be very careful and cautious. They said that I ought to get away from London soon and be out of England that month.

"The first thing we must do for you," Dr. Copshrews said, "is to get you a name; I would offer you mine but it might draw attention to you. I would suggest that you keep your first name of Edward or Ned; you would find it easier to answer to. Have you any sort of preference for any name?"

I said : "Yes; I have always liked the name of Torrance or Torrens."

They agreed that that was a pretty good name and would have my linen marked by it. They were then busy for a while taking my main measures, so that they could procure me a kit of clothes. Sir ——— was the next to speak.

"You are safe here," he said. "I've often had patients lying quietly here for private treatment. You are now one of them. Still, harbouring a condemned felon is against the law, and there are such things as informers who receive reward for their reports. And no public man can be really safe in London. You are known to thousands, remember. Patients never forget those who minister to them in sickness: their faces are stamped on them. You have treated hundreds, nay thousands, of Londoners; any one of them who might happen upon you would infallibly recognise you and betray you. The thief-takers talk to everyone; it is astonishing how they come to know things. Young Mr. Copshrews will take you to his place in the country tonight. You had better stay a week there, chiefly in bed getting your strength, and only going out of doors at night. In the meantime I have written to a friend in Liverpool, a rum and sugar merchant, who trades to the West Indies and knows the ships sailing. I have asked him to help you to a passage as a ship's surgeon. I do not doubt that in a few days' or, at most, in a few weeks' time, he will be able to fit you with a ship. Now you may know that the ships in the rum and sugar trade make other passages. They go to Africa."

"Yes," I said, "I read only the other day, that they are slavers, and take slaves to the West Indies."

"Yes," he said, "and for those reasons they always need surgeons, and sometimes find it very difficult to find them or to keep them. You will be employed at once; you need have no fear of that. It will be a bad five or six months for you; but at the end of that time you will be in the West Indies or the Americas, one or the other. You will be well paid in the outward and middle passages, and will have an equipment of drugs and instruments in the ship. Dr. Copshrews and myself, who believe in you, will fit you with a purse for your start. Now you have your name, Edward Torrance. Will you think out a past for yourself? It is not an easy thing to do. You speak French, Dr. Copshrews says, and have been in Paris. Well, it may help if you invent a father who practised medicine in Paris and lived a wandering life abroad, teaching you as he went. You will have to be very reticent. Then, for your writing; you have hurt your arm; you must use your left hand. It is hateful to have to lie and invent thus; but life has so treated you that you have no choice. Dr. Copshrews is sure that though this is not a grand start in life, it is one that you will improve. It is the first step that counts."

Since I was not to die and had had enough of England for the time, exile seemed a blessed thing to me. In any case the belief and the kindness of these two men was blessed to me. I thanked them, and prepared for my future with reviving hope.

Young Mr. Copshrews lived in the country in the pretty village of Hampstead. I drove out there after dark as a sick man, swathed in coats and rugs, and bearing with me as baggage a trunk marked "E. Torrance," full of new clothes. I went to my room on arrival and went to bed. It was a very pretty room, for young Mr. Copshrews had an eye for elegant things. I was told that I was to play the sick man, and to pass the greater part of my time in bed-

"getting my strength." This was agreeable enough. I was
worn out, and found that I could sleep for the greater part
of each day. But on the third day, as I woke, I found the
elderly maid in my room, looking at me very curiously,
and asking: "Did I please to ring?" I had not rung; I
thanked her, and said so; she said she was sorry, but had
been sure she heard the bell. After she had gone, I sat up
in some uneasiness. She had come in to have a good look at
me; I had no doubt of that. In the day or two before we
had passed each other, or seen each other at some little
distance. Now, for some reason, she was curious about
me; and this was alarming to me, for her face was somehow familiar. It was a pale face, like a sponge for its want
of expression, but with a pair of shrewd eyes. I had seen
hundreds of just such faces in Dr. Copshrews's surgery;
could it be that she had been one of them and now recognised me? Where had I seen her? Where had she seen
me? Her curiosity was shrewdly roused, no doubt, or she
would not have crept in to see me as I slept. I felt it the
more, as Dick Copshrews and his wife were to be away
that day, till late in the afternoon. Of course, I agreed, she
is in charge of the house, and may have thought that I
rang; or may have thought fit to remind me that it was
time I had breakfast; but . . . I was scared, now; such a
woman, such a look . . . no, she had come in because she
recognised me, and wished to be sure; or because she was
suspicious and wished to be confirmed; or because there
was someone outside who had traced me there, and had
sent her up to see and report. What if that were the case?
What if Dennis, or some thief-taker or other had suspected, and pursued? Dennis might well have suspected.

Nay, Dennis must have suspected. By this, he must have opened that grave in St. Giles's, and in spite of the lime, seen the imposture, and come after me. It would be easy to trace me. Where could I go, save to some relative or friend of Dr. Copshrews? He still hoped for the twenty thousand pounds, or such share of it as would fall to him as the informer.

You will think I was mad. I was a little mad. That was a terrible morning.

My first thought was to get away from the house, with what clothes I could make into a bundle. But where was I to go? Even if I went, I should have to return to hear the result of the letter to the Liverpool merchant, and to beg money. I crept quietly from bed and dressed myself. I was in no case to defend myself. The marks of what had been done to me were plainly on me, and would be for some days more. Anyone throwing off my neck-cloth could see what I was. I dared not even be challenged. Then, it had been arranged that I was to play the part of a sick man, to stay in the house, not to venture out of doors in daylight. I reflected that I had better keep to that plan, until the danger forced me from it. What was the danger?

Well, the danger was Dennis, as far as I could see. He, or someone, had brought suspicion to that servant, who was in charge of the house. Or had the servant known who I was? My case had made a stir; it had been talked of all over the town. I had treated thousands of humble patients, who knew me by sight much better than I could know them. They, the patients, had looked at the man, their saviour. I, the doctor, had only looked at the symptoms. Now that I reflected on her face, this woman's face seemed familiar. I was sure that she had been a patient, but when, and for what and where, I could not remember.

I was in a room which looked out upon one of the many lanes of the Heath. I judged that if the thief-takers were after me, they would have watchers on the back of the house. I crept to the side of the window, and very, very carefully peeped out from behind the edge of the curtain.

From the first peep I had no result. I saw a sweep of the barren hill of the Heath in the bleakness of an autumn morning. A donkey was standing, nosing at the last of the grass; a few hens picked and scratched not far from him; no people were there. Going to the other side of the window, I tried again; and this time had a sad shock.

I could see across and along the sandy lane for some distance. It was an open track, without hedge. A brook ran across it about fifty yards from me; there was a little bridge across the brook, of plank and hand-rail. Sitting on the hand-rail, facing in my direction, was one whom I took to be Dennis. He was so stooped that I could not see his face, but the figure was his, I felt sure.

I had long before observed that to look at a man will call his attention to the looker; I kept my eyes from his face, but stared at the figure. I was scared to the depth of my marrow. I had had moments of hope since my death, but now it seemed sure that death was to come to me again, and not only to me, to those who had befriended me. The man seemed to be biting his nails, in great anxiety. He was staring down at the water of the brook going under the plank at his feet. It seemed to me that he wasn't seeing the water. He was trying to solve some problem not easy to solve. He looked up at last, towards the house; it was Dennis beyond a doubt. There came a tap at my door; my heart sank down and down. I had locked the door, to prevent any other visit. I thought, "If these are the thief-takers, I'll leap through the window for it." Going quietly to the door, I asked:

"Who is it?"

The maid answered: "It's a tray of breakfast, sir."

I thanked her, and said that if she would leave it I would take it in. She asked, should she take it down, to keep hot? I told her no. As soon as she had gone, I listened in agony. Was someone waiting outside for me to open? I must say that I expected a rush upon the door as I turned the key. No one was there; the tray with my breakfast lay there. I had no appetite to eat; but I pocketed a piece of bread, in case I had to run for it. Dennis was now walking up and down by the brook. His problem seemed no clearer to him; he was plainly perturbed about something. And after watching him a kind of hope did spring up in me, that he was not sure of me, that his thoughts were not on the house where I crouched behind the curtain. Yet, why was he there? Why had the maid come in and looked so strangely? It was only eleven in the forenoon. Dick Copshrews was not to be back before dark, say five in the afternoon. I had to do nothing, except wait and fear, for six hours. If it would only fall dark, it would be something. As I watched, it seemed to fall dark; a little rain began to fall in that light, close, specking drizzle which tells of the beginning of a storm. The day, at the same time, seemed to close in and become hopeless. Dennis, down in the lane, turned up his coat collar against the wet. He seemed to be expecting someone now, for he

looked up and down the lane, which was a bad sign to me,
who had every reason to dread whoever might join him.
The rain grew worse, and Dennis, who, as I know, hated
being wet, stayed out in it, perturbed and waiting for
someone; why?

I watched, to find out why. At about noon, I saw a man
on horseback drawing near, from the direction of London. He was swathed against the wet and rode the unmis-
takable, fine chestnut horse, "The Bonco," belonging to
Dennis. I thought: "He has been waiting all the time for
his servant with the horse; now he'll mount." The man
rode to Dennis and spoke with him, but so turned from me
that I could not tell who he was. I was certain of the horse,
and supposed the rider to be Henery; he had a look of
Henery. To my astonishment, the man did not dismount
and leave the horse to his master; he turned, and the two
set off together, Dennis on foot, the man riding, going
slowly, in deep talk, towards London. The rider seemed
to be Henery; but Henery would have dismounted. Who
was it, then? After that the rain began to come down in
earnest.

I could not understand what was happening. Presently,
I went downstairs in the muffled and sick man's way,
which I had adopted. I sat by the fire in the sitting-room.
Nobody seemed to be gathering near the house, as far as I
could see. The rain was driving down and down.

From where I sat I could hear the occasional footsteps
in the lane, each step made me shudder, and whenever a
step stopped at the house, my heart sank.

There was a little sharp pen-knife on the writing-table.

I took this, thinking: "Well, they shall never get me into Newgate again."

The servant tapped at the door and came in presently. She looked at me curiously, and, as I thought, with some compassion.

She said: "You haven't eaten your breakfast, sir. Dr. Copshrews said you ought to eat. Is there anything that you could fancy?"

No, there was nothing that I could fancy. I was in too great a terror. I longed to ask her, had anybody called to ask for me? But I dared not. I knew too surely that she would say: "Yes, sir, and the gentleman is going to come again later with some friends."

The day dragged slowly on. It grew dark early, owing to the rain. Four o'clock struck, and the maid came in with candles and drew the curtain.

"A pity for this rain, sir," she said. "It'll make Mr. Copshrews late."

This was a shocking remark to me, that Dick might be late. However, time passes: it always does pass. Even that day passed, and Dick came in alone, letting himself in with his key and shaking the rain off himself on the mat outside the door. He came in presently to see me, and as soon as I could, I told him of my terror, how I felt that the maid suspected me, and that Dennis had been outside the house that morning. He was puzzled about the news of Dennis, and presently went away to ask the maid if anyone had called there during the day.

She said, yes, a very strange-looking man had come to the door about half-past ten that morning, and had asked to see Dr. Copshrews; "But," she said, "I didn't like the man's look at all. I told him that Dr. Copshrews was in London; that he'd come to the wrong house."

Dick came back to me after this, and said: "I'm puzzled. I don't understand it. Dennis did come here; but I have other things now to say to you: that merchant in Liverpool can give you a post as a ship's surgeon, if you can come to Liverpool at once, before the end of the week. The ship is the *Albicore,* Captain Ashplant."

"Captain Ashplant," I said, "that terrible fellow, who was tried for murder: I saw him in Newgate."

"Would he recognise you?" Dick said.

"I should hardly think so, but I should recognise him."

"I should risk it," Dick said. "Anyhow, you'd better get away from here to Liverpool to-night. I don't like what you have told me about Dennis. You'd better get away. We'll make a cross-country run. We could pick up the Liverpool coach at midnight. I'll go see about post-horses. And see here, we have some money to start you with, and my father specially tells me, that you're not to thank him for it, for it is less, much less, than you have earned for him in any of the years that you have been with him. Your pay as the surgeon in the *Albicore* will be five guineas a month, and you can leave her at the end of the middle passage, either in Jamaica or the Americas. One thing let me caution you about. My father doesn't know, but being what they call a failure, I've knocked about the world more than he has, and I speak from knowledge. Captains in the African trade are Devils from Hell. Don't give your Captain a chance to sell you. He'll try it, if you give him the least handle against you, or let him suspect what's happened. Trust no one in the African trade, not for one minute. And I'll give you, before you start—I'll get about it now—letters to the Governor of Jamaica, and the Governor of South Carolina."

"Do you know them?" I asked.

"Not I," he said, "but I know the kind of men you're going with, and if you leave these letters in your chest they'll read them, and they may make them a little cautious."

Dick had been a sad trial to his father, and had been the main cause, in a way, of all my own troubles; but he risked his life for me, in those trying days, without seeming to think twice about it. Sir —— and Dr. Copshrews had both sworn to preserve life when it was possible to do so. I could understand them straining points in my interest. Dick did it, as he would have put money on a horse, because he liked a flutter.

We set out in the post-chaise an hour later. It was a dark night, with the rain pouring; we had a long way to go; and I must say that I thought there would be a great likelihood of finding the coach full when it came up, at about midnight. However, Dick was certain that it was never full at that time of the year; there would be room for me; if there weren't, I should just have to post it, a stage or two more, and catch the Marathon. On arrival at "The Trumpet" I had a handkerchief over my eyes, and all the appearance of being a very sick man unable to walk much. Afterwards, in a little, smelly, cold private parlour, lit by two tallow candles and a fire which would not burn, Dick and I played a simple game of cards, of which he never seemed to tire. He said that "the French call the game 'Le Rouge et le Noir,' which means 'The Red and the Black.' " It is played by two players. One turns over a pack of cards, laid face downwards, the other guesses, before each card is turned, whether it will be red or black. We played this till about midnight, when a waiter came to tell us that the horn of the approaching coach had been heard at the lower bridge, and would be in in about three minutes. Dick gathered up his cards; he always carried cards; and totted up the score.

"If we'd been playing this for money," he said, "you'd have won £3 15s. 0d. Now we'd better go out to the coach."

We went out, to find the rain stopped and a clearing heaven above us. The coach was just coming up to the door, amid a bustle and clatter. A deep-toned and a tin-toned chime were answering each other from different towers for the quarter-past midnight. Dick was right about there being room; I could go inside.

There was some delay at the inn; the horses were being changed; outside passengers were getting hot drinks. We stood in the doorway of the inn for a few minutes, amid the noise and the push, the horses stamping and blowing and scraping, men and women calling for this or that, and a guard giving directions. "Is that box in for the two outsides?" "Yes, sir, in the boot, sir." "The brandy will be ninepence, sir." "Ninepence. What d'ye take me for? Ninepence for a brandy. Take your damned brandy." "Ninepence is the price, sir." A young woman was seeing her mother into the coach. "Be sure you let me know about Tuesday," the mother was saying. The mother was an inside passenger with me.

Dick spoke to me as to a patient, as he helped me in.

"You must not talk," he said. "Rest your throat in every possible way, and keep well covered up. You can be quite easy in your mind, madam, the gentleman is not infectious, but he must not talk, and is still very weak. It would be a Christian deed, madam, if you would help him at the stops, for he ought not to be without assistance."

The good woman said that she would help the poor gentleman gladly. She filled the window, saying farewell to her daughter, and bidding her not forget about Tuesday. Dick stayed on, to see the coach away. I had glimpses of him when mother or daughter held back from the window for an instant. He was well lit by the lamplight from the door. He must have had a poor night's rest that night, there he stood, with his queer, pale face, so strong with courage, waiting in the cold, so that I might have cheer at my going.

"You're going to be quite all right now," he said. "You're going to be a great success in life."

I said, weakly: "It will be due to you, if I am."

"Not a bit," he said, "it will be due to your future wife, you'll find."

The coach was just about to start when there came a little stir. A man strode up, with "By your leave, please. I must just have a look at who is going." He was a man whom I had often seen in Newgate. I do not know his real name : the prisoners always called him Shackles. He was a noted thief-taker, who had a great acquaintance among the knaves of England. He was often in the prison, talking with them, and getting information from them, more probably from what they screened, than from what they told. But he was shrewd as a frost, and many a man had gone to the gallows through him. He had a terrible memory, which was said never to fail.

"And who is going here?" he said, gaily. He had the bill of the passengers, and clambered up the steps, to look at the men on the outside. One of them asked what and who he was looking for. "Ah," he said, "there's been a bad business out at Chelsea, and we've reason to think the man'll be making for the north." He looked at the people outside, and then clambered down. Just as he reached the ground, Dick came to the window.

"Oh, Ned," he said, "I declare, I forgot my father's lozenges. Here they are," he said. "Just suck one whenever you feel the irritation."

The thief-taker was now beside him. "Ned Torrance," he said, peering in.

"A patient of my father's," Dick said.

"A quinsy case, eh?" the man said. "Well, I don't want you, Mr. Sore Throat. Keep covered up, sir. And Mrs. Summerfield . . . right . . . none of my birds here. Right away, coachee."

The coachman was waiting for the word, so was the ostler, so were the horses. The coach surged forward. I saw Dick wave and heard him cry: "Good luck and health"; then we were off, with four good horses, on the first stage.

When I opened the box of lozenges it was broad daylight, and I was alone in the inside of the coach. I found that the box was Dick's agate-topped snuff-box, from which Dick had emptied the snuff. Instead of snuff, he had put a little packet of paper, which seemed to have been

torn from a parcel at the inn door. The paper contained
five guineas, and the words "Good luck" scratched with
the inn pen.

I reached Liverpool safely, but with plenty of misgivings and forebodings. In London, I had had friends to advise and to lean on; here I was by myself, with no past,
with no story that could deceive a schoolboy, and with
such a terrible anxiety to be gone, that I feared all would
see it, and know from it what I was. Dick had said:
"Trust no one in the African trade, no, not one inch"; and
now I was to be in the African trade under that awful
Captain, whom I had seen at Newgate. I was to be at the
mercy of that man, who had escaped hanging for murder
by keeping the witnesses out of London.

And suppose that this terrible Captain recognised me?
We had not been long together, near Newgate's grim door,
and the light had not been good, but I knew, too well, how
poignant all the memories of Newgate are. His mad yellow eyes had rolled upon me; he had seen me; people had
whispered to him: "This young bird is in for murder."
Possibly, he would recognise me.

And yet, supposing his ship had sailed? What if I were
too late? It were better, certainly, to run the risk of being
recognised by Paul Ashplant, than to be kept longer in
England.

And then, suppose that I was even now being pursued
by Dennis and the thief-takers, all coming hot-foot on my
trail? They would guess what I was trying to do: I was
trying to fly the country. Some would go to Chester after
me, perhaps, but some would come straight to Liverpool.
How could they fail in this?

With this supposing, all my old terror returned: Dennis was on my track. He had come to Dick's door; he had been hot on the scent then; depend upon it, he was not far behind him now. Suppose that this ship should not be ready to sail, or suppose foul weather in this late autumn season should keep her from sailing, even a few days longer? Possibly one day would be too much for me. The thief-takers would be in Liverpool by then; and where would they go first to look for me? It was quite plain, they would go to the outward-bound ships, to ask to see their doctors, their passengers, their new hands. No, the hounds were after me, and I had little hope, only a crazy longing, which I kept telling myself was crazy.

I found Sir ——'s friend, the merchant, at his tavern. My throat was all muffled up still, and I looked sick and anxious, no doubt; he had misgivings about me.

"You don't look quite the man for the Coast," he said. "I'm in two minds about shipping you."

I said that I had been ill in bed, but was mending, and that the sea air would soon heal the weakness in my throat.

He growled something about weak throats meaning weak bodies. I told him to feel my pulse; since that would show him if I were weak or not. I believe that he was not pleased with my answer any more than with my look, but an acquaintance hailed him at that moment, and called him to drink something. While he was out of the room the waiting girl said to me:

"Sir, if you're a doctor, don't you believe him. He's crying for a doctor. His ship can't sail without one. He's only trying to do you down. Stand up to him for more."

When he came back he was in a rosier mood, and I am

glad to think that in spite of my terror I took the girl's advice, and gave her a guinea from the proceeds. Often and often I thought of that girl later. Her name was Jane; and the man who married her got a good helper.

In our bargaining, I undertook to be surgeon to the ship *Albicore,* bound from Liverpool to the Coast, and to continue in her till she discharged at a West Indian or American port. I was to have seven guineas a month; I was to be berthed and fed with the officers; and to have two months' pay in advance. As the ship was almost ready to sail, it was necessary that I should go on board her at once and overhaul her medical stores.

"I'll come down with you, doctor," the merchant said. "She's in the Pool there. I'll introduce you aboard her."

I asked when she was to sail?

He said: "She'd be out by to-night's tide, if the sailors understood their own interest. But when they've got a penny to spend on rum, you cannot get them, no, not if you pray them. Government ought to make it a felony for these dogs to hold up commerce the way they do. There are good crews within half a mile of us at this moment, sotting themselves with drink, while we merchants are offering them good ships and prime wages. They just sit still and laugh at us. Government'll be forced to act presently, willy-nilly, but by that time commerce may be ruined."

Growling thus, so as to make my heart sick, for I felt that I might now be kept in the port till I could be traced and taken, we came down to the foot of the hill, to the Pool, where the shipping lay. As the tide was ebbing, some of the ships were on the mud. Three lay in the deep water in the midst of the Pool.

"That's the *Albicore*," the merchant said, pointing to one that seemed deeper and dingier than the rest.

Soon we were on board her.

By this time, my heart was in my mouth, with fear lest the Captain should remember me, and lest these dogs, the seamen, who plainly could not know their own interest, should have money for a few days more in their inns. Then, I had the horrid thought, that I had not only the Captain to fear. Doubtless, his officers would have been in Newgate with him. A good many men had been with him when he went out of prison. I might happen on three or four of them: why not? They must all have been there. They would all have stared on the young doctor who had killed an Admiral; one of them, at least, would quite certainly remember me. I seemed to have leaped from a frying-pan directly into the fire. Worse than this was an inner conviction, which sometimes came to me in those anxious days, to tell me that a thing was happening. I knew within myself, from this inner prompting, that the hunt was after me, that I was being pursued. The scent had been doubtful, but was now strong.

The *Albicore* was filthy from weeks in port without hands to clean her. Her decks bore a clutter of stores not yet stricken below; she was in disorder everywhere. If I were lucky, I was to go in her into endless exile; if not, I was to be dragged from her to a swift end.... But by this time Captain Ashplant was coming forward to greet us, with his lowering, pale, evil eye and downward scowl; he had the real Newgate look.

"Good day to you, sir," he said.

"Good day, Captain," the merchant said. "I've brought you your surgeon; this is Dr. Torrance."

The Captain gave me a scowl, in which there was no shadow of recognition. I would have known him among ten thousand.

"Pleased to meet you, Doctor," he said. He turned from me to the merchant. "Will you come below, sir?" he asked.

He ushered us aft and then down the ladder to the close little cabin.

"The Doctor will need to overhaul his medical stores," the merchant said. "While he does that I'll have a word with you."

"Right, sir," the Captain said. "Steward, there. Show Dr. Torrance the medicine-chest and fetch swizzle. Oh, and fetch Dr. Torrance's trunk to his room from on deck there."

The steward said : "Certainly, Captain Ashplant."

The medicine-chest was cleated to the deck in a tiny cabin off the main saloon. The steward produced a key from half a dozen such hanging round his neck from tarry strings.

"You see, sir," he said, "I have to keep them round my neck or they'd be stolen from me." He unlocked the medicine-chest and said : "The book is in the left-hand till. Dr. Torrance; but now, sir, if you'll excuse me, I must go to the Captain."

Though I was shut in the little cabin from the main room, the door was only thin wood, with ventilations of jalousies on it. I could hear much of what was said, and remembered how Dick had said : "Never trust anyone in the African trade, no, not an inch." What if they were to talk about me, and say that I was an escaped murderer, who was to be used as a surgeon till the ship reached the West, and then to be denounced or sold? You will say that this was pushing ungenerous suspicion too far. It was. But when you are hunted, you had better suspect; no pack is more grim to its quarry than the pack of men.

However, my task was to check the medical stores in the noble chest, made, as I judged, in the East Indies, of some very hard, bright wood and bound with brass. I opened it and hooked back the lid. There in the till lay the account-books. As I took them up I heard the Captain call a health and the merchant say:

"I've got you your doctor. You'd better haul out into the stream and get your powder. It'll be alongside by one o'clock with a gang to stow it."

"Very good, sir," the Captain said. He dropped his voice and said something, which seemed to be about me.

The merchant said: "No, he's strongly recommended. And comes in the nick." Here he dropped his voice and seemed to utter a warning about me.

The Captain laughed his evil laugh and said: "No fear, sir."

I wondered what it was that I was not to have or not to be allowed to do. But I had to work at my stores while the men had their glasses refilled and drank to the success of the voyage.

It was soon very clear to me that many surgeons had had charge of the *Albicore's* medical stores. She was now seven years old, and in that time had had nine surgeons, of whom the two last had been in the last year, Dr. Carvy and Dr. Tuohy, both of whom had died on the Coast to which we were bound. The latest surgeon was a certain Trace or Tracy, if that were the name, who had been there only a fortnight before me. What had become of him? And had the medical equipment gone with him? If not, where had it gone? Much was gone. The instruments, unguents, purgatives, bark, balances, splints, tents, bandages, all were gone; the chest had been pillaged.

I heard the merchant saying: "Well, here's to to-night's try. I've got them all squared and I don't think Ginger Dew will cross me. So let's drink to-morrow's tide, Captain."

They drank it down, whatever they meant by the toast. Presently, after a lot of talk which I did not understand about eyes, cops and talliks, and how old Mollee of Little Massa would soon get something he wouldn't like if he stood in the way of honest trade, the merchant had a last drink as I finished my list and brought it out. By that time both the men were somewhat flushed with drink. I showed my list with the deficiencies marked upon it and said that the chest had been pillaged.

"That's my damned mate and that damned surgeon," the Captain said. "They went through the ship as soon as my back was turned."

The merchant took the list. "I'll send these things aboard to you this afternoon," he said. "Now, Doctor, have you all your sea-store? A sea bed and blankets; a tarred hat and coat, and so forth?"

I said: "No."

"Well," he said, "you'll need them. The ship's going to tow out into the stream in a few minutes. You'd better

give me three of those guineas you had from me and I'll
send the things off to you with the pilot."

I asked if I might not go ashore to buy them.

He said : "No. You're moving into the river now. You're
aboard now ; no man can go ashore now till you make the
Coast. I'll send the things off to you."

Dick had told me never to trust these follows, but I had
no choice but to trust him ; so I gave him the three guineas,
which he took. He shook hands with me, knitted his shaggy
brows at me, gave me a glare, and went off with the Captain.

The steward, a little, frail, elderly man, appeared at
my elbow from a hole in the floor. "Perhaps, Dr. Torrance," he said, "you'd like to see your cabin ; it is this
way."

It opened off the side of the saloon. It was a cupboard
measuring about eight feet long by four and a half feet
wide, by about six feet, deck to beam. It was lit by a bull's-
eye of glass in the ship's side. A locker under this light was
the bedstead. I opened the locker, and was much surprised
to find it almost filled with small swivel-guns, well-
greased and stoppered, and their mountings.

"Can I have these things away?" I asked.

He did not much relish the question, saying that these
things were part of the cabin equipment. "We'd never be
safe without them on the Coast."

I said that that might be, but that I could not store my
clothes while the guns were there.

"Well, I'll have to ask Mr. Pegg," he said. "I can't take
so much on myself, sir."

He recommended me not to use the bed on the locker-

top, but to sling a hammock from the hooks in the beams. I
asked him if he had known the other doctors in the ship.
He said that they were all dead, except the one who had
run. Dr. Carvy, he thought, had been given something to
put him away by old King Mollee, who may have feared
that Dr. Carvy would have refused some slaves that Mollee wished to sell. Dr. Carvy had swelled up terrible on
that very locker-top. So had Dr. Tuohy, in a way; but
Tuohy was not like Carvy; he was a very kind gentleman.
Tuohy had died of a suffumigation; all purple in the face.
Then young Dr. Timothy had got the small-pox from the
slaves; some very poor lot of slaves who ought not to have
been allowed on board, only poor Dr. Timothy was drunk
at the time and let them pass and then died of their infection. At this time, as we chatted and tried to make the
cabin comfortable, there was much noise forward in the
ship, and I became conscious of movement. We had un-
moored from the buoy in the Pool and were now slowly
towing out into the river, so the steward told me, meaning
to anchor there until we got our powder on board. He
talked always in a little low voice, hardly more than a
whisper, and seemed pathetically eager to have me on his
side. He said that if I wished a hammock instead of a bed,
he would speak to the Captain about it for me, and Captain Ashplant would issue one from the slop chest. I asked
if all the doctors of the ship had died in that cabin. He
said No; only Tuohy and Carvy; the rest had died ashore
"of the climate." Presently, as we anchored in the stream
amid a good deal of shouting, he said:

"I wonder, Dr. Torrance, if you'd be so very kind as to
look at my sore leg?"

There was no doubt about its being sore. I said I would
dress it as soon as my stores come off.

I was some little time in the cabin trying to make tidy.
The steward caused the removal of the swivel-guns from
my locker. When a sickly-looking lad had carried these
away, the steward came in with a bucket and clout; he
washed out the locker and left it open to dry. It could not
be dry till the morrow, so nothing could be done about the
stowing of my clothes. There was to be no dinner, the steward said, for the Captain had to dine ashore, and the mates
were having something on deck; however, he brought me
some bread and cheese and a bottle of beer. After this,
there came a hail from the deck for Dr. Torrance, and the
steward reported my medical stores, and would I check
them at the chest as they were brought below?

The lad who had helped to carry down the drugs told
me that among them was a package addressed to me, he
supposed by the merchant, whom I called Eyebrows and
the rest called Old Sokdollijer. I judged that these might
be some of the sea-stores which he had promised to buy
for me. However, I saw at a glance that the things came
from London. It was a package of books, mostly medical
works likely to be useful to me, but one or two devotional
works, Smith's *Private Prayer*, Ellison's *Christian Practice* and Docking's *Quiet Christian's Hymnal;* with these
were L'Estrange's *Fables*, Gay's *Fables*, Pope's *Odyssey*,
and five *Ramblers* for general reading. There was a letter
with the books. It was written on fine parchment and
sealed with an imposing seal; it certified that Dr. Edward
Torrance was duly qualified to practise medicine; it was
signed by Dr. Copshrews and by Sir ———. Undoubtedly,

the gifts came from Dr. Copshrews. I did not know what dangers he had incurred by sending me the certificate, nor how far it was lawful; but its effect on me was one of light and joy. I might study and practise my profession, and perhaps even yet become known and blessed as a healer of the pains of life. My grief was that I could not write to thank him; however, such a flood of thanks went out to him from me that he must have felt it, and known that his gift had come like manna in the wilderness.

After putting these books inside my cabin, I turned to the work of checking the drugs by the list. I had hardly begun when the mate, Mr. Pegg, came down in a great taking to explain that the bastards had sent a double dollop of castor-oil-bean, whereas they'd enough bean for a thousand slaves already in bulk below. Captain Ashplant, who was dressing for the shore, told him to send the bean back and not make such a row. Mr. Pegg was a youngish man, fair and fattish, with a habit of puffing out his chest. "I'll dump the bean back all right," he said, and went on deck to do it.

I was intent upon my work in the dark stern-cabin, memorising the amount and the position of every drug and article so that I could go to it with certainty in any emergency, and hearing the Captain swearing at the steward as he shaved him in the cabin alongside, when I became aware that I was being watched. My nerves were not in a good state. I had suddenly a shocking thought that the thief-takers had run me down and were just behind me to take me back to Newgate. I turned, and there, behind me, was a big black negress in a green dress. How she had come there and how long she had been there, I could not guess. She seemed pleased at having startled me; but not pleased at my being there.

"You no to do so," she said.

I answered: "Yes, but I have to do so."

"No, no," she said, "I say not to do so."

I repeated: "Excuse me, madam, I shall do so."

She seemed very much disturbed, and said: "No, you shall not do so. Paul, Paul, Paul."

Now the Captain was being shaved inside his cabin within six feet of her. Her sudden screaming of his name startled him, so that the steward's razor nicked him. I heard the Captain swear, and strike the steward, kick over the basin, and open his door.

"Paul," the negress cried, "he insult me. He not do so."

The Captain had a lot of lather on his chin; blood trickled on it. He caught the negress by the throat and said: "I'll teach you to come yelling at me, you jade, on a sailing day." There was some old rope on the cabin floor; it had come as the lashing to my bale of goods. With incredible speed and certainty the Captain snatched some of this, twisted it about her throat, flung her down and then beat her with the bight of it. He beat her and beat her till he wearied; then he pulled her to her feet, kicked her out of the cabin and said: "Any more of it and I'll cut your throat." I remember the look she gave me to this day. The Captain went back muttering to his toilette, and presently went on deck and ashore. He gave me an evil glance as he passed.

When the negress was kicked out of the cabin, she did not utter a sound; she was silent afterwards. I hoped that perhaps she had left the ship, for I judged that hell was raging in her.

It began to be darkish presently; the work on deck and aloft ceased, and the two mates came below to wash for supper.

Mr. Pegg said: "Dr. Torrance, you must meet Mr. Tulp, our second mate."

Mr. Tulp came forward into the lamp-light. He was about eighteen, but having been at sea for six years, he seemed twenty-five. He was a young man with a permanent tooth-ache and soul-ache. He looked as though his parents had cursed his coming, and he had lived to curse them for begetting him.

"Steward," Mr. Pegg called, "can we have a swizzle on tick to welcome Dr. Torrance?"

The negress put her head suddenly into the cabin and said: "No swizzle; no tick. I not allow. I tell de Captain."

I said that it was for me to stand treat, if the steward could sell me a bottle, and if the lady would join us. This changed the state of affairs, so we had our drink, in fact, all the bottle, and the lady had the most of it. When we had finished, the mate said:

"By the way, Doctor; did I give you your letter?"

"Letter?" I asked. "No. I had no letter."

"Well, one came for you with the medical comforts. I left it in my pocket."

He went to fetch it, while I wondered who could have sent me a letter. I asked Mr. Tulp, the second mate, if my things had been sent to me, my sea-store of blankets, and so forth, which were to come by the pilot.

"Pilot?" he said in some amazement. "We have no pilot. We can enter and leave the river without a pilot, I hope."

"No," I said, "but the merchant said that he would send the things by the pilot."

The mate had rejoined us. "What?" he said. "Old Sokdollijer said that? Did you give him the blunt, too?"

I said: "Yes, three guineas."

The mates looked at each other as though it were a good joke.

"Well, if that don't beat Newgate," Mr. Pegg said. "You can't beat Old Sokdollijer. 'Send the things by the pilot.' That's a good one."

"Do you mean," I asked, "that he won't send them?"

They looked at each other again, as though this were another joke.

"Why, no," he said. "Send them, not he. It's a chowse; but here's your letter."

I took the letter and got away from them on the plea that I had to read it. The address had been printed, not written, with a bad pen: "To Dr. Edward Torrance, in the care of my shipowner in Liverpool." I opened it under the tallow candle in my cabin. I judged that it must be from Dick. I think that it was, but the note was printed in the same way, so that I could not tell the hand. It said: "Dear Ned, Henery is following you to Liverpool." There was no signature, no indication of how soon Henery might be expected, but it seemed to me probable that Henery would be in the coach which had brought the letter, and might be even now gathering men to come to take me. It only needed this to complete my misery. I went up on deck and looked at the river, the shipping and the city lights. I must say that I had little pleasure in life at that moment. Here was I, a condemned and half-hung felon, certain to be hanged if caught, living in a queer world, with a captain who seemed to be a criminal maniac and a negress who seemed to be his mistress, whose anger I had incurred, who yet would get drunk with the mates, and endure the utmost savagery of brutality. Here I was in a slave ship bound to the unknown coast. The Coast, as they called it, to which sailors could not be tempted and where a doctor died every voyage; but I was only there while my luck held: it might not hold; I was being pursued and might be caught at any moment.

I dropped the letter into the river in little pieces, lest it should be found and incriminate the sender. I was called presently to my supper, which we ate in the cabin. The negress sat at table with us. She treated the two mates with the utmost insolence, and they submitted to it. I did not. Thinking that it might ease the situation, I proposed another bottle of rum. Mr. Pegg said that this was not fair, that I had stood them treat and that it was their turn, but that the fact was they were both outward bound and hadn't got a tosser between them. So we had another bottle from the steward, and although no rum on the market could have cheered my heart much, I was the better for it, for the negress became stupidly drunk and had to be put to bed by the steward.

"You'll excuse my giving you a warning, Dr. Torrance," Pegg said, "but you'd ought to be careful with the judy. It's best to keep in her good books."

"But what is she?" I asked. "Is she a slave? What position has she in the ship?"

"Who?" he said. "Old Black Mantacaw? She's a slave, yes, and one day she'll be treated like a slave and be kicked from Hell to Hackney and back again and then again the long way round. Then the next day she'll be the Old Man's fancy girl; and then she's the queen of this good ship; and we never know which she's going to be from day to day— the queen or the door-mat."

"And what is the Captain like?" I asked.

Mr. Pegg looked at me; Mr. Tulp looked at me. They supposed that I had seen the Captain, and that if I hadn't seen him, his fame must have gone round the world and reached my ears.

"I'll just take a turn on deck," Mr. Pegg said. He came back immediately. "You were asking about the Captain," he said. "I just took that turn on deck to be sure he wasn't on board. Now, you want to know about Captain Ashplant. I'll tell you in two words: the finest Captain in the trade, bar none. Bar none, ain't that so, Tulp? Ain't it so, mister?"

Mr. Tulp said: "Yes, certainly."

"Mind you," Mr. Pegg said, "if he don't go to Hell when he dies, there's no truth in religion."

"Tell me," I asked; "I see from the stores books that there have been eight doctors in this ship, and that they've all died."

"No, nine doctors," said Pegg. "You're the tenth; the other one ran."

"Tell me then," I said, "is the Coast very unhealthy that they should die like this?"

"I'll tell you a secret," Mr. Pegg said. "I've been seven voyages to the Coast. Look at me, now. I never have a touch of fever, nor anything else; never a touch. The Coast's not unhealthy. It's poison you have to watch. Never you touch any food or drink that those black fellows have handled. Full of poison, the Coast is. All those blacks are up to poisoning—juju, massa-massa: all sorts. Nothing they like better than to wash a white man away with one of their drugs. The Coast's no more unhealthy than an English summer day, except for sunstrokes. Apart from sunstrokes and poison, the climate's fine. And you look out for Black Mantacaw here. She has wafted many away, I'll bet. 'Send him home to him he lub'—that's her motto. You watch that dame; she needs it."

"What poisons do they use?" I asked. "I might have antidotes."

"They've got a lot of poisons," Mr. Pegg said, "and they've got the antidotes too, but we've not. Ain't that so, mister?"

Mr. Tulp said that it was so, but that their great thing was a little powdered bamboo, that ate through the bowels.

As we were on these medical topics, I asked what sort of health the slaves had when they were once on board. Mr. Pegg looked at me with some suspicion.

"They get all sorts of healths," he said, "the same as any other body of men. Too good health for our comfort, a lot of times. Ain't that so, mister?"

Mr. Tulp said that it was so.

Mr. Pegg then said that he would sing if he weren't so damned dry, and as this was a hint that the bottle was out, I called the steward to ask for another. Mr. Pegg said that this was not fair, as I'd already stood them treat, but the

fact was that they were outward bound and hadn't a
tosser, and would make it up to me out on the Coast.
"Ain't that so, mister?"

Mr. Tulp said that it was so. So we had the other bottle
and Mr. Pegg sang. Mr. Tulp said he would have sung,
only he was too down-hearted. So Mr. Pegg sang instead.
Presently Mr. Pegg said that he'd better turn in to get
some sleep, as he would have to be up to welcome the crew
at three in the morning.

"But I thought you couldn't get a crew," I said.

The two men looked at me with some pity. Mr. Pegg
jerked his right thumb towards his left shoulder, which is
a gesture to indicate amazement at any depth of ignorance.

"Crew," he said. "Why, the Old Man's gone to get one.
And if they're anything like the last, they'll need some
welcoming."

"Then are we likely to sail soon?" I asked.

"Yes," he said, "we sail to-morrow morning, if the
crew's fit to stir."

And at last he broke up our evening party; the two
mates went on deck, took a turn forward, had a word with
the watchman, and went below to bed. I went on deck, too,
and stayed there, wondering how soon Henery would
pitch upon me. I had had such harsh turns from fortune,
that I supposed, that just as we got under weigh the magistrates would stop us and take me to prison. Anything too
bad for another would be my fortune. Then I thought:
Why should I endure such fortune? If it be not fit fortune
for a man, why bear it? If this be life, why bear life? What
can be the good of it? If it be punishment, for what is it

punishment? What sin have I committed to deserve it?
How can I offend if I refuse to bear an injustice? If this
be the working of Providence, why, I will defy any such
Providence, so crude and so cruel, so stupid and so unforgiving. I looked down at the water gurgling along the
sides; there was plenty of it there; all of it promising a
peace. I looked up at the night; there were some stars
there; I must say that they did not seem to mind what I
did. Of human links, I had almost none. Old Copshrews,
well, I should never see him again; Dick I should never
see again. The two or three lads with whom I sometimes
foregathered for chess or music, they had turned from me
at the very first coming of my trouble. As to the girl, well,
I could not blame her; she obeyed her mother, no doubt.
"Ah," I thought, "I must indeed be a poor specimen, since
all believed that I was a murderer directly the charge was
brought; all except Dr. Copshrews and his son; and that
old surgeon who knew my father." Then I thought that
here in the river and down below in the chest were death
and poisons enough to remedy any evil fate that might
threaten. "If it be true that Henery is after me," I
thought, "I can defeat him. If I stay here on deck, I shall
hear any boat that comes, and can slip into the river before any thief-taker can seize me. If I sleep, and am surprised, I can have poison about me and so escape. But even
so, I am going to a place where poison will be my end in
any case."

I slipped down to the cabin, which was lit for the night
with a battle-lantern. I could hear the heavy breathings of
all the sleepers near me in their different dens, Black
Mantacaw, who talked in her sleep, Pegg, who snored,

Tulp, who whined, the steward, who wheezed. I wondered what notes the Captain and I would add to the music. I opened the chest with the key and carefully took out a small poison bottle. With that I felt secure. Not all the law in the land would be able to cheat me out of that. I closed the chest, locked it, and stole on deck again. I meant to watch till we sailed; no man should lay hands on me, to drag me to a gaol again.

On deck I found a seat from which I could watch the lights along the river-bank. These were the sailing marks of the port, burning all night long. From my perch I heard the sweet bells of a church chiming the quarters. Two ships in the river, at some distance from us, kept the time by the striking of bells throughout the night. I did not, at that time, understand their reckoning. One o'clock passed, then two, then three, with nothing stirring; a small boat went past under sail at about half-past three. After four the river seemed as still as the grave.

It must have been six o'clock or past when there came a noise from the Pool, as of men shouting, screaming and singing. The watchman slipped hurriedly aft to call Mr. Pegg, who came on deck within a minute. He seemed surprised at finding me on deck.

"What, it's you, Doc?" he said. "Give us the lantern, steward." The steward, who had followed him up with the lantern from the cabin, handed it to him. I saw then that he had a slim little club or bludgeon in his hand. "See my Tickler, Doc?" he said. He handed it to me. It was of some very heavy, hard African wood, so that for all its slimness and the slightness of the swelling at its head, it was a dangerous weapon. "I'll need it with some of these birds," he said.

He went to the gangway, where he carefully lashed the battle-lantern so that it could not be dislodged by kick or blow. Meanwhile, the noise of screaming and yelling drew nearer. I could make out a biggish boat lurching towards us under sail. She was full seemingly of wild beasts.

"These are the growlers," Mr. Pegg explained. "The Old Man's late with 'em; he's had a job to get 'em, likely. It'll cost guineas a man, sometimes, to get a crowd. That's the fruits of liberty, that is, letting seamen choose and pick. We offer good wages and the best of treatment, and that's the result; they'll let the ship rot rather than go in her. I'd make it felony in any seaman to refuse a ship that wants him. But here, here they come. You'd best stand from under, Doc; you might get a rap else."

The boat drew nearer. I felt that perhaps Henery and his thief-takers might be in her, too, with every hope of finding me asleep. There was a place up above the gangway, near the mizen-rigging, where I could see and hear. If anyone in the boat were after me, then I could know in time. I could be in the water on the other side of the ship, in the clutch of the current, before they could lay hand on me. That I vowed I would do.

As I took my place with this resolve, the boat's sail shook and came down in the midst of an explosion of blasphemy and obscenity. The boat bumped and ground herself alongside. A man just under me caught the mizen chains with a boat-hook and Mr. Tulp, running up, flung down a line. The boat was fast alongside in two turns.

Then within the boat, among yells and snatches of song, curses and screams, a barge-load of wild beasts began to seethe and stir. Craning over the side, I saw Captain Ashplant and two stalwart-looking men. They had a dark lantern among them; one of them opened the slide, to light the mob up the ladder. For a flash of terror I thought that these men were the thief-takers. Then I decided that they were boatmen, by their instinctive swaying to the motion of the boat. Then one big man from among the mob, being fighting drunk, struck the lantern out of their hands into the river with an oath. He was at once hit on the head with the tiller, I thought. All the time Mr. Pegg was saying:

"Come up, boys. There's hot drinks all ready for you. Come up and have one on the ship."

Captain Ashplant called: "Up on deck, sons. Rum hot for all hands. Up and get forward to it."

The noise of the men fighting, swearing and cursing was like nothing I could have imagined. One or two of them were trying to get up the side. One had, I think, reached the deck and fallen prone, when suddenly an Irish voice cried:

"Holy Jasus, boys; she's a slaver. I smell the stink of her. Out of it, boys. It's a trick; she's for the Coast."

Ashplant leaped at him and struck him a blow. "Will you shut your head or will I cut your throat?" he said.

He knocked the Irishman down, but his words had been heard, and cries rose.

"None of your slavers. Out of it, boys."

But now the boatmen joined in. "None of your lip," they said. "Up that ladder. Up the side with you."

They were armed and ready; the others were unarmed

and drunk. There was a free fight. The Irishman jumped overboard, but a boatman knocked him senseless and dragged him back. Mr. Pegg, who was never backward in the restraint of human liberty, came down into the boat with Tickler.

"Up the side with you," he said. "Up the side with you. Get up."

The poor, drunken wretches had no chance. They were beaten, and banged, seized, dragged and kicked up the side. Seven sober, resolute men had overcome three times their strength. The last ten gave no trouble. For a few minutes a heap of bodies lay on board the *Albicore* just inside the gangway. I thought that they might be killed. The boat being now cleared of them, cast loose and shoved off. Her boatmen called: "A happy voyage, Captain," but Ashplant did not answer this. Thinking that some among the bodies might be living, and might be needing my help, and being for the moment quit of my fear of Henery, I went down to Mr. Pegg, who was unlashing his battle-lantern.

I said: "May I have the lantern a moment? Some of these fellows may be hurt."

"Hurt?" he answered. "You can't hurt a drunken man, that is well known. These aren't hurt, they're drunk; drugged, too, most of 'em, and the fresh air's been too much for 'em, same as it always is." He strode to the heap and kicked into it. "Rise and shine," he said. "Out of that. Get to your own sties, pigs; no sleeping aft. Up you get."

To my astonishment, the heap did rise, but it did not exactly shine. Man by man, groaning, deadly sick, in pain, in stupor, drugged, knowing not what they did nor where they were, they picked themselves up and staggered and swayed their way forward, where two arch-fiends, the watchman and the boatswain, helped by the boatswain's mate and perhaps by Mr. Tulp, kicked them into the forecastle, shut the hatch on them, and left them to sleep it off. I heard Ashplant say to Pegg that in another year or two it would cost five pounds a man to get any crew at all, unless Parliament did something. It was just ruin to commerce and the country.

As my fears were strong upon me and my dangers likely to grow with daylight, I moved aft, away from them, thinking of the scene. I judged that I was not dead and not in hell: yet surely, I was in a company of devils. And yet, why was I complaining? I was lucky to have even that fate. "Yes," I told myself, "I am lucky, beyond all my dreams, to have this fate. In Newgate, only so few days ago, this would have seemed Paradise. It is life, in a sense it is freedom; it is bliss. . . . Oh, I ought not to growl, but be thankful unspeakably."

I noticed that the Captain and Mr. Pegg remained deep in talk of a very secret kind close to the gangway. Something had gone wrong, and the Captain was not best pleased about it, for he went past me snarling and down to his cabin. He'd been up all night doing deeds of devilry, and one or two of the deeds did not bear examination. Pegg hailed me in a little voice:

"Hey, Doc there, just a minute."

I went down to him.

"Anything I can do for you?" I asked.

"No, it's not me," he said, "it's the Old Man again. Ye

see, he's the finest Captain in the trade, bar none, but the trouble with him is he never knows when to stop. Ye see, getting a crew isn't like gathering rosebuds, some of them you have to hit; and he always will go for the head, the Captain, and he rather thinks he got a man too hard at the 'Eight Bells.' "

"You mean he killed him?" I said.

"Well, he doesn't know," Pegg said. "They were working on him to try to bring him round; but you see, somebody might get hold of it, and then there'd be hell to pay. So he wants me and you to swear he wasn't out of the ship all night; that's in case it should come to anything."

"You think the man is killed?" I said.

"Well, he will go for the head," Pegg said, "and the head's only a thin shell, when all's said. If he'd only hit him in the wind, it would act just as good for the moment, and the man would be well next morning. So if the man's dead, and the widow gets to the magistrate, they'll be on board in no time; it's light now. And the Captain wasn't out of the ship all night, remember. Tulp will bear you out. But the trouble is, the Old Man's got such a mug on him, no one could mistake him."

"How have you got your crew?" I asked.

"There's roguery in all trades but ours," Pegg said. "You go round to the inns where there are seamen or suspect there are seamen, and you say to the landlord: 'Now, how much for a man?' Then you make your bargain, and he gives them something in their drink, and then presently you can get them down to the boat. You aren't used to a seafaring life."

I said I wasn't.

"Ah," Mr. Pegg said. "Well, you're like a young bear, all your troubles still to come."

I felt that if this were true, my life would be a very doubtful benefit. The heaven was beginning to show signs of light.

"And here," Pegg said, "here comes a boat."

It was true; a boat was rowing out to us from the shore. Only one man was in her. He rowed hard, came alongside and said:

"Is the Old Man there?"

Pegg said: "No, what is it? Are you from the shore? From the 'Eight Bells'?"

"Yes," the man said. "We had a doctor on him. He's gone. And the widow and her friends are gone to the magistrates. We can't stop 'em; they're too many. So you'll know what to expect. Forewarned is forearmed." And with that he rowed away.

"Poor Old Man," Pegg said. "If he ain't had some trouble lately."

I thought it was a queer way to describe the case. The Captain had done one peculiarly dirty murder, and had now added to this a sudden and brutal one, and now the ship would be detained, and all on board her would be held as witnesses. All my hopes of escaping from Henery were gone.

"Well, I must break it to the Old Man," Pegg said. "He won't be too well pleased."

He went below, while the light grew upon the river, and shone upon the distant hills. It was a fair morning, with a brisk, pleasant breeze. There wasn't much beauty in my heart nor aboard the *Albicore*. Pegg came on deck with the Captain, who had been cheering himself and still held a bottle.

"Call all hands on deck," the Captain was shouting. "I want to see them. I want to cut their throats. Boot 'em up for me to kill a few."

There was no delay when he gave an order; the boatswain, his mate and the watchman leaped down to beat up the ghosts of men whom they had so recently beaten down. Some were unable to move, but an abject dozen did come tottering aft, all bruised, drugged and cut, some of them reeling sick, and most of them now aware that they were for the Coast, that Coast of Dead Ned, from which so few seamen returned. The arch-fiends beat them into a line in front of the Captain, who walked up and down the line threatening them with his bottle.

"You didn't want to come with Paul, did you?" he said. "No. But you're coming with Paul, and I'm going to cut your throats, every throat you've got. Hey, I'm going to be happy cutting your throats. I'll use the lot of you till you're dead pork and cut you up for fish-bait. I'm Captain Paul, who flogged Maggot Williams dead. Nothing to how I'll flog you dead."

I cannot imagine anything liker the welcome of Satan to a few unhappy damned than that awful harangue. I watched it, and listened to it, nor can I forget it; but I had an eye on the river all the time for a boat drawing near with Henery and the magistrates. That boat was coming; it could not be long delayed.

I knew nothing of the magistrates, nor how they proceeded against ships in the river. I supposed that they would send out some armed and manned boat from the Pool; I, therefore, watched the entrance to the Pool. There, sure enough, while the Captain harangued his victims, a boat shot out under sail and made straight towards us. She had several men in her. I could not see who nor what they were, but had little doubt that this was to be the end of me. This would be Henery and the thief-takers coming to drag me away. I looked at the distant hills to the south and to the water streaking past the ship. Putting my hand into my pocket, I fingered the cork of my poison bottle. I would drink the draught and then leap overboard; for I had tried life and it was not worth the having, not by any computation.

"There's a boat coming," I said to Pegg.

" 'Deed, there is," he said, pausing; "and well I know her; it's Sokdollijer and Barney what brought us the hands just now. And . . . say . . . I must tell him." He touched the Captain's arm and said: "It's the owners, Captain Ashplant."

The boat dropped her sail so as to pass slowly by us; she did not close. I judged that she was the boat which had brought our crew. Old Eyebrows, the merchant, was in her. I thought: "Can he be bringing my sea-stores?" But, no; he hailed, and said:

"What are you staying for? Are you daft or drunk? The man's gone. Get to hell out of it. Get to hell out of it. I'm off fishing."

The sail went up as he finished and the boat shot ahead. I leaped up into the rigging and cried:

"You're a dirty, cheating, thieving skunk; where are my sea-stores, you filthy, lying knave?"

He heard me, I am glad to say. He did not pay any attention to me, but looked back at Pegg and the Captain and waved us imperiously to sea.

"That's orders," Pegg said. " 'Get to hell out of it.' That's 'Get to sea,' sir."

"Who's to get to sea?" the Captain asked.

"Old Sokdollijer's orders, sir," Pegg cried. "And you'd best consult your safety, sir, since the man's gone. Man the windlass."

Paul stared stupidly at him and at the line of seamen. Then he sprang at them with his bottle, striking right and left.

"Did you hear the order?" he shrieked. "Get forward; man the windlass."

If he had said: "Ghost the windlass," it would have been apter, for a more sickly set of disembodied spirits never tottered. However, from somewhere or other a second set appeared, and got to the work in earnest; these were the permanent crew of the carpenter and his mate, the sailmaker, the blacksmith and blacksmith's mate, the cook, and the two boatswains, all steady, strong men, who knew what had to be done. With these, helped by Tulp, and such of the ghosts who could move at all, the windlass was manned. There were yells and moanings, plenty, from the sick in the forecastle. I said to Mr. Pegg:

"Let me heave, too, will you?"

"Dammy, Doc, you'd oughtn't to," he said, "and you a doc; but a man's weight is a man's weight."

I took my place on a bar and hove all I could.

"Sing, you bastards," the boatswain called. "Put your weights on; heave; and start a song."

He went down into the forecastle and drove up two more unfortunates to heave. When he reappeared someone had cut him over the eye with a neck of broken bottle; he said it was one of the Micks done it, but it was nothing at all. He continued to call people bastards, to heave, and to kick the sick, though the blood kept trickling into his eye.

It seemed a weary age to me, but after a long, long time, Mr. Pegg called to loose and set a sail or two; then after heaving again, the anchor left the bottom; we were slowly moving from our berth. In a moment more we had the anchor in sight and scattered to sail-making. More and more sail was set, till we were gathering way, and seeing the shore slip by. Suddenly a big Irishman appeared from below. He was white as chalk. He held a neck of broken bottle in each hand. He cried: "Annyone want his face combed can get it done here." He searched the deck for the Captain, caught sight of him, and called: "You and your Coast, you murdering dog; don't think you'll get me to it. Ye can give me share of the Coast to me Aunt Sairey. Good-bye, my bucko-boy." He flung one bottle neck at the Captain, the other at the boatswain; then, leaping on to the rail, he dived from it and struck out for the shore.

"Heave that topsail aback, mister," the Captain cried. "Jump into the boat there, you; I'll have that man's backbone stripped for that."

Some men ran hither and thither, as though obeying orders. Mr. Pegg went up to the Captain and pointed out a boat, full of men, which had put out from the shore some distance ahead of us.

"See, you, Captain," he said, in a low voice, which I heard plainly enough, "there's the magistrates come for you. They'll board us, sure as a tick, if you heave-to. Keep all fast with the braces. Get out of that boat."

He spoke too late. Two unfortunates had run to the boat at the davits, cast off the gripes and let go the falls. They slid into her and had her cut adrift before either Pegg could get to them or the ship could tow them under. I had not thought that we were moving so fast; they seemed to spin away aft from us; I saw them shake their fists at us. There was going to be no Coast for them.

"They've done us," Pegg said. "Well, we can't stop to pick 'em up, worse luck."

He had a telescope in his hand; I took it from him and turned it on the boat towards which we were swiftly rushing. She was waiting there for us. She was going to board us, for her bowman had laid in his oar and was standing with his boat-hook ready. Her crew wore red jackets. "Port-master's crew," Pegg said. There were four persons in her stern-sheets besides her coxswain; one of them, as I could plainly see, was Henery, another was the thief-taker, Shackles, who had looked into the coach that night. "Them other two are beaks, beaks from up the Hill, magistrates," Pegg said.

One of these magistrates now rose in his place and hailed us through a speaking-trumpet: "Check your head-braces. Heave-to. Heave your ship to. Surrender in the name of the Law."

"With a wet fore-sheet," Pegg muttered, and glancing forward along the deck of our rushing ship.

I could not know it, but we were at the end of a board, and at the point of altering course. Tulp was steering; we were going nippily along.

"Up with her, mister," Pegg cried.

Tulp shoved the helm up; the ship trembled, shook and seemed to delight in it, then lifted and turned upon her heel. There were sudden yelled orders from Pegg, a crying from a lot of racing men, amid a flying and a rattling of rope. For a half instant she checked perhaps; then she was running free.

"Round like a bird," Pegg cried. "She's the handiest bitch of a little ship in all God's ocean."

A sheet of spray rose up from her bow and shone like flying-fish. The boat or barge was already far astern. Turning the glass on her, I saw her men hurriedly stepping her mast.

"They've got one sail: I've got forty," Pegg said, "not to mention save-alls."

Mr. Pegg conned the ship and saw all trim. He sent a lad aloft to loose more sail. He looked at the now distant boat and spat towards her.

"Paid her with the fore-topsail," he said. "I didn't rightly hear what they said. They was wanting to sell us some red herrings, wasn't they; if we should ever be asked?" He winked at me.

"Yes," I said, "they were offering us some red herrings."

"They'll not sell us any herrings, nor anything else now," he said. "They've lost their market. No ship'll catch the *Albicore*. But I marvel the beaks could have thought they'd stop the Old Man with a warrant; he's too downy a bird. The finest Captain in the trade, bar none."

The wind freshened; our ship quickened her going as she felt the new sail. All about us, mewing and poising, came the Mersey gulls, whom I envied from the very depth of my heart. They were free; they were happy; they were not devils to each other, or, at least, not such devils as men. Soon, we were surging through the bar, in the midst of a rain-squall. On the sandspit near the bar was an old gibbet, bearing an iron frame, in which part of an old pirate still swung. He was my brother, I thought; but had had no luck. I was one of the lucky ones; one almost in a hundred thousand. I could begin again. As we drove on, the sun came out and lit this sailing-mark. It shone out and gleamed against the purple of the cloud, till at last it was dim astern, then out of sight. I who was Dead Ned was bound for the Coast of Dead Ned, to what Fortune who could tell?

I shall tell you in the second volume.